STETSONS, SPRING
AND
WEDDING RINGS

Jillian Hart,
Judith Stacy,
Stacey Kayne

 MILLS & BOON®

First published in Great Britain 2010
Harlequin Mills & Boon Limited,
Eton House, 18-24 Paradise Road, Richmond, Surrey TW9 1SR

STETSONS, SPRING AND WEDDING RINGS
© Harlequin Books S.A. 2009

The publisher acknowledges the copyright holders of the individual works as follows:

ROCKY MOUNTAIN COURTSHIP © Jill Strickler 2009
COURTING MISS PERFECT © Dorothy Howell 2009
COURTED BY THE COWBOY © Stacey Kayne 2009

ISBN: 978 0 263 87586 7

Printed and bound in Spain
by Litografia Rosés S.A., Barcelona

CONTENTS

ROCKY MOUNTAIN COURTSHIP

Jillian Hart

Dear Reader

You may remember the Brooks brothers of Moose, Montana Territory, from my last anthology story, ROCKY MOUNTAIN BRIDE, in the *Western Weddings* collection. This time Clara Woodrow arrives in town, hoping to find employment with the Brooks family, and is mistaken for a mail-order bride by youngest brother Joseph. Clara is immediately taken by the handsome Brooks brother, but is his profession of love and his tender courtship sincere?

I hope you enjoy accompanying Clara as she discovers true love. Oldest brother Gabe's story is next!

Thank you so much for choosing ROCKY MOUNTAIN COURTSHIP.

Happy reading

Jillian

Chapter One

Montana Territory, 1882

The January snow beat with a fury against Joseph Brooks as he reined his trusty bay to a stop in front of the train depot. Gosh, it was coming down so hard he couldn't see past Don Quixote's nose. The stallion picked his way to the hitching post and Joseph swung down, swiping the snow from his eyes. How was he gonna see his new bride in all of this? He would bump into her before he ever set sight on her.

Don Quixote blew out his breath, as if he were warning his master to be cautious. Joseph looped one rein around the log post and rubbed his buddy's nose. "Don't you worry. Sure, I'm a sight overeager, but I sure would like a girl of my own. Watching my brother so danged happy is about to do me in."

Don Quixote stomped his front hoof, as if he had an opinion about why brother Nate was so happy these days. Joseph gave his hat a good tug. The stallion wasn't wrong. Sure, his brother was happy; he'd married the most beautiful woman in Mountain County and he went to bed with her every night. Not to be disrespectful, but at twenty-two, Joseph sure would have liked to be able to do the same with his own gorgeous wife.

And soon he would. He plowed through the deep snow on the platform steps and felt the rumble of the train through the soles of his boots. Hadn't his ma and pa been real busy writing and receiving letters the last few weeks? That's exactly the way it had gone when they had found his sister-in-law Savannah. Ma and Pa had been the ones to bring her out to marry Nate. Nate hadn't known a thing of it. He thought he was picking up a package for the folks—that was until Savannah stepped foot off the west-bound train.

And guess what? His ma had sent him to town to pick up a package. As he tromped closer he could see the faint splash of the train's red boiler through the snowfall. The westbound train. He wouldn't be surprised at all if an unbelievably lovely woman stepped off that train and into his arms. With no mar-riageable females his age in these parts, a person could under-stand why he was so eager.

"That you, Joe?" A voice called out from one of the package cars.

Joseph squinted. He could just make out a form in the shadowed compartment. "Howdy, Roberts. It's good to see the train is still running."

"So far." The baggage man swung into sight with a box under his arm. "You never know what's up ahead of us. The summit might be snowed over and we'll be backing down the grade to spend the night here."

"I hope you get through." It was a problem whenever the snow fell so hard: the trains stopped coming until the tracks could be cleared. He thought of the "package" likely to get off the train. Good thing she hadn't been stranded some-where. He might not know anything about her, but he knew one thing. Ma wanted pretty grandchildren, so she was likely to pick out an awful pretty gal.

No complaint there. Joseph knocked snow from his hat brim. "Good luck to you, Roberts—"

"Don't forget this." He gave the box he carried a toss.

Joseph caught it. A package. How about that?

"For your ma," the baggage handler explained. "Give her my respects."

"Sure thing." Joseph hiked the box under his arm. How about that for a coincidence? He hardly gave it much thought because he saw a slim shadow up ahead of him. The snow veiled her, but she was a petite, delicate lady with one of those fashionable ruffled skirts. She wore a bonnet that hid most of her profile from him. He knew it was her. Joy lit him up down deep.

Now, most fellas didn't go about letting their ma pick out a wife for them, but he had bought one of those heart-in-hand magazines not long ago and read all the advertisements from women looking for a new life. He had scratched his head, not knowing where to start. Looked like now he wouldn't have to puzzle it out.

"Howdy, miss?" He used his most polite voice. "Are you looking for the Brooks family?"

"Why, yes I am." She turned toward him in one slow swirl. He made out the sweet oval shape of her face, a delicate chin and a rosebud mouth before the snow gusted between them, leaving her once again veiled to his sight. If she was half as pretty as her voice, then he was one lucky man.

His heart rocketed around his chest. He fumbled for his hat brim, but his fingers felt stupid and he had to reach for it twice. He swept it off, using what manners he had. "I'm Joseph Brooks. I've come to take you in to town."

"Joseph." She said his name with a smile.

He liked how that sounded. His blood warmed just thinking of hearing his name on her voice in the dark of night. His chest filled with satisfaction. Gee, but this kept getting better and better.

"I read about you in your mother's letters."

"I expect you have." That pleased him. Ma was good at writing long-winded letters, so it had to be a good sign that this woman knew so much about him and was *still* glad to meet him. "I'm at a loss, miss, seeing as how I don't know your name."

"It's Clara. Clara Woodrow."

The snow thinned, allowing him a better glimpse of her face. Big, wide-set eyes stared up at him, unguarded and blueberry blue. A man could lose all common sense staring into those eyes. Air lodged midway in his chest, and he felt the earth tilt. "That's a pretty name for a pretty lady."

"You are a flatterer, Mr. Brooks, but I shall forgive you." Her voice was gentle with a smile in it. "I can see I will have to have my wits about me whenever you are near."

"Yes, but I am harmless, I swear it." A cold arrow of snow slapped against his cheek. He shook his head, suddenly realizing he was standing in the middle of the train platform in a snowstorm. The rumbling idle of the engine, the crunch of passersby in the snow and the bite of the wind had faded and remained in the far distance. All his thoughts and senses seemed held by her.

"Are those your bags?" he asked of the shadows slumped a few paces beyond. When she nodded, he squared his shoulders and did the manly thing: he took care of her. "Let me fetch those for you. I suppose you'll be staying at the hotel here in town?"

"The hotel? Why, no. I was led to believe Mrs. Brooks had a separate living area for—" She hesitated. "For me."

"A separate living area?" He hefted up the two rather tattered satchels, careful not to drop Ma's package. "She must mean the maid's quarters."

"Yes, that's it."

"Well, if that's what she said, I had best get you home." He flashed her a grin. "Come with me. I have a horse waiting.

It's too bad it's so late or I could hire a sleigh from the livery stable. Is horseback all right?"

"Yes, I am simply grateful that you have come, Mr. Brooks. I had fixed in my mind that I would have to ask directions of some kind soul and simply walk until I found your home."

"Walk? No, it's much too far. We live miles out of town."

"Then I'm doubly grateful you are here." She bowed her head against the resistant wind and followed the wide-shouldered, strapping Mr. Brooks through the drifted snow on the wide platform, a question troubling her. "How did you know I would be here?"

"My mother knew." He held out his hand. "Careful here, the snow is deep and it's hard to see the steps."

"Thank you." What a kind man. She was not used to this brand of treatment. Her gloved fingertips brushed his broad palm, and through the leather of his driving glove and the wool of her mitten, electricity jolted up her arm and straight to her heart. The step beneath her shoe felt strangely buoyant and she was glad for his steadying hand helping her to keep her balance.

"Are you okay there?" he drawled in his pleasant, smoky baritone.

"Y-yes." She had no explanation for what had happened. The moment passed and she was on the ground without remembering getting down the rest of the steps. All she could register was Joseph Brooks taking her by the elbow. He guided her through the hail of driving snow and into the wind shadow next to a big bay horse.

"Ma should have told me to bring one of the geldings for you."

Now that she was close enough without the snow between them, she could see he was charmingly handsome. The broad rim of his Stetson framed his rugged face to perfection. He had a high intelligent forehead, or at least she imagined so behind the fall of his longish brown hair. His eyes were dark and full of good humor. His nose was a masculine slope, not too sharp and not too big, just right for his granite face.

He would look imposing, she decided, if not for the warm ready grin that seemed to permanently shape his mouth. A dimple sat in his chin like a cherry on a sundae, topping off what was perfection. Not that she should be thinking this way about her possible employer's son.

At least, she hoped she had a chance for the job. *Desperate* was a word she didn't like to use, but with less then ten dollars in her pocket she could not be called anything else. She had come here on chance alone, and she wasn't the most optimistic of girls.

He hung the handles of her satchels over the saddle horn. "Do you know how to ride, Miss Clara?"

"No, sir." There had been no need living in Chicago, where she could easily walk wherever she needed to go. Walking was probably not something she could easily do here. There had been so many tiny towns along the railroad line through the western territories, she had done her best to imagine what it might be like to live in a place like this, remote and wild, surrounded by nature instead of people and buildings. Trees were everywhere she could see, tall, white-mantled sentries guarding the street.

"Do you at least know how to keep your seat?" His eyes had slight, pleasant crinkles in the corners as if he spent a lot of his life laughing. He must be the sort who looked on the bright side of things.

She liked that in a man. "Mr. Brooks, I have to confess. I've never been on a horse. I don't know how to drive, either."

"Then I shall teach you." He secured the satchels and package to his saddle. "You are going have to get used to riding and driving if you plan to spend any time with me."

"Then I'll look forward to it." Why she said such a thing, she couldn't rightly say, but he didn't seem to think less of her for agreeing with him. She wasn't flirting, although it felt that way when Mr. Brooks grinned at her. Surely the fine man was not interested in a housemaid or such a plain girl. She had no illusions about that. Her mother had told her often enough, and there had been Lars who—

She tamped down that thought. Do not think of him, she ordered herself.

"Give me your hand." Mr. Brooks had swung up into his saddle and looked mighty imposing on the top of his powerful horse. He removed his boot from the stirrup. "Put your foot here and I'll help you up. We'll make a western girl out of you yet."

"How do you propose to do that? Surely there is more to it than horseback riding."

"Why, who knows? I just might have to marry you."

That surprised her. She gasped, not knowing what to say. Perhaps he felt this, too, this unusual and instant pull between them. She blushed furiously. "You must stop teasing. I'm not the kind of woman who just accepts any man's proposal."

"No, I don't suppose you are." He laughed, and the warm rich sound was as cozy as butter melting. He held out his hand. "Proposals aside, think you would like to come home with me?"

"I suppose. I need to stay somewhere." She tried to keep a straight face but somehow they were laughing together.

Snow tumbled against her face as she laid her hand against his palm. His fingers wrapped around hers, vibrant with strength and vitality. Longing filled her as she hiked up her skirt ruffles and slipped her toe into the leather stirrup. Suddenly she was airborne, the ground falling away and the snow blinding her. She settled on Mr. Brooks's lap, safely tucked in his arms. His grin was wide and tempting and her heart gave a little flip-flop.

This was not what she had in mind when he'd offered to share his horse with her. She shifted, but that didn't seem to improve the situation. Surely this was not the way to impress her future employer, by showing up in her son's embrace. Perhaps it would be prudent to push him away, but something prevented her. Maybe it was the worsening beat of the storm making it impossible to speak, or the howling wind that would drown out her voice.

A warm sweep of rightness wrapped around her. She had been lonely for so long, and what a relief it was to finally feel in safe hands. There was something about Joseph Brooks she liked very much. It was almost as if she knew him from somewhere before. She didn't, of course. It was quite an odd sensation, but not as strange as the rock of the horse's first step that jarred through her. She gasped and reached out for something—anything—to hold on to.

Mr. Brooks. His arms held her tight and kept her from falling. "You're safe with me, Clara."

She didn't doubt that one bit. She blinked the snow from her lashes, leaned against the hard plane of his chest and felt the smallest seed of hope. The snow sharpened, driving at her like needles, and the wind blasted ice all the way to her bones. Let the wind blow, she thought, for here in his arms she felt as if no amount of cold or storm could diminish her chance for a new start.

"Look up and tell me what you think of your new home." His voice rumbled through her intimately, as his warm breath brushed her temple.

Home. Coziness bubbled through her, and she couldn't rightly say if it was due to the notion of having a place where she might belong. Perhaps it had more to do with the handsome man who was kissing-close. Her heart lurched. Her lips tingled, simply from his nearness.

"You can hardly see much because of the storm." His baritone vibrated pleasantly, invitingly. "But come dawn, you'll open your curtains to the prettiest sight in these parts. Next to you, of course."

"There you go, being charming again." What was she to do about the bold man? Oh, he was a gentleman, she could tell that about him. He had been nothing but proper on their long, unchaperoned ride together. He had held her politely and cordially, always respectful, even if she was seated on his lap and pressed dangerously close to his chest.

And if a measure of warmth flushed across her face, probably reddening her cheeks, she decided to stay in firm denial of it. She certainly was not attracted to her prospective employer's son. Really, and there was no reasonable chance he would be interested in her. She thought of her carefully patched dress and coat, and felt shabby.

There was nothing shabby about the view spreading out before her. Buffeted by snow, cloaked by night, the forest gave way to a stunning sweep of fenced meadows and gardens on a gently rising hillside. On the crest of that hill glowed the lamp-lit windows of an impressive home with the hint of a veranda and gables and two stories. No curtains covered the glass, and from where she sat in Joseph's arms she could plainly see a well-appointed parlor, a fire roaring in a river-rock hearth. A kindly looking salt-and-pepper-haired man reclined in a wingback chair, obviously enjoying the fire's warmth, studying his open newspaper with great seriousness.

"Is that your father?"

"Yep, that's my pa." Love warmed his voice, revealing him. This was not the kind of man she was used to, she suspected. Although she hardly knew him, it was plain to see the honest affection for his sire. "I suspect you know enough about him to know he would spend all day just like that if he could get away with it, reading newspapers by the fire. He cares about politics and the nation's happenings."

"I remember reading in your mother's letters that he receives quite a lot of newspapers by mail." One of her duties, should she get the job, would be to keep the newsprint piled in the parlor to a minimum and to fetch the mail when she was

in town on house errands, which would include several newspapers.

It was a lovely house, and she suspected it would be a
pleasant job. When she'd read Mrs. Brooks's letter of inquiry,
she hadn't imagined something so down-to-earth. The big
house looked comfortable rather than fancy, a family home
rather than a showy palace. This was not a wealthy family,
she suspected, but they did prosper.

"You look disappointed," he rumbled against her ear. "You
were expecting something better?"

"You mean richer?" She blinked snow from her eyelashes,
because the burn in her eyes could not be from emotion. "Yes.
I was afraid of not meeting expectations. Of not fitting in. The
last job I had was cleaning for several taverns near my house."

"We're normal folk. You'll see that when you meet my
ma."

The seeds of hope within her took root. This was truly a
chance for bettering her life, much more than she had dared
to imagine. She could see the polished, sensible dining table
through the pristine windows, and candlelight flickering off
gleaming crystal and silver. What a boon to work in such a
room, rubbing wax into the lustrous cherry wood and taking
care of this family's beloved home.

*Maybe I have a chance here. Maybe I can find happiness
here.* Her head felt fuzzy as she realized Joseph was pressed
against her, his hands encircling her upper arms. Heat blazed
through the layers of his gloves and her garments, and again
she felt that strange blast of electricity telegraphing down her
spine and into her toes.

"I won't let you fall." His promise shivered through her,
and the icy chill fled from the wind as did the sting of the
snow on her face. He lifted her powerfully from his lap and
for an instant she was airborne, anchored only by his touch.

Chapter Two

Her patched shoes landed lightly in the snow, and she sank to her ankles. Joseph's touch remained like a brand. His lips brushed her hair as he spoke quietly to her, as if they were in a crowded room instead of alone in the night. "Let me take you to your rooms. I should introduce you to Ma straightaway, but maybe you would rather get settled. You seem anxious, Clara."

"I'm trying not to show it."

"You have nothing to worry about here." He dismounted, landing beside her, an impressive shadow in the deepening twilight. "Aside from the occasional mountain lion or bear, that is."

"That's something I haven't had to worry about before." Her skin tingled strangely where his touch had been. She rubbed her arms, but it didn't leave. Snow tumbled from her cap, however, and slapped against her cheek. "Are my rooms far?"

"Down the path on this side of the house." He looped the horse's reins around a garden post. "It's hard to see from here. Don't worry. I will lead the way."

"Thank you." She felt breathless and her knees were strangely weak. When he touched her sleeve, a signal to follow him, her stomach flip-flopped and fell down to her toes. Surely she was not affected by the man. She had grown too sensible to be attracted to the male gender. Surely this was all simply the aftereffects of traveling long endless days on very few meals.

She trailed after him in the snow, stepping into the footprints he left. Snow soaked through her shoes, and the wind groaned and creaked through tall, dark trees, almost invisible in the storm. Surely this was not a portent of things to come, a sign she had made a mistake.

"This is where we spent many a warm summer's evening." He paused, fondness warming his voice and chasing away the chill in the night. "My ma has a fondness for the roses that bloom here, up against the house. I like the cooling breeze off the mountains. Keeps me comfortable while I whittle."

"What do you carve?" She caught a glimpse of the shadowed railing of a wide porch before they passed beyond the house. She imagined a family pleasantly gathered there. "How many of your brothers are still at home?"

"I'm surprised Ma didn't tell you. There's just my oldest brother and me, now that Nate has moved out and married."

If every one of them were as nice as Joseph, then what a lucky girl she would be. *If* she got the position. She tried to picture what it would be like working in the comfortable house. Much better than in a saloon, that was for certain. "Could you tell me if there have been many other applicants?"

"Applicants? That's a funny way to put it." He continued along the pathway, with the tall house on one side and tall trees on the other. "I don't rightly know, as my ma is the one managing all this. But you are the only woman who's shown up."

"Truly?" What a relief. She released a pent-up breath and swiped a cold snowflake from her forehead. Perhaps not many women would want to travel so far into the remote wilderness for a job. That might work in her favor when she approached Mrs. Brooks for employment. "I've come so far. You have no notion what good news that is. I feel like the luckiest person on this mountain."

"No, that can't be true. I'm the lucky one. I'm lucky because you're here."

Now that was truly puzzling. Her step faltered. Why, it was almost as if he thought she was someone else. How strange. "Me? Mr. Brooks, surely you are not trying to charm me again?"

"Can't blame a fellow for trying, can you?" His boots thudded on wooden steps and scuffed across a snowy porch. The darkness was too thick here, where a porch roof blocked even the hardest snowfall. "Come on in. Careful of the steps. They are a tad slick."

A match flared, guiding her way. She hardly noticed the quaint little porch before she glided through the opened doorway, drawn by the sight of Joseph touching the flame to a crystal lamp's wick. The light caught and grew, tossing a golden glow over the snow-dappled man. In full light, he was highly pleasing. His hair was raven, not brown as she'd first thought, and his eyes a dazzling midnight blue. He stood straight and strong, tantalizingly manly and crowned by his Stetson. His wide shoulders cut an impressive line.

All reason slid right out of her head at the sight. A lifetime's worth of vocabulary vanished. A strange longing blew into her as if borne on the wind. Never had she been affected by a man like this. Not even Lars, whom she had once hoped would propose to her.

She would be wise to remember how that turned out.

"Don't stand there in the cold." He replaced the crystal chimney with a *clink*. "Come in out of the draft and explore a bit. I reckon you will want to look around while I get a fire started."

"Yes. Thank you kindly." Perhaps she sounded so breathless because she was worried. What if coming here out of the blue was a mistake? What if Mrs. Brooks didn't want her? Then where would she go? How would she be able to improve her life? If only those worries would fade as easily as the shadows. Joseph lit a second lamp, bathing the room in a golden glow.

What a cozy cabin. She gaped in wonder at the smooth honeyed log walls and the green gingham curtains at several large windows. A horsehair sofa looked deliciously comfortable and faced a well-cushioned wingback chair. Either would be a perfect place to do her needlework at the end of a long day. A small round oak table, sporting one of the gleaming lamps, tossed light into the recesses of a tidy kitchen, where a cookstove sat dark and silent in the corner. Sunshine ought to come in through the window, making it a good place to sit and read in the morning. She closed out the remembered image of the dirt-floor shanty she and her mother had rented last. It was hard to believe that she might be able to live in such a fine and pretty cabin.

Joseph knelt by the stone hearth in the sitting area and struck another match. She couldn't explain why her eyes kept him in sight as she spun in a slow circle, taking in the empty shelves on one wall and the cushioned window seat next to the open door. It was as if her senses wanted to stay firmly on him and against her will.

"It won't take long until the cabin is toasty warm." Joseph stood, blowing out the match. Fire crackled in the hearth and the orange light danced over him playfully, accenting his high cheekbones and carved jaw. "You stay here and thaw, and I'll go fetch your things."

"No, I'm fit as a fiddle and perfectly able to—"

"Miss Clara." His reprimand came kindly. "Do I look like a man who lets a woman do the heavy lifting to you?"

"No." The truth was, she thought he looked like the best kind of man, who stood for what was right. Maybe that's why her pulse pitter-pattered as she watched him tip his hat politely and hike into the bitter cold. She circled around the sofa toward the fireplace to keep better sight of him. Hard not to notice his good-natured stride as he shouldered into the dark storm and disappeared into it.

Fine, so I like the man. There was no harm in liking him.

She stripped off her gloves, hardly aware of the blessed heat, and held her hands out to the growing fire. But liking him was as far as she was prepared to go. She was too practical a woman these days to believe in love.

While greedy flames pressed away the icy cold air, she took time to study the room. There were details she hadn't noticed at first glance. Now with the firelight, she could see empty shelves along the inside wall waiting to be filled with knickknacks and books. There was a window seat beneath the nearby window.

When she peeked into the bedroom, she spotted a real feather mattress on a carved, four-poster frame. A mirror attached to a bureau reflected faintly back at her.

Why, I look a fright. She hardly recognized herself. Her wool hat drooped with melting snow, her hair was falling from her pins and tangled dreadfully, her face chapped pink from the hard cold and rough winds. Wet patches of snowmelt clung to her threadbare coat as if someone had tossed a bucket of sludge at her. Her shabbiness showed. She could not expect to be hired looking like a ragamuffin on a street corner.

Ashamed, she removed her hat and her hairpins. Her honey-gold hair tumbled past her shoulders in disarray. Her fingers itched for her brush and comb, but they were tucked safely in one of her satchels. She pocketed her pins and ran her fingers through her hair. Maybe she would have enough time to freshen up and look more presentable before—

The door banged open, answering her question. Joseph tromped in, snowy and strapping, her satchels in hand. He closed the door with his foot, his gaze raking over her with such force it was hard not to feel self-conscious. Her hand went to her hair and she blushed. Breathless again and her knees going weak, she had nothing else to blame it on this time. Nothing, that was, save for Joseph.

"You have to forgive me," she found herself saying, stepping away from the bedroom. "I'm a bit windblown."

"That happens a lot around here, too." He lumbered closer, his gaze never leaving her face. "I hope that doesn't change your mind. I would hate to think you're eager to catch the next train out of here and head home."

"I cannot do that. I have no home to return to." Too honest, she admonished, but it was too late to take back the words. Spoken, they hung in the air between them like the crackling cold.

"I'm sorry to hear that. My sister-in-law, Savannah, came out here to marry my brother because she had lost her family and her home. I reckon something like that has happened to you?" Caring gleamed in his dark blue eyes like a rare jewel.

Compassion. That wasn't something she found often in her world. That made her like Mr. Joseph Brooks even more. He clearly had a big heart. "My ma ran off the day before our rent was due. I had to sell everything she left behind, even my best clothes."

"That had to be difficult." He set the satchels down near the bedroom door, but he only had eyes for her. "Were you put out on the street?"

"A neighbor lady took me in, although I paid her in trade."

"What kind of trade?" he asked.

"She needed dishes, and Ma hadn't taken the ironware with her." She hung her hat to dry on a nail on the mantel. Firelight washed over her, highlighting the worn places on her coat. "If not for your mother's letters, I'm not sure what would have become of me. Work is hard to find these days, and to have a place to come to, why, I can't tell you what that means."

"I'm glad, too." He couldn't remember anything meaning so much. His heart had surely never ached like this before. The trip home had certainly affected him. Nothing in all the world could ever be nicer than holding Miss Clara Woodrow in his arms. If he had ever known anything closer to perfection, then the memory of it slipped from his mind, paling in comparison. He was close enough to see the melting glisten of snow in her silken hair and to breathe in her feminine, rose-water scent. She had perfect creamy skin, delicately formed cheekbones and a cute sloping nose. Eyes sad with hardship met his.

He'd caught enough of a glimpse of her on the shadowy platform to know she was pretty, but right here in full light, he was arrested. Captivated as if she had cast an enchantment upon him. The most beautiful woman he'd ever seen, beyond all doubt. No, in fact, beautiful was too mild a word to use. Amazement left him speechless; all he could do was to drink in her splendor.

A wisp of honey-blond hair caressed the remarkable curve of her cheek. Her lips looked as soft as rose petals, and, why, the rest of her! Not to be disrespectful, but she sure made a lovely figure with the firelight caressing her womanly curves. The air whooshed out of his lungs. A whole bushel full of caring tied around his chest like a great big red ribbon. By golly, he was the luckiest man in all of Mountain County. There was no doubt about that.

"That was one cold ride." He liked being close to her. The fire's warmth licked at his trouser legs. "Are you getting warmer?"

"A little."

"Let me help you with your coat." He reached to loosen her top button. "I want you to be comfortable here."

"Thank you, Mr. Brooks." Her voice was breathy and tremulous.

"Call me Joseph."

"Joseph. Aren't you being a little—"

"Improper?" His knuckle grazed the coat's fabric, not far from the swell of her bosom, and he blushed and carefully worked at the next button. "I'm simply trying to take care of you. Least I can do, because you came so far. I'm glad you're here, Miss Clara."

"I am, too," she admitted. He mesmerized her, that's what was going on. This man had so much wholesome charm and manly charisma that a girl like her with little experience would, of course, be captivated by him. Who wouldn't be? Judging by his easy manner, he probably had beautiful women falling at his feet right and left. It was a wonder he wasn't married. Perhaps he was the sort who enjoyed being a bachelor with many girls on a string.

That explained why he was a tad forward. "I desperately want your mother—Mrs. Brooks—to like me."

"No need to worry." He loosened another button.

Why was she breathing so fast? Her heart fluttered behind her ribs as if it had dissolved into a dozen butterflies. "You sound awfully certain. She must have gone through many letters of application."

"That's a funny way to put it, but I'm sure she did." He loosened another button. "Ma will be enchanted with you."

"You sound far too certain. She hasn't met me yet." *That's* what she should be concentrating on, getting this job and not on the man before her. She stepped away, intent on breaking his strange effect on her, and worked the last button free.

"Ma is the kind of lady who loves everyone." He circled behind her, unrelenting.

"I want this to work out, I truly do." Her confession rolled off her tongue before she could stop it. She winced, hearing the ring of her far too honest words in the stillness between them. Now she was the one being too forward, speaking as if she already had the job.

Joseph did not seem to mind. His leather gloves gripped the back of her neck. His was a tender touch; his voice when he spoke was like satin. "I have a good feeling. I want this to work, too."

They must be sorely hurting for a maid. And Joseph Brooks was too charming for his own good. There was something amiss, something out of place she could not put her finger on because of his touch. He smoothed her long hair out of the way, his touch almost like a caress. Very inappropriate, and she opened her mouth to say so, but not a single word emerged.

As he tugged her coat off her shoulders, she was aware of every solid inch of him. The strange jolt returned, zinging through her like a lightning strike. Her pulse screeched to a halt, and it was as if her heart would never beat again.

Whatever this strange, emotional pull was, she had to resist it. She pressed away from him just a tad, steeling her spine. Her face heated and she didn't know where to look. It would be very easy to come to care about Joseph.

"Are you blushing?"

"I'm not used to such attention."

"Then you had best get used to it, pretty lady." His baritone knelled rich and intimate. "I know you are worried, but I'm not. I'm glad you came, Clara. I can't think of anyone better."

How sweet. "Except for the fact that you don't know me at all. I could be a laze-about."

"Beauty and wit, too. I think you and I are going to get along just fine." His hand brushed her cheek. "I will be good to you, I swear it. I'll build us a place of our own."

"What?" A place? As in, a house? Had she heard him correctly? And why was the floor spinning? The cabin seemed to tilt at an odd angle. "A place of our own?"

"Yes, I know it's soon to talk of such things, but we both know why you're here, Clara." His gloved finger folded a lock of hair behind her ear, the gentlest of all touches, and he towered over her, pure gentleman and dazzlingly tender. "I'm already sweet on you. I know it in my gut. I just know. We are going to be the happiest married couple in these parts."

"M-married?" she stuttered. No, surely there was something wrong with her hearing. Perhaps it was the aftereffect of train travel or from choosing to skip the noon meal to save the cost of the food. Any moment now her mind was going to stop sloshing around and settle down to working correctly, and Joseph was going to start making sense to her. "Why would you think that?"

"You're right. I'm getting ahead of myself. It's a fault of mine." He took her coat from her; bits of melting snow shook loose and fell to the floor. "I promise to give you all the time you need. If I'm not mistaken, here's Ma now. I'll let you two get acquainted while I stable my horse. He shouldn't be left standing in this weather."

"No, of course not, but—" The long last look he threw at her felt like stardust's gentle glaze. She felt a magical warmth surround her, something she could not touch or see but felt all the same. Places in her heart came alive, places she never knew were there before.

Transfixed, she watched the wide-shouldered man hang her coat on a peg by the door and open it to a pleasant, apple-faced woman with her hair piled loose and tall on her head. The two exchanged words; Joseph strode out into the dark. Clara stood as still as an end table in the parlor, her pulse thumping bizarrely. His bold comments rang in her mind. *I just might have to marry you. I'll build us a place of our own. We both know why you're here, Clara.*

"Miss Pennington? Hello, there. I'm Mary Brooks." The pleasant woman tapped closer, wrapped in a fine cashmere shawl and wearing a tasteful brown velveteen dress. Nothing but kindness and happiness marked her round, pretty face. "I saw Joseph walk past the kitchen window with you in tow. I'm delighted you decided to come a bit early. How lovely to meet you."

Miss Pennington? Suddenly it all made sense. They *were* expecting someone else. Someone else had already been hired for the position and, by the sound of things, had some relationship with Joseph. He'd simply mistaken her for Miss Pennington. That was why he behaved far too familiarly. Her ears began to buzz, disappointment settling like a weight in her chest. "Mrs. Brooks, I'm so pleased to meet you, but my name is—"

"That Joseph, putting you in the maid's quarters. What was he thinking?" Mary Brooks threw out both arms and wrapped Clara in the sweetest, tightest hug she'd ever imagined. A mother's embrace, welcoming and comforting. "You must come to the main house with us immediately. I've had the cook set an extra plate at the table. Your room should be ready in a bit, as we are currently without a second maid. How were your travels? My, you are such a dear thing. As pretty as a picture."

Overwhelmed, Clara could only search in vain for words. A terrible falling began somewhere in her midsection, and it felt as if it took all her hopes with it. Mary Brooks was not expecting a maid. No, not at all.

"What did you think of my Joseph? Isn't he a dear?" Mary squeezed Clara's hands gently, telegraphing both need and joy. The mother's love sparkling within her was impossible to miss. "I think you two would be perfect together."

"I'm sorry, but you were expecting a bride for him?" She couldn't say why she felt desolate, but at least some of the pieces were starting to fit.

"Yes, dear. Of course. Isn't that what those months of corresponding between the two of us were about?" Mary's face drew into a perfect visage of concern. "Don't tell me we are not what you expected, that you're disappointed in us? I know you are used to many conveniences, Boston is surely a fine city, but I assure you, a remote location like this has much to offer. And there is no finer man anywhere than my son."

"I'm sure that is all true." Her voice sounded wooden. All Joseph's kindness toward her and this woman's motherly concern would vanish as soon as she said the words. But they must be said. "I am not Miss Pennington. My name is Clara, and I've come for the maid's job, if it's still open."

"The maid's job? I don't understand, child."

Her knees wobbled, and beneath her mittens her palms went damp. She refused to let herself wonder what Joseph would think. She refused to acknowledge any feelings toward him at all. This was the moment of truth. The reason she had sold everything she owned to travel far from everything she knew. "Nan Woodrow is my mother. You had been corresponding with her about a position in your home."

"Yes, of course. Where is she? Did something happen to her?"

"You could say that. My ma isn't the most reliable of people. I'm afraid she ran off."

"Ran off? You've come all this way, and alone?"

She nodded miserably. What Mrs. Brooks must be thinking! Shame crawled through her, but she firmed her chin. "I assure you I am nothing like my mother. I work hard and I need this job. Please, would you consider hiring me?"

Chapter Three

Joseph swiped the towel one last time across Don Quixote's withers. "What do you think of Clara?"

The stallion stomped his right hoof and tossed his head.

"That's what I think, too. Woo-wee." He patted his horse's neck. "Looks like there are going to be a few changes around here."

Don Quixote whinnied low in his throat as if in complete understanding.

"I wonder how things are going up at the house." He closed the stall gate and pried open the grain barrel. He grabbed the scoop and filled it, pleasantly recalling just how good it had felt to cradle his betrothed against his chest. Mighty fine, indeed. "I bet Ma has Clara warming by the fire and talkin' her ears off."

Don Quixote didn't comment as he dove into his trough and gobbled up his tasty grain. After all, first things first.

"Yep, I bet that's how it's going. Clara and Ma are probably fast friends by now." He hardly remembered tossing the scoop back into the grain barrel and getting the lid down tight. Because every thought in his head centered on Clara—his wife-to-be. Emotion filled his chest, a feeling that was too embarrassing to say out loud. Recalling how she looked with the firelight caressing her skirts and the melted snow in her hair glistening like diamonds made the emotion in his chest double. Was he already in love with the girl?

"See you later, buddy." He couldn't remember ever being so eager to get back to the house and it wasn't because his stomach was grumbling, either. He buttoned up and grabbed Ma's package before heading outside. The cold blast of night air hardly troubled him as he closed the stable door tight and started the hike up the hillside. He felt as if he walked in summer sunshine. That's what love could do to a man.

Why, he couldn't remember a better evening. Hazy moonlight penetrated the thinning clouds and threw silver across his path like a hopeful sign. This late-season storm had nearly blown itself out. New leaves rustled on tree boughs as he trekked past, and snow dropped in chunks to the ground. He followed the darkly gleaming snow along the garden gate toward the house, knowing Miss Clara was inside.

Clara. What a fine lady. His chest puffed up with pride and something buttery warm and too wonderful to name. He couldn't say his boots touched the ground as he hiked along the wind shadow of the house. He almost turned around to see if he left any tracks in the snow behind him, but his attention turned toward the lit windows. Already his eyes hungered for her. His whole body tingled, remembering how dandy it had been to hold her in his arms. He sure would like to do that again.

He took the porch steps two at a time, already making plans in his head: the log house he intended to build with an appealing view of the Rockies' peaks and the mountainside below; all the fineries he wanted for his wife. No doubt she would want a fancy kitchen and a sewing room with a newfangled sewing machine and all the pretty things a woman required. He shook the snow off his clothes and stomped his boots, determined to take the best possible care of Clara, when he spied her through the kitchen window.

Golly, but she made a pretty picture standing there at the counter. He drank in the sight of her, as fragile as a porcelain doll but all woman. No doubt about that. Not to be disrespectful, but she had a very fine bosom. He tried not to think overmuch on her bosom for his face heated and he fumbled with the doorknob. He tumbled into the mudroom, losing sight of her. His heart, however, clutched the image of her close. As he peeled off his boots and coat and hung his hat up to dry, every fiber of him ached to see her again. The low melody of her voice rumbled pleasantly through the wall as she spoke with the cook.

What a fine lady, to be so polite to the help. She was down-to-earth. He liked that about her. That, and every single thing he knew about Clara Woodrow. Sure, he was falling awfully fast, but he had been looking forward to this day for a while. He hadn't expected an instant attraction to her; he had never experienced the like of it before. As he pushed open the door and burst into the kitchen, his gaze went only to her, to his Clara, turning from the steeping teapot to offer him one perfect smile.

His heart squeezed so hard it brought tears to his eyes. He had never beheld such perfection. In full light, her beauty paled next to the gentle goodness he saw shining within her. It outshone her significant outward beauty and made the faded pink calico dress she wore look like the finest gown. His entire being changed in that instant, heart and soul forever surrendered to her.

So this is what love is. He closed the door behind him, his world forever changed. Commitment and devotion filled him like water in a well, rising up until he brimmed with it. Fierce protective urges rolled through him, making him feel ten feet tall. He would do anything for her, give his life for her if he had to. He set the brown-wrapped package on the counter, a stone's throw from Clara. "I can't believe Ma let you escape her. I expect she's waiting for you in the parlor?"

"Yes, I believe she's taken up her needlework." Her shy smile touched her soft mouth, and she averted her eyes, turning to fuss with the tray on the counter in front of her. "Would you like some tea to warm you?"

"Why, I surely would." He was touched that she would be offering. Already she had slipped into the woman-of-the-house role. His chest swelled with happiness. That had to mean she felt this attraction, too. "Let me carry the tray for you."

"Oh, no. I couldn't let you do that. Let me wait on you." She might be soft-spoken, but she was no wilting flower. Determination deepened her blue eyes and sharpened the dainty curve of her finely carved chin.

"Fine. Have it your way." He would do anything to please her, and he liked that she wanted to take care of him, too. He could see their future, each taking care of the other. "I aim to please, pretty lady."

"There you go, flattering yet again." She added a third cup to the tray.

"I can't help myself." He chuckled, following her through the kitchen. "You bring out the worst in me."

"I suppose I shall simply have to get used to it."

"Yep, because I reckon it isn't going to get any better." For instance, there were plenty of flattering things he could offer as they strolled through the house together. The sway of her hips, subtle and terribly feminine, drew his gaze. She had tied back her hair into a single loose braid, and it framed her face like a golden cloud. She held herself with an inner grace, which made the serving tray she gripped with both hands look out of place. She was like a thoroughbred in a herd of donkeys.

"You seem more relaxed than when I first spotted you on the train platform." He had a thousand questions for her. He wanted to know everything about her. "I hope you come to feel at home."

"I already do," she confessed.

"Now that you see my folks are good people, and you've met me, you have to know—" He caught her elbow and drew her to a stop. "I'm going to do my best to make you happy."

"Happy? No, not me," she denied gently with a shake of her head.

"I would like to take you for a sleigh ride tomorrow." He kept right on talking. "Just you and me. Now, I know for your reputation, it is best if we're chaperoned, but I think we need to get to know each other better. After all, we have a future together, you and I—"

"Mr. Brooks, there's something I must tell you." The tray she held quaked enough to rattle the cups in their saucers. "I'm not who you think I am."

"What do you mean?" Tenderness rang in his voice. "You think I can't see who you are? A fine lady, fallen on hard times. The same thing happened to my sister-in-law, as I told you. I care about you, Clara, and I—"

"Joseph!" Mary interrupted, calling loudly from the next room. "Is that you? Have you finally come in from the stable? I've been waiting for you."

"I'm finally here, Ma." He rolled his eyes, looking sheepish. "She still scolds me as if I'm twelve. She can't help it. Come, let's go sit with her."

"Yes, she's no doubt waiting for her tea." She had no time to explain as he had already started in the direction of the parlor, only a few steps away. His fingertips around her arm seared through her garments like flame.

Why did this man affect her so? Whatever the reason, she would do best not to consider it. Joseph was now her employer's son, and the moment he realized it, his charming nature toward her would vanish. The bright admiration would dim from his eyes. She may as well brace herself for it.

She broke from his touch and carried the tray straight to the table beside Mary's rocking chair. The china clattered; the tea sloshed. As hired help, she tried not to listen to the con-

versation between parents and son. She lifted the teapot with
wooden fingers and poured.

"…what luck Clara came instead," Mary was saying.

Her face heated. She was not ashamed to work as a maid
for her living; it was a far better job than her last one, which
for all the long hours she worked barely paid the rent.
Stubborn pride held her up as she set down the pot and carried
the full cup, without sweetener as ordered, to the older Mr.
Brooks, who gazed over the top of his newspaper, listening
to the story.

"Come all the way from Illinois, did you?" he asked,
peering at her through his reading spectacles. He was a man
who worked hard for his living with callused hands, a burly
frame and a weathered face.

"Yes, sir," she murmured, trying not to listen to Mary's
final explanation. She returned to her tray and stirred two
sugars into the woman's tea.

"So that's how Miss Woodrow has come to work for us."
As quietly as those words were spoken, they thundered like
dynamite in Clara's mind. "She will be a fine addition. You
mind your manners, Joseph. We haven't had a young lady on
staff for quite some time."

"Yes, of course, Ma." His baritone sounded strained and
hollow.

Was that his disappointment she felt, or simply her own?
And why was she disappointed? She did not come here looking
for a charming man to romance her. She served Mrs. Brooks
her tea, careful to keep her back to the man standing near. Was
it her imagination or could she feel his gaze scorching her?

It's your imagination, Clara. It has to be. Now that he
knew who she was, he would not be trying to charm her. She
stirred honey into the final cup, per Mary's orders, hurting
strangely. She was not interested in a courtship. Love had not
treated her well. It was certainly not a consideration here. So,
why was her heart aching? Why couldn't she keep her head

down and her attention fixed on the cup and saucer she served him, instead of meeting his gaze?

Because a tiny, forgotten part of her wanted the fairy tale. Deep down, there lived a kernel of hope that there might be a true love meant only for her, a man who could see something special in the plain girl she was.

That man could never be Joseph, she reasoned. Surely, for now all he saw was a serving girl.

That's what she was, and she was proud of it. She grasped the empty tray, curtsied and padded out of the room. Glad for this job, she closed her ears to the rising conversation behind her. Sure, she liked Joseph. He was a likable man. But she had to be practical. She could not believe in impossible and foolish fairy tales.

She gladly left the room and bustled into the kitchen, ready to help with the rest of the meal preparations. It wasn't disappointment eking into her like frost in the night. She wouldn't let it be.

Joseph couldn't get over his shock. As he blew on his tea to cool it, his mother's words taunted him. "After all the letters I wrote to her mother, you'd think the woman would have shown more courtesy. That poor girl, with a mother like that! I'm sure Clara will suit us just fine."

So that's what all the writing and mailing of letters was about. A slight wind could blow him over. Stunned, he retreated to the sofa and settled on a cushion, stretched out his feet and took a swallow of hot tea.

"Seems like a girl in need," Pa said as he set down his paper with a crinkle. "I noticed three patches on her dress, and I was hardly looking."

"That's why I hired her on the spot, the poor dear. I didn't even check her references." Ma took up her embroidery hoop from her lap and began to stitch. "Can you believe she came the entire way by herself? And just eighteen years old."

"A shame she has no one to look out for her." Pa shook his head from side to side. "You did right in hiring her. She has an honest look. She'll do fine."

"I think so, too. She makes an excellent pot of tea." Ma squinted at her needlework, fussing with thread and needle before fastening her all-seeing gaze on him. "You will behave yourself, Joseph? Don't think I didn't notice you speaking alone with her."

"I will be nothing but a gentleman." His vow was a sincere one, but he wasn't sure if he had masked the disappointment weighing on him. Gosh, but he had been sure Clara had come to marry him. Well, the joke was on him. He had leaped to the wrong conclusions—him, and no one else.

"I hope you didn't leave my package in the barn again." Ma glanced up at him, censure still on her face, but a smile, too. "I have need of the embroidery thread I ordered."

His ma was a softy. Which was good luck for him. "I'll go fetch it from the kitchen. I—"

"No need." Clara's melodic voice surprised him. She padded nearly soundlessly into the room and set the small box on the table next to Ma's chair. Her skirts swirled at her ankles as she turned neatly. "Your cook said supper is ready for the table."

"Excellent. Thank you, Clara." Ma's needle dove through the fabric. "We'll be right along. Joseph, go—"

He knew that his mother was speaking to him, but could he make his ears work? No. They had seemed to malfunction right along with his eyes. His every sense felt harnessed to Clara as she waltzed from the room. The rustle of her petticoats, the lamplight turning her hair to spun gold, the remembered feeling of her in his arms and protecting her from the brunt of the arctic winds. He knew her skin smelled like freshly budding roses.

"Joseph!" Ma's admonishment was pure warning. "What did I say about that poor girl?"

"My thoughts were gentlemanly, Ma. Honest." Gee, a guy couldn't win. Was it his fault he was already sweet on her? He pushed off the sofa. "What did you want me to do?"

"Go fetch your brother. He's in the library."

"Figures." When he was in the house, Gabriel was hardly ever anywhere else. Joseph strode from the room, just as his father muttered, "Five patches, Mary. That girl is in hard straits."

Why hadn't he noticed the patches? And why was it bothering him? He couldn't accept that Clara wasn't meant for him. The steely devotion in his heart was real. The lightness he felt from her smile was no fabrication. Instead of heading down the hall, he back-trailed and pushed open the kitchen door. The clatter of pots and the clink of dishes met him, along with a lot of steam as the cook poured the water off a kettle of boiling potatoes.

"Hurry, girl!" Mrs. O'Neill, the cook, screeched. "I'll not get blamed if the potatoes are mealy!"

"Yes'm." Clara was a flash of pink as she raced toward the basin with a bowl for the potatoes.

He let the door swing closed. He doubted she'd noticed him. Doubted she would appreciate an interruption. Pa was right. Judging by the look of things, she needed the work. He remembered how anxious she'd been when she'd asked about his mother and the letters of application. It all made sense now as he trekked down the hallway. Maybe he had imagined Clara's sweet interest in him right along with everything else.

His knees went weak, and he grabbed the wall for support. His senses, attuned to her, made out the pad of her nearby gait. Probably carrying the potatoes to the dining room. More footsteps joined her. The other maid and the chef's assistant, both hurrying.

Maybe now was as good a time as any to pull her aside. He poked his head around the doorway. The sight of willowy Clara placing a second bowl on the table next to the steaming potatoes made the devotion residing within him double. Yes, there were tidy patches on her dress made of the same fabric, and the cuffs of her sleeves were threadbare and the edge of her collar starting to fray. He could see that now.

But there was something else. Something he could not deny. He had never seen a lovelier sight. She stuck a serving spoon into the bowl, positioning it just right. Lamplight framed her like a blessing, and his heart gave one final, slow thump before it tumbled out of his chest, falling endlessly.

She was the one. He wanted to earn her love. He wanted to be the man who took care of and provided for her, who made her smile all the day long. And as for other things he wanted to do with her, well, that made him blush. As he'd promised his mother, he would be a gentleman. And he would, even in his thoughts. But that didn't stop his blood from heating or the tenderness from doubling within his soul.

Clara whirled on her heels to return to the kitchen, but she must have sensed his presence. Her eyes went wide and her rose-pink mouth shaped into a surprised O. High color swept across her porcelain features. Was she angry with him? Could she somehow know what he'd been thinking—or, rather, trying not to think? Dark nights spent together, tucked cozily beneath the bedclothes, peeling off her nightgown and leaving a trail of kisses—

Hell, that is not gentlemanly, Joe. He squared his shoulders, drawing himself up straight. He could control his thoughts better than that, right? He focused on her pale face, weary with exhausting travel. She appeared vulnerable and more fragile than he'd realized. He wanted to brush a stray curl behind her ear and gather her in his arms. She was a mere slip of a woman, petite and frail-boned, and he tried not to notice her lush womanly curves. Gosh, it wasn't easy to stay mannerly when it came to her.

"Perhaps we could talk." She broke the silence, circling around the table with a swish of her skirts. "I think it would be best to clear the air between us."

"Gee, that doesn't sound good for me."

"No, and I'm sorry for it." As she waltzed nearer, he spotted the tremble of her chin, and her hands, terribly small when compared to his, clenched into fists.

Perhaps she had been able to sense the direction his earlier thoughts had been taking. Embarrassed, heat stretched tight across his face and he let his chin sink a notch. He couldn't say he didn't notice the gentle curve of her neck, lovely and elegant, and the rise of her bosom which was deeply fascinating, or the tiny cinch of her waist—

"Joseph, I know what you're thinking." Her hushed alto caressed over him, as if with understanding and not censure.

"I doubt it." If she did, she wouldn't be so calm. He fought the urge to reach out and stroke his thumb along the satin of her cheek.

"I can only apologize. I knew something was amiss." She stopped, her hands uncurling at her sides in a helpless gesture. "You were there to meet the train, for one thing. I knew your mother wasn't expecting me, but I let myself think perhaps you met prospective employees at the train as a matter of course. Perhaps I was unsure of being alone in a strange town, and you were—"

"Accommodating? Friendly? Eager to help?" He offered her a smile.

"Yes." Relief slipped off her in a visible wave. "I'm relieved it's all been straightened out, and you know the truth about me. I know I'm just the hired help, but I don't want any strain between us. You have been kind to me, even though you thought I was someone else."

"I only ever thought you were you." He shrugged helplessly. "I'm glad I was there to fetch you from the train, Clara. I would hate to think you would have made that long walk here alone and in the cold. I'm sorry for how forward I was. I reckon you think the worst of me."

"Not even close. I understand." Her shy smile said more

than words ever could. The pinch of sadness around her eyes, the way she took a step backward, putting distance between them, the hitch in her words as she turned away. "Goodbye, Joseph."

She didn't mean goodbye, as in she was leaving. But in that she thought there would be no further contact between them. She had a job to do and a position within the house. And his mother would not be happy if he started courting the hired help.

But his heart had already chosen. When she walked away, she took his whole world with her. Standing as if in the dark, he had never seen his path in life more clearly.

Chapter Four

This was truly a good job, Clara realized as she stopped scrubbing the outhouse floor—the fifth of the morning—to dunk the brush into the nearby bucket of sudsy water. While this wasn't the most pleasant of tasks, she was happy working for Mrs. Brooks. She stretched her back as she dunked the brush again, taking a moment to glance over her shoulder at the white-capped mountains spearing straight up into a cloudy sky. Truly a beautiful sight. Tiny snowflakes danced and swirled nearly weightless to the ground. A great peace filled the vast spaces of mountainside and valleys. Joseph had been right when he'd told her it was the prettiest sight.

Joseph. Her chest gave a strange hitch whenever she thought of him. He had charmed her with his kindness, in spite of her better judgment. She grasped the brush, bent over and returned to her work, rubbing circles on the floorboards until her shoulder hurt.

You don't want romance, Clara, she reminded herself, so why was she missing him? There was nothing left to say. His flattery had always been meant for another woman. No doubt the mysterious Miss Pennington was an accomplished, lovely young lady from a good family. Just as she should be, for

Joseph was a kind man. He deserved a nice wife. That's what she wanted for him. Really.

So why did loss weigh inside her, as cold as the morning's wind? On her hands and knees, she backed out of the outhouse, scrubbing as she went. Her shoes hit snow, then her shins, then her knees. When visions of Joseph Brooks entered her mind, she polished them right out the same way she buffed the floorboards with a clean towel.

Her work done, she gathered up her supplies. The scent of soap and the dried lavender sprigs she'd hung on the wall made it pleasant. Pleased with a job well done, she reached for the door to close it. This was the life she had, and she was glad for it. She wasn't lonely for a certain man's low-throated chuckle, she thought as she turned on her heels and heard the steely *clink-clop* of horseshoes.

Through the snow-laden evergreen boughs she caught sight of a bay horse and a small black sleigh. Her spine melted vertebra by vertebra even before the driver came into sight. Joseph with his brawny shoulders and dependable smile.

The youngest Mr. Brooks, she reminded herself stubbornly. Seeing him again was like the daylight bleeding from the sky, leaving only darkness. She straightened her shoulders, digging deep inside for as much dignity as she could muster.

"'Morning, Miss Woodrow." He drew the horse to a halt and tipped his hat brim. "How are you on this fine Saturday morning?"

"Miss, now, is it?" She gripped the pail's handle tightly and waded in his direction. "A little more than twelve hours ago you mentioned marriage."

"True. I'm the sort of man who likes to get right to the point." How dashing he looked seated in a small sleigh. A black wool coat hugged his magnificent shoulders and emphasized the manly strength of his chest. His Stetson caught tiny, airy snowflakes, and his dimpled smile shone as confidently as it had last night. It was just as well that everything between them had changed.

"A mistaken point," she corrected him, coming to a stop beside his sleigh. "As I was not your betrothed."

"Not yet."

Why was she laughing? "So, is that why you've come? To practice your charm on me until your fiancée arrives?"

"Am I charming you?"

Only by the flash of his midnight eyes. Clara steeled her spine and set her jaw with determination. "I don't find you charming in the least."

"Oh? Then I shall have to try harder." He hopped to his feet, so that all six feet of him towered over her, impressive and breath stealing. "Are you wondering what I'm doing here?"

"Yes, as I've sure you have plenty to keep you occupied. Don't you help your father with the ranch?"

"Yes, and my morning work with him is done. I have some spare time." He strode toward her, taking from her the bucket heavy with brushes and soap. "You said you didn't know how to drive a horse, and I vowed I would teach you."

"You promised a lot of things I hardly expect you to keep."

"Why not? Do I seem like a lout to you? A liar?"

"No." She smiled shyly.

"Then let me help you, Clara." He set the bucket behind the seat, where covered baskets sat, huddled together.

"We should not be on a first-name basis, Mr. Brooks." The wind chose that moment to catch the placket of her unbuttoned coat and ruffle the skirt of the full apron she wore, issued by the housekeeper. A reminder, of sorts. "I have work to do."

"Yes, and do you know what that work entails?" The charm faded, leaving only kindness on his chiseled face. Goodness radiated from him unmistakably as he held out his hand. "You are to deliver the noon meal to Pa and the ranch hands. Three times a week you must drive into town for the errands and the mail."

"Oh." Things she could not do, for she had never handled a horse. She had never been able to afford one. "You have come to help me, and I thought you were trying to—"

"Flirt with you? You have the entirely wrong impression of me, Clara." His gloved hand caught hers, cradling it as if tenderly. Maybe it was nothing more than kindness. "I know how I seemed to you last night, practically proposing to you, a complete stranger, in a snowstorm."

"You thought I was your Miss Pennington."

"Who?" He blinked, surprise twisting across his forehead. He helped her onto the sleigh seat, his touch powerful and gentle at the same time.

"Perhaps it's not my place to say." She thought of what his mother had told her, and could not remember if the older woman had shared that information in confidence. "You should speak with your ma."

"I tried, believe me. She has been very quiet on the subject." He leaned closer, bringing with him a winter wind and warm man scent. She shivered, stunned at her reaction, as he drew the warm bear fur and spread it over her lap. "There is no reason why we can't be friends."

"Are you always friends with your household maids?"

"No." Humor stretched his mouth into an amazing smile.

She didn't remember settling farther over on the seat to make room for him, only that suddenly he was beside her. Her skin tingled with awareness of him. His big, capable hands were gloved, and when he took up the reins she did not feel a shiver. Really. She did not remember how his touch had been as hot as a branding iron. Honest.

Fine, maybe she remembered a little. Okay, more than a little. Sometimes hope was a terrible thing, making you want something you couldn't have—something you were afraid to have.

"This is a first for me, Clara. You have to believe it." His big hands gathered the thick leather straps. "You have to understand. Surely this has happened to you before."

"What has?"

"Captivating a man so he can't see anything else save for you."

"Why, yes. It happens constantly. It's such a bother, really, how men fall at my feet. I can hardly walk for tripping over them." How could this man be serious? "I know what your problem is. Your mother has to write to larger cities to hire household help and to marry off her sons. You aren't used to being around women your own age."

"Not true. In school, there were three girls in my grade. The trouble was, they fell in love with other fellows and married before I could snatch any of them up." Although he tried to hide it, she could sense a hint of sadness. He inched closer and presented her with the thick leather straps. "You take the reins. Go on, grab them right behind my hands."

"You have never beaued a girl?" She leaned closer into his heat and breathed in his fresh man-and-winter-wind scent. Her fingers closed around the reins inches behind his, and her shoulder bumped the warm iron of his arm.

"Got turned down when I tried." When he tried to grin, it didn't reach his eyes. "Lara turned around and let Chuck Thomas court her. They married right after she graduated from school. I guess that smarted for a while."

"Being cast off by someone you care about hurts."

"You sound like you know something about that."

"Yes. Of course. There have never been any men falling at my feet. Only one, and he was not falling, believe me." The big bay stallion shook his head, as if he did not approve of the switch of drivers.

"Don't worry about Don Quixote. He's a gentleman, too. You want to tell me what happened?"

"No, but I have a feeling you will pester me until you have the truth." Dimples framed her mouth, a hint of the smile she held back. She nodded toward the horse. "I can feel him through the lines."

"Yep. See how I keep the reins light, but not too light? That's the tension you want. Each horse is different, but my boy likes a gentle hand." He did not want to talk about his horse. She captured his interest. He had to know why she held herself back, as if reserved, as if she were even more wary than before. Her heart was a puzzle he intended to solve. He gave the reins a quick snap and the horse and sleigh shot forward. "Feel how I did that?"

"Yes." She nodded, her wool cap brushing against the side of his jaw. "This is like flying!"

"I take it you haven't been in many sleighs?"

"Not once." Wispy tendrils escaped from her knit hat and framed her face perfectly. If sweetness could be caught in an image, hers would be it. Bright blue eyes sizzling with excitement, her petal-pink mouth stretched into a tantalizing smile, her cheeks rosy. But there was more. A beautiful joy radiated outward from her heart. She could have been a winter sprite soaring with the snowflakes.

"You surely are a city girl. Hold on." He snapped the reins lightly, clicking to Don Quixote. The stallion swiveled his ears, nodded his head and stretched out into a fast trot. The sleigh felt airborne, hardly deigning to touch the top layer of snow. "What do you think now?"

"We should slow your horse down. We could crash."

"Hardly." He kept hold of the reins long enough to direct Don Quixote toward the next hillside, nestled with snow-mantled trees. "See how I tugged on the right rein?"

"Yes, I see. You would do the same to turn left." A crinkle of worry cut into her porcelain forehead. "How do you slow down?"

"No more worrying." He released his grip, leaving her in

charge of the horse, and settled back, relaxing against the seat. "You're driving, Clara. It's that easy."

"Sure, you can say that because you know how to stop." But she was laughing, beginning to see that they were as safe as could be. Don Quixote, well aware of where they were headed, obliged by cantering along the cut trail. The fence line rolled by, a foraging moose looked up in disgust as they blew by and her musical laugh rang as clear as the truest bell. "I think I've stepped off the train into a wonderland. Storybooks are this magical—not real life."

"Glad to hear you like this corner of Montana."

"Oh, I do. It's like a slice of heaven dropped to earth. I've never heard such peaceful quiet or breathed in cleaner air."

"There's no one back in Chicago who would miss you? A few old beaus, perhaps?"

"I thought we had already been plain about that. There were no beaus. Just one. Once."

"Sometimes that's all it takes." He didn't need to read the sadness that slipped across her face, for he could feel it square in his heart. That man, whoever he was, had hurt her. "What was his name?"

"Lars. He worked at the livery stable close to where I worked." She set her delicate chin, a show of strength and not defeat. "And because you seem to think it's your business, no, I don't miss him, and I doubt he even remembers me."

"How can that be?" He couldn't imagine it, for he would never forget her. This moment, with the warm softness of her arm against his, was emblazoned on his soul forever. He would always recall the faint scent of roses, the silk of her hair against his jaw and the beat of desire rising in his blood. The desire for something he knew not—he might not know much about love and all the intimacy that went with it, but he knew one thing. He wanted more than what could be found at night with her. He wanted to wake each morning with her in his arms and her cheek resting on his chest. He wanted to go about his day's work with thoughts of their closeness keeping him warm. Coming home to her in the evenings, to her smile, her embrace, her kiss. "You are too beautiful to forget."

"There you are, trying to charm me again." She shook her head as if to scold him, but her words were falsely light. Perhaps she was trying too hard to hide her sadness. "Joseph, you should try telling the truth for once."

"But I am."

"You *think* you mean that." Snow clung to her face like tears. "You shouldn't call me beautiful. It's not true."

"Is that what this Lars fellow told you?" Now things were making sense. "If he did, then there was something wrong with that man."

"He met another woman, who was actually very beautiful, and he proposed to her instead." She blinked hard, as if troubled by the snowflakes caught in her eyelashes.

He wasn't fooled. "You fell in love with this man?"

"I cared for him very much. A huge mistake, as it turned out." She nodded up ahead, where the trees lining one side of the slope gave way to snowy meadow and fence line. "Are we here? You never told me how to stop your horse."

"That's easy." He covered her hands with his, not because it was necessary but because he wanted to. She was much smaller, her bones and muscles fragile when compared with his own. Stinging tenderness bruised him from the inside out, both a painful and a healing emotion at once as he gently tugged at the reins.

"Whoa, boy," he crooned, and the sleigh slid to a halt. His heart went right on soaring. Clara turned to him, glowing with accomplishment.

"Thank you, Joseph. Driving was a lot more fun than I thought it would be. Don Quixote was a true gentleman."

The stallion nickered, as if pleased with the compliment. All Joseph could hear was what Clara hadn't told him about the man who had left her for another. He knew what that felt like. What it was to be found wanting, and how it could knock the starch out of you.

"Grub's here!" Pa's right-hand man, Grobe Sutter, called out over the sounds of hammering and sawing. The half-dozen ranch hands put down their tools, left their fence mending and started to amble over.

He had no more hopped out of the sleigh and offered Clara his hand to help her, than he caught sight of the men nearly running. They were mighty quick for fellows who had been at work before sunrise. Aiken Dermot shook the snow from his hat brim, ran his fingers through his hair and drew himself up full-height. His old school buddy had eyes only for the willowy woman in the worn gray coat. Jealousy nearly blinded him.

"Let me get the baskets," Joseph told her. Not his job, but he didn't like the way Aiken was sizing up the woman and nodding slowly, as if he thought he might try to nose his way in. "They're mighty heavy. You wait for me in the sleigh."

"I should be doing this, Joseph." She paid him no heed, unaware of the way another hand, Lew Burton, tossed her an interested wink. With a smile and interest glinting in his eyes, he beat Aiken to the back of the sleigh.

"'Afternoon, miss." Lew tipped his hat as if he were the finest of dandies. "You must be new around here. I heard word that Mrs. Brooks had brought a new gal from back East. What I didn't hear was that you were so darned pretty."

Clara appeared shocked, as if she didn't know what to say. Well, Joseph surely did.

"Enough of this." He hadn't anticipated every ranch hand they had making moon eyes at Clara. He stepped in between them. Red, racing jealousy flared through him like cannon fire. He jammed a basket in Lew's direction. "You take this and get away from her."

"Guess that answers my question. She's his fiancée, boys,"

Lew called out, looking danged disappointed. "Knew the rumors I heard from Zed at the depot couldn't be right."

"Yeah, Zed never gets it right." Aiken's chin went down. "Shucks. Why are the prettiest gals always taken?"

"I'm not—" She tried to explain.

"I'll be back for the baskets," Joseph interrupted, before his Clara could correct any of the men's notions about her. There was no way he was letting a single one of them think she was on the market. No way in hell. Protective fury raged inside him, and he felt like a pawing bull ready to charge a rival. He handed off the last food baskets to Old Man Riley.

There. The meal was delivered. He whipped around, surprised to find Clara a few steps behind him. Shock marked her innocent face, and she took a step back.

"You interrupted me, Joseph. Why didn't you tell them the truth?"

He seized her by the elbow, gritting his teeth and doing his best to ignore the flare of another emotion. Desire coursed through him like a newly sprung river. "Are you lookin' to marry one of them?"

"What kind of question is that?" She tried to wrench her arm free.

Not going to happen. He could feel the curious stares of the men nearby, unable to take their gazes off Clara. He wanted to punch every one of them for it, but he couldn't seem to let go of her. "Just get in the sleigh."

"And who are you to boss me around?" She kept her voice low, perhaps aware, too, of those watching them. "Let go of me, Joseph. And no, I don't want to marry any of them. I don't want to marry anyone."

"Why not?" He released her and held back the blanket so she could settle more easily onto the cushioned seat.

"Because I don't want someone plying me with false compliments on one hand and commanding me on the other, trying to win my heart and then running off when someone better comes along." Her chin went up, all fight, all pride. She gathered up the reins in her slender hands. "I'm here to work. I need this job, because I have nowhere to go and little money left to get there. You, why, this is all simply amusement to you, isn't it? Biding your time until your mail-order bride arrives."

"There isn't a mail-order bride coming for me."

"I wouldn't be too sure about that." Her eyes shadowed, growing darker, and for a moment he saw behind her anger to the hurt and the fears beneath. "You never did mean to be friends, did you? You meant to try to romance me for amusement, did you?"

"For amusement?" That was the furthest thing from his mind. How had things gone so wrong so fast?

"The next time we meet, Joseph, you had best stick to our agreement."

"What agreement?" What in blazes was she talking about? And why was his head in such a muddle that he couldn't make sense of anything? All he could read was her unhappiness, the pain pinching in the corners of her soft mouth, the pride that kept her slim back straight and her elegant chin set. How had this gotten so out of control? Why wasn't she making a lick of sense to him?

"The one where we agreed I was simply the hired help?" She gave the reins a snap, and Don Quixote, the traitor, pricked his ears, nickered as if in apology and stepped out, drawing the sleigh away.

"I thought we were at least going to be friends."

"This is an official end to our friendship," she called over her shoulder.

He stood, boots planted in the snow, heedless to the men's murmurs behind him and the buffeting wind and snow. All he saw was the sleigh growing smaller with distance, leaving him hollow inside. As if she were taking a piece of his heart with her, and there was not a thing he could do to stop her.

Chapter Five

Every time she thought about it, anger speared through her. Whether she was dusting Mary's knickknacks in the parlor or drying dishes in the kitchen, any mention of Joseph by the other staff made her blood heat with fury. The mere sound of his footsteps in the hallway could make her remember the claiming brand of his fingers on her arm.

He's not like Lars. She swiped the last dish dry and placed it carefully on the growing stack on the counter. If Joseph had known at the train depot that she was not speaking with his betrothed, he never would have said those things to her about marriage. He never would have charmed her or behaved so familiarly.

"Girl, you keep your mind on your work." Mrs. Baker, the housekeeper, reached for a dry towel to wipe her hands. "Mrs. Brooks does not pay you to stare blankly off into thin air. Now go throw out the dishwater."

"Yes, ma'am." Clara draped the dish towel over the wall rack near the cookstove, her face heating. She had heard the censure in the woman's tone. Mrs. Baker was the type of woman who enjoyed finding faults, but this time she was not wrong. Thoughts of Joseph had distracted her. She unhooked her coat from the peg by the kitchen door and heard a stair squeak in the stairwell behind her. She recognized Joseph's gait. She wasn't proud of it, but she already memorized the rhythm of his step.

Don't think about him, Clara. She drew in a breath, fortifying herself. As she slipped into her coat, she did her best *not* to wonder if he was heading to the library to choose a book from the collection of leather-bound volumes, or if he would retreat to the parlor to chat with his parents.

"After you bring in a bucket of water, you are done for the night." Mrs. Baker lifted the stack of dishes without a single clink of porcelain and stowed them on overhead shelves.

"Thank you, ma'am." Clara hefted the enormous washbasin from the counter, careful not to slosh dirty soapy water all over the front of her. The scorching sides of the basin seared her fingertips, but she kept going. Suds bubbled and frothed at the basin's rim, and every step she took, she didn't take her eyes from the water line. It sloshed with her gait, and a soap bubble lifted and popped in midair.

"Let me get the door for you." Joseph's baritone rumbled as if out of a dream.

Not that she had any. No, she had given up dreaming years ago. Her chin shot up, her gaze lifted and her breath caught at his grim expression. He towered over her, taller than she'd remembered, his face dark with shadows and his big, impressive body tensed, as if poised for a fight. This was a side of Joseph she had not seen and had never imagined was there. Gone was his easygoing charm and friendly good humor, replaced by a stoic strength she hadn't guessed at.

"Th-thank you." She feared her stuttering and wispy voice betrayed her. Head down, she slipped through the door he held and into the welcoming dark of the porch, but even that disappointed her. There were no shadows to hide in as the door shut with a crisp click. Frost crunched beneath his boots as he followed her to the top of the steps.

She had done her best to avoid being alone with the man.

As she scurried ahead of him, her mind wandered. Why had it been him who had happened to be going outside at the same moment she was? How was she going to face him, after leaving him to walk the quarter-mile distance home in the snow?

Shame burned through her like a fire's blaze, remembering what she had done. Acting more like a spurned schoolgirl than an employee. The water sloshed over the front of her apron, the hot water soaking through her coat, dress and corset to wet her skin. Shoot. She repositioned the basin, wishing she could refocus her concentration as easily. Her every nerve attuned to the man trailing down the steps behind her, his presence as unmistakable as the snowmelt dripping off the roof and onto the back of her neck.

Silence fell between them, uncomfortably loud. It drowned out the singsong dripping of buildings and tree branches. It muffled the watery munch of her shoes on the slushy snow. It penetrated her like an arrow, invading tender flesh. Her hands quaked, sloshing hot water everywhere, as she bent and placed it on the ground. With every breath, awareness of him ebbed through her. Wordless, he halted on the pathway and his big shadow fell across her, hands braced on his hips, emphasizing his magnificent shoulders, and planted his feet, legs spread.

The shadow before her on the moonlit snow drew her gaze, and she upended the basin, hardly aware of the water pooling too close to her shoes. What fascination held her to him? Why couldn't she pretend he was nothing to her, nothing at all?

"I'm waiting for your apology." The low notes of his voice struck with displeasure. "You left me standing in front of the other men like a fool."

She hung her head, feeling the weight of an uncertain emotion, a burden she could not name. Yes, she certainly knew this moment between them would come. Why else would she have avoided him so well the last few days?

Her stomach twisted tight and she straightened, the empty

basin banging against her kneecap. She did not feel the bite of that pain, since a greater one grasped her with sharper teeth. Any moment now Joseph was going to say the words she dreaded. The ones that would hurt like nothing she had known. This is what she had wanted to avoid.

"Your being a fool was not my fault." She faced him, unable to see what was on his countenance, whether it was anger or dislike of her. "Leaving you behind, that was a mistake. I can only apologize. I am sorry. It was wrong."

"You apologize, and yet you blame me."

The perfect round of a blinding white moon climbed the velvet black sky behind him, casting him in silhouette. It was a kindness, because she would not have to see that his regard for her had vanished. A regard she had not been able to accept. "You acted as if—"

"As if I were sweet on you? As if I wanted to punch any man who looked at you the way I did?"

His use of the past tense was not lost on her. Pain cracked through her chest. She did her best to ignore it. To draw herself up straight and to pretend she felt nothing for him, nothing at all. "You were acting strangely, Joseph. As if everything you said on that first night were true. We both know it isn't. It can't be."

"I admit I thought you were someone else. Is that what you wanted to hear?"

"Yes, thank you." The crack of pain within her carved deeper into her tender heart. Why was she hurting? It made no sense. She was not sweet on the man. She had not been charmed by him. And if she said that enough times, she was sure to make it become true. "And what is it you wanted to hear, Joseph? That when I met marriageable men like Aiken and Lew, I would try to gain their interest?"

"I've hated knowing you were delivering their meals without me there." A corner of his mouth twitched, but he remained as if in darkness. The only hint of levity was the lilt of his voice. "Maybe I was mistaken. You've come back each time without an engagement ring."

"You're teasing me now?"

"No. Just myself." He eased closer, one step at a time, a solemn man of strength with a faint hint of humor crinkling the corners of his eyes. Moonlight graced him, hinting at the straight blade of his nose and his square-cut jaw. "I don't understand how any man can take a first look at you and not see what I see."

"What do you see?"

"A cozy fire in the hearth when I come through the front door after a hard day's work and you waiting for me. A meal on the table and you to talk and laugh with over it." He pulled the basin from her fingers and tossed it in the direction of the steps. It landed with a distant thud somewhere in the deep shadows.

"You see your own personal maid to tend fires, keep house and cook for you?" Her eyes pinched with honest emotion. "This is why I came for a job, not for a husband. I feel sorry for your betrothed."

"There is no betrothed. Not yet." He bit his tongue to keep from telling her the truth. He had already found his bride. Telling that to her only seemed to make her push him away. He laid his gloved hand against the side of her face, and immeasurable adoration glowed within him like the silvered moonlight. "You think I've been insincere."

"Yes. Perhaps you didn't mean to be."

"No." He had been telling her his heart. He let her step away from him, breaking his touch. Nothing could break the emotion glowing within him like an eternal flame. "I haven't been around a lot of single women my age. I'm short on experience, but you have to know I meant no disrespect."

"That I do." Her eyes looked impossibly dark and deep. Her beauty must have enchanted the moon, for its pearled light followed her. "I suppose I can stop trying to avoid you?"

"Good idea, since the house isn't that large. I might not see you, but I can hear you in the next room. I reckon you can do the same with me."

"Perhaps." Noncommittal, she dipped her hands into her coat pockets and pulled out home-knit mittens. She seemed to concentrate overly on the task of fitting her fingers into the warm wool.

Her silence was revealing. A whole range of feelings had moved through him from the moment she had taken Don Quixote's reins and left him looking like a fool. Humor had been the first one, striking him hard. Impossible not to like a woman who could hold her own against a man. The others had chuckled, calling out advice to him on how to handle a woman, all good-natured stuff about how complicated they were and how smart the city girl was compared to a high-country mountain man like him.

But more feelings, ones easily hidden at the time, had crawled to the surface. Rejection was one, reinforced whenever he heard but didn't see her in the house. Sure, he might have caught sight of the swirl of her skirt as she left the room or the hint of rose water in the air when he entered the parlor. But emptiness was another emotion troubling him, carving out a hollow place within him that hadn't been there before.

Hurt—that was something else he'd felt in the dark of night, in his room at the end of the hall. He'd sat at the window and looked out over the garden where Clara's front window shone with lamplight, and he'd wondered if she felt as lonely as he did, more than *she* had ever known before. She had changed everything in his world—what he wanted and what he thought about. His sense of well-being was gone, blown to bits as if with a rifle's bullet. He couldn't lay his head on his pillow without wondering what it would be like to have her lying beside him or how sweet it would be to draw her into his arms and love her fully, the way a husband ought to love his wife.

He'd come to realize what he had done wrong. Romancing a woman was harder than it looked. The one thing he did not want was to be the reason she kept turning away from him, the way Lara had done long ago in his school days. That had stung at the time, sure, but this pain he felt right now hit powerfully enough to bring him to his knees. The one thing he couldn't stand would be to lose the chance to love Clara for all the days of his life.

"I'm not looking for a housekeeper, just so you know." He fell in stride beside her as she crunched and slid along the worn path away from the house. "I said it all the wrong way. I've got to get better at that. I meant I would be eager to come home to the woman. Her coziness, her laughter, her presence."

"Oh." She said the single word low and hushed, making it hard to know what she meant, if she understood or if she still thought him insincere. The wind tugged loose airy curls from her coiled-up braids to swirl invitingly against her face.

Everything within him ached to capture those fairy curls in his bare hands, to cradle the dear curve of her chin in his palm and taste her kisses. He longed to savor her heat and her every texture, to unbutton her, layer by layer, and lave kisses down her long, graceful neck and farther still. Blushing, he tried not to think about how much he craved to know more of her, to know all of her. The softness of her bosom, the flare of her hips, and what it would be like to lie intimately with her, to feel her legs entwined with his, to be joined as one.

Need, both sweet and vital, punched hard until it hurt. *Just take it slow, Joseph.* He veered off the broken path when she did, following the iced-over trail to the water pump. The moonlight fell at her feet, as if privileged to light her way. Feeling the same, he grabbed a bucket from the stack before she could, hung it on the notch and covered her hand when she reached for the pump handle.

She stiffened at his contact and his closeness. "I ought to do this, Joseph."

He stood his ground. "It might be frozen. Let me get it started for you."

"It does seem to be stuck." Her words sounded strained.

Strained or affected? He had to find out. He pressed closer to her until her shoulder blades brushed his chest. The luxury of her hair tickled the underside of his jaw. *Please feel what I do,* he wished, gathering up all the forces of his soul. *Please want me the way I want you.*

Was it his imagination or had her fingers nudged his? He relaxed his hand, waiting spellbound and breathless for the smallest movement. It came quietly and sweetly, the tiniest acquiescence as her fingers widened to allow his to entwine with them. His breath caught and held, his heart tumbling irrevocably. In the kiss of moonshine, she was exposed. Wide-eyed, she watched him with both fear and hope, emotions he could feel hovering in the crisp air between them and with his every breath.

"Joseph, the water?" A shiver rolled through her, and he could feel every nuance, every worry and wish.

With her fingers between his, he put some muscle into it, and the pump handle gave. Water splashed, drumming into the tin pail as he savored her summery scent. He fought the need to press against her more tightly, enfold her in his arms and never let her go. For whatever reason, she affected him deeply and he was grateful. He'd taken to her from first glance, but every time they met his affections for her expanded like stars in the night sky.

"I've got it now," her gentle alto reminded him, but instead of notes of censure in her voice, there was something hidden.

Something only his heart heard. He did not move. "Maybe I want to help you, Clara."

"Maybe you are trying to charm me again."

"Charm you…no longer. My aim is to show you the man I am." The pail was full, and it was like dying a little to release the handle and take his hand from hers. To step away from her softness when every instinct he owned shouted at him to get closer until there was no way to know where he ended and she began.

"Joseph, surely you know we cannot be friends." Her plea sounded frail on the inclement wind, as fragile as the ice forming at his feet, cracking beneath his boot as he took a step.

"I do not wish to be friends, pretty lady. Wait here." He took the pail from her, tossed her a grin and left her standing alone in the star shine. The world around her transformed. Ice crusted the snow and shone like diamond dust. Icicles dangled overhead as he hurried up the icy path to leave the water bucket on the top porch step. He would take it inside later. But for now, he had more information to gather. Did he have a chance? Was he right, did she have hopes and feelings for him, too?

As predicted, she did not wait as he'd asked. She followed him as far as the trail's fork, one leading to the stables and the other to the maid's quarters. "I never asked what brought you out in the cold this time of evening."

"I intended to pay Don Quixote a visit. He and I haven't gotten in as much talking as we usually do." All he could see was her. The swish of her skirt. The sway of her hips. The pearled light on her skin. "I was also thinking of sledding."

"You? Aren't you too old to play in the snow?"

"Playing in the snow is ageless." He matched her pace, taking the unbroken edge of the trail and leaving her the cleared pathway. "Surely even a lady as proper as you, Miss Clara, knows that."

"I've rarely indulged in such silliness." She tried to hold back a smile and failed. "The truth is, I've never had much time for play."

"You have always had a serious life?"

"I ran errands for several businesses in town, swept store floors and boardwalks and cleared snow for most of the day when I was a child."

"What about school?"

"I never made it past the third grade. I was kept out, to help make what living I could. But one of the hurdy-gurdy dancers at one of the saloons liked to read and taught me what she could. I doubt you can understand how I was brought up."

"With little to hope for, so it seems to me. With a ma you couldn't count on, a pa who'd abandoned his responsibilities. I can see why you don't believe in me, Clara." His hand settled on her shoulder, drawing her around. He towered over her, both a stranger she did not know and a dream she'd never been brave enough to wish for, all at once. His thumb brushed the dip in her chin. "But you will."

How did she tell him she was beginning to believe? She felt dazzled by his caring gaze, captivated by his branding touch. This man could enchant her, when no one ever had. His fingers blazed on her skin like the first star in a winter sky, bright enough to light her way. His gaze settled on her mouth and lingered, and the contours of his rugged face changed. His mouth softened. His eyes darkened.

Alarm tripped through her veins. She bit her bottom lip, afraid in a way she didn't understand. Surely he wasn't thinking about kissing her. She steeled her spine, gathering up her will. How easy it would be to throw off caution and lean ever so slightly toward him, let her eyes drift shut and know the feel of his kiss.

The wind gusted hard, slicing through her layers of clothing like a blade. Her head cleared. *You do not know this man enough. You have not seen enough of his character.* The commonsense reminder whispered through her mind, giving voice to her doubts, which life had reinforced. Men did not stay. And if they did, they did not stay for her.

Again she withdrew from his touch and the allure of his intent gaze. Whatever he was asking, she could not agree to. Something deeper than disappointment and darker than regret slammed against her rib cage, but she ignored it. "If you will excuse me, it's time I went home."

"Your workday is done?"

"Yes, although there is much to be done in the cabin." Minor things, like refilling the kerosene lamps and darning her socks, which had worn through again. But he did not need to know that. Let him think she had pressing tasks that could not wait. It would be best for both of them, best for her heart. Her shoes slipped a bit on the icy path, and the crunch of her footsteps echoed in the great hush of the night.

"Are you settled in all right?" His question followed her when he did not. "Are you liking the place?"

"Liking is too small a word." Her confession rose across the platinum span of snow separating them. Heat flooded her face and embarrassment across her heart, for she was not only speaking of the cabin. Afraid he knew that, too, she continued on, walking as fast as she dared until the shadows surrounding the garden hid her from his sight.

Chapter Six

"I'm tellin' you, I think she just might like me more than a little." Joseph's steps echoed in the stable as he wrestled his sled out from behind Gabriel's collection of saddles. "She had a look on her pretty face, one I've seen before. Back before Savannah married Nate and she was sweet on him and didn't want him to know it. That was the same look Clara had tonight."

Don Quixote inhaled the last granules of grain from his trough, swiveling his ears as if he were listening intently. He whinnied his opinion low in his throat.

"I'm glad you think so, too." He dragged the old sled out of the tack room and squinted at it.

Don Quixote lifted his head from the grain box and did the same.

"Not too impressive, all covered in hay dust like that." He hadn't reckoned on their boyhood sled looking neglected and battered, but the runners were in fair repair. "Good thing it's dark out. With a lick of luck, she won't be able to tell."

Don Quixote whinnied with a shake of his head, sending his sleek black mane swinging. It was plain to see the stallion didn't agree.

"It's the only plan I've got. If you have a better one, speak up." Joseph stopped to run his hand down the horse's nose.

"You and I have a trip to make into town tomorrow. Things ought to get interesting with the snow melting, so rest up. You might need all your energy. Then there's always the Johnsons' filly in town to impress. Either way, it's bound to be a big day."

He intended to time things right so he could volunteer to escort Clara on her first drive to town. Whistling, he yanked the sled by its rope out into the night. Don Quixote nickered a cozy good-night. He closed the doors tight against the cold wind and high-mountain predators.

Clara's light drew him across the hillside, with heart pounding and his palms damp beneath his gloves. Dang, but he was nervous. Courting a woman was sure tough on a man. By the time he got up the courage to rap his knuckles on her front door, his nerves were atumble. He could hardly suck in enough air waiting for her to answer. A thousand rejections took form in his imagination. Clara saying a fast and very adamant "No!" Clara slamming the door in his face. Clara looking horrified at the thought of spending time with him. Clara laughing in mirth at his tender assumptions.

His knees were knocking as he waited. He knew down deep that she would never treat him that way, but what a man knew and what he feared were two different things. A wolf howled in the nearby forest and others answered, echoing across the mountaintops, nearly masking the sound of the door opening. Lamplight spilled over him like hope, and she looked beautiful as always with her braids uncoiled and without her proper white apron. He couldn't help but notice how her green calico dress made her look like summer in full bloom, lush and ripe and tempting.

"I know you said you had things to do," he began, trying to banish the nervousness plaguing him. "But I thought you might like to try your hand at sledding."

"How did you know I've never been?"

"Just a guess, from what you said." It stood to reason.

She'd worked as a child, instead of learning to read and cipher at school, and hadn't had much time for play. "It's a lot of fun."

"More so than sleigh riding?"

"I promise you the time of your life." Was that interest sizzling in the blue of her eyes? He surely hoped so.

"The time of my life? My, that is a big promise."

"One I intend to keep." He unhooked her coat from the peg by the door. "This might be your last chance until snow flies again, probably in October. That's a long spell to wait for some of the best fun you will ever have on a downhill slope."

"You are outrageous, Joseph, claiming such things. I have a suspicion you are not only speaking of sledding."

"It takes one to know one." He held out the garment for her. A challenge dazzled in his eyes along with something else, something far too serious and too frightening to believe in. So why was her arm sliding into her coat sleeve as if of its own accord?

"And what if my sledding experience is not as stellar as you claim?"

"Life's experiences come with no guarantees," he answered smoothly, easing her coat over her shoulders. So close, she inhaled the fresh air, hay and his pleasant male scent. Awareness tingled through her. His lips brushed her hair as he spoke. "But you will never know if you don't give it a try."

Why did it feel as if he were no longer talking of the act of sliding down a hillside in the dark, but something much more perilous? When he circled around to catch her top button in his callused, working-man hands, his humor was gone. His easy-going friendliness vanished. The lamplight found and caressed the intensely masculine muscular curve of his shoulders bulging beneath his coat. She felt every inch of his power to protect, to defend and to provide. She recognized an immeasurable tenderness as he worked the first button through the buttonhole, his knuckles grazing her chin.

Her body betrayed her, her heart hammering fast and hard, her breath coming in shallow, quick puffs. Could he feel her reaction as he drew the coat over her breasts and secured the button? His touch felt shocking, for all its properness and the layers of clothing separating her skin from his touch. She felt as vulnerable as if she stood naked before him. What was happening to her?

"You'll need your muffler and hat." He stole both from the wall pegs and draped the length of knit wool around her neck. His smile had changed. No longer jovial, intensely serious, it emphasized the sharp planes of his face, his high cheekbones and the firm square cut of his jaw. He plopped the knit cap on her head, and her hands caught his of their own volition, feeling the hard ridge of muscle and bone beneath his smooth, hot skin.

Little fires flared through her, an awakening of both body and spirit. A stirring of heat and gentle feelings she'd never known before. *This is not love,* she told herself, stubbornly willing it to be so. She defiantly fought down the strange new affections. But they were so overwhelming, she might as well have been butter melting on a hot stove.

"Will you come with me?" He held out his hand, palm up, waiting. His question rang low with a deeper meaning. A meaning that made her soul shiver and private places within her come alive. His baritone dipped, unfailingly intimate. "The night is waiting."

This is not love, she repeated, caught between wanting to stay safe alone in her cabin and needing to find out what awaited her on the starlit snow and in the chambers of Joseph's heart. How did she choose? Both were perilous. Both would end in heartache. She bit her bottom lip, aware that it drew his gaze there. Was he thinking to kiss her? Her stomach dropped at the notion of kissing him back. Her lips tingled, craving something she did not know.

Did she stay here and always wonder what if? To spend her days never sure what would have happened it she had accepted his offer? Or did she go with him, fearing it could not last? Did she seize what time she could, stealing happiness beneath the light of the moon?

She didn't know what came over her. "Let's not keep the night waiting," she said, and took his hand.

Joseph steadied the sled at the crest of the slope, quaking in a way he never had before. Clara noted his every move. He could sense her gaze on him like a touch to his shoulders, to his back and to the side of his face. That she agreed to come was a hopeful sign. Kneeling down, he held the sled steady. "All aboard."

"The hill looks steeper than I remember." Her skirts swished against his knee. "And far too rugged. Are you sure we won't crash like a runaway train?"

"No, I'm not sure at all. Crashing is a risk we are both going to have to take." He took her hand, savoring the smile curving her mouth. "Sit right here. Feet forward, and hold on to the side here."

"This can't be comfortable. I'll fall off."

"I'll hold you so you won't." He eased behind her, doing his best to keep the sled steady. "Are you starting to see how this goes?"

"You're going to put your arms around me, aren't you?"

"As long as you don't object." Sure, he could have let her slide down the hill all by herself, but how was he going to get closer to her that way? His legs embraced hers as he cradled her between his thighs. More intimate than on their horse ride the first evening they had met, and he couldn't complain about that. No, not one bit. Her rosewater-and-soft-woman scent tantalized him as he wrapped one arm around her waist. The underside of her breasts rested against his forearm.

You're a gentleman, Joseph, he reminded himself, but his blood heated anyway. He might be refusing to imagine having the right to unbutton her dress and worship her breasts, but his body responded anyway with a desire so strong, his vision blurred. All common sense fled.

"Are you ready?" he murmured against her ear. The silk of her hair and the satin of her skin captured him like a spell, binding him to her with a tie so fierce it could never be broken.

"You'll hold on tight to me?"

"I won't let go." He pushed off with his free hand, and the sled bumped over sharp rises and dips before hovering on the brink of the hill's edge.

"Maybe I'm thinking to change my mind about this." She gripped the worn wooden sides tighter. "Could you stop?"

"I could, but then you would miss this." His words puffed against the side of her face, intimate and tantalizing. "Look up."

Silvered light drew a path down the hillside, making the snow gleam like a dark opal. Shades of navy blue and purple made the shadows mysterious and beautiful, transforming the landscape. Joseph's arms around her could not be the reason she felt as if she'd walked into a fairy tale. Her world had never been so beautiful. Dark stands of snow-capped trees towered like watchful sentries as the sled dipped downward, gathering speed. Time paused right along with her heartbeat as the sled bumped upward and took flight.

"Whatever happens," Joseph whispered, "keep your eyes open. You don't want to miss a moment."

Gravity grabbed hold of the runners, hurling the sled downward, and downward still. She lost her breath. Airless, she clung to the sled, safely wrapped tight in Joseph's arms and tucked against his thighs and chest. Wind snapped against her face, burning her cheeks and blurring her vision. A single bump rocked through the sled as the runners hit the ground again. Tiny airy wisps of snow whirled up from the blades, and the rush of wind filled her ears.

"Isn't this fun?" Joseph's lips brushed her cheek when he spoke.

Thrilling. Exhilarating. Safe. She felt the tiny coils of

tension at the base of her skull release. Common sense left her as simply as the hillside behind them. She felt weightless as the stars hovering in the flawless sky, as free as the sled speeding down dips and over bumps in the hillside, sending them into midair again.

"Hold on!" Joseph called out, laughing. His deep chuckle rolled through her, one ocean wave after the next, beating at the gates to her heart. The moon brightened in the sky, dancing and twirling as the sled listed to the left, unseating them, and they were falling together, she and Joseph. The snow seemed to reach out and welcome them, cushioning their landing. His laughter shivered through her as he hit the ground first, taking the brunt of the blow with his shoulder and rolling to keep her in his arms.

She came to rest on his chest, laid out over him. His hat was gone. Her cap was falling into her eyes. Was that her laughter floating on the silent wind, joy warming her like midsummer?

"Are you all right?" Joseph asked, concern on his face and love in his eyes.

"I'm great." Tiny shards of ice melted against the back of her neck and seared her face. Although Joseph cocooned her, his arms holding her firmly on top of him, she still felt as if she were soaring. Her laughter mingled with his. "I'm fantastic."

"I told you, didn't I?" His words were deep, layered with meaning. "You are beautiful in the moonlight, Clara. More beautiful than any woman could ever be."

"I don't know what has become of my common sense. I think I left it on the top of the hill, or how else would I have wound up this way?"

"In my arms?"

"Crashed a few yards away from the garden fence."

"At least we didn't crash *into* the fence." He pulled off his glove and gently brushed tangled wisps from her eyes. "We ought to be counting our blessings."

His touch scattered her senses and made it impossible to think straight. She ought to pull away, but his tenderness mesmerized her. Held captive, she savored the brush of his fingertips on her temple. The sweep of his thumb as he chased bits of snow from her cheek. It took all her effort to force her tongue to work. "Which blessings should we be counting?"

"That we are here together." His thumb grazed her bottom lip.

"Yes. Together." Awash in sweet sensation, Clara sighed when his thumb scorched a trail along the bow of her upper lip. His gaze settled on her mouth. Desire quaked through her, the wish for just one kiss.

"And since you are here with me like this…" He paused to draw his thumb down the center of her lips to her chin, tilting her face toward his. "There is one thing I must do before I let you sled down the hill again."

"You think I'm going to want to do that again?" She meant to be coy, to tease, but her words came out breathless and vulnerable, betraying the sweet pulse of want filling her in slow, steady beats.

"Sure," he mumbled, slanting his mouth over hers. "If we want to land just like this."

His lips claimed hers in a brush of a kiss, a velvet-warm promise of more to come. Dazed, she clutched his coat, holding on. A little dizzy, a little captivated, she fought to catch her breath. He pulled away to search her gaze, and she read a depth of caring there in his eyes, a powerful caring, one that she had never known in her life. He wasn't assuming; he was making sure that she wasn't merely accepting his kiss but hungering for it, too.

Again, her heart pleaded. As if his heart clearly heard, his eyes deepened to a shade darker than the sky. A hint of a smile was his only answer. This time when his lips found hers, there was no tentative caress, no thoughtful introduction. Her fingers curled into his woolen jacket, and it was as if gravity loosened its hold on her. She was airborne once more, lost in the explosive stroke of his mouth to hers.

With only his arms to anchor her, she fit her lips to his, her heart afire. Sweetness filled her, as weightless as a summer cloud. Never had she felt so much before, as if she were about to come apart at the seams. The tenderness she felt for him was too large to keep inside her, so beautiful it brought tears to her eyes. Hot and salty, they slid down her cheeks, uncontrolled, and still she could not bear to let his lips leave hers.

"It was my first kiss, too." His confession shivered through her, spoken as they breathed the same air. She felt as if their hearts were synchronized; as if nothing could ever go back to being the same without him.

"Do you want to do that again?" he asked.

"The kiss or the sledding?"

"I have a mind to do both." He took her hand in his, so big and sheltering, when hers was so small.

This was the man she never dreamed she could find. The man she thought she would never have. Both strong and tender, both fun and serious, but there was more to the dream. If Joseph were truly meant for her, if there was such a thing as one true love, then he would be forever committed to her. His love for her would be greater than a single kiss, but grand enough to last eternally. Was it possible any man could love her that way?

Doubt crept into her. She felt the air cool on her skin. The moonlight seemed to fade a notch. Dampness blew on the changing wind and she felt a drip in the middle of her back followed by a second.

"It's a warming wind, the Chinook." He sounded as surprised and as breathless as she.

All around them the forest came alive. Snow dropped from thousands of tree branches and the merry sound rolled through the mountain valley like a celebration. Ice began to melt in joyful melodies. An owl swooped past, gliding on widespread wings.

"We might be lucky to get one more run." He helped her up and brushed a chunk of snow from the hem of her skirt. "But it looks like that's the last we can expect."

"Too bad. I think I like sledding."

"Me, too. The end of one thing is the start of another. How about a buggy ride tomorrow?"

"I believe I have plans. Or, rather, Mrs. Baker has plans for me." The top layer of snow felt soft around her shoes. Things were changing in the night and in her heart as Joseph drew her into his arms.

"Just in case the sledding is a bust, I had best collect my kiss now." His smile became hers, slanting over her lips, stroking sweetness through her, leaving her breathless. With every slow caress of his mouth to hers, great tenderness built within her. Tucked against his chest, enfolded in his arms, hope began to stretch as wide as the sky. Love, whole and unbidden, bloomed within her, bringing fresh tears to her eyes.

A distant sound registered somewhere at the back of her mind, growing louder as Joseph ended the kiss. He left her sparkling from head to toe, aching with new love for him. Nothing was dearer than the grin dimpling his mouth or the contented sigh rumbling through his chest as he drew her more tightly against him. The reliable, fast *thump-thump* against her cheek told her what he couldn't say. He was carried away, too.

The distant sound became more clear to her as her senses returned. Someone was calling Joseph's name.

"My pa." His smile faded as he released her. Taking his time, he righted her hat and kissed her forehead sweetly. "He must need me."

"Go." She hated stepping away from him. She despised drawing in the strings of her heart and letting him leave. Her common sense would surely kick in any moment now, and she would stop aching for the sensation of another kiss and the intimate, wonderful shelter of his arms. "Please, don't keep him waiting."

"I wish—" He didn't finish that thought, but he gazed to the east, to some unseen place where stars shimmered and snow-capped mountains glowed. "Tomorrow, I'll be coming for you. Don't forget."

"But I have work to do."

"Yes, I'm well aware of that, beautiful." He captured her hand in his and lifted it to his lips. He brushed a kiss to her knuckles, as courtly as the best prince in the most romantic fairy tale. "Let me walk you home."

"No, you go to your father. I can find my way." Perhaps on the short path around the stand of cedars and between the garden fence she would find the practical young woman she had been less than an hour ago. With every step she took on the moon-washed trail, she hoped to find her good sense and the plain girl who would never have fallen in love over a few kisses.

Great kisses, true. No, fantastic kisses, she corrected as the lamplight from her front window came into sight. Her nape prickled and, feeling Joseph's gaze, she spun, her skirts swishing, her feelings rising to a crescendo as their gazes met and melded. Across the span of opalescent snow, she felt treasured. As if she were the most beautiful of women, the most beloved princess, cherished above all things. That was how Joseph made her feel.

Impulsively she blew him a kiss before dashing into her warm home. Even in the stillness, she no longer felt alone.

Chapter Seven

❦

"Aren't you supposed to be out checking on the herd?"

Joseph winced at the amusement in his mother's voice. Just how much did Ma know? And did she know it or simply suspect it? He glanced around the parlor for any sign of Clara and, finding none, went to glance down the hallway.

Ma watched him thoughtfully from her chair, where she was sorting through her new embroidery threads.

"I went out early." Truth was, he had been up before the chickens, riding in the wet, harsh mountain conditions. Rain might be falling, but it was snowing in the higher pastures. There was no sign of Clara in the library. "I've got a few things to do in town before the branding starts."

"A few things?" Ma arched one brow and her face looked as if she were fighting to hold back a grin. "Last I heard, you and your pa had more than that planned. You two were thick into it when I headed to bed last night. Guess you and he had a discussion about your land?"

"I guess we did." Truth was, it was a long discussion. He stopped at the base of the stairs. Was Clara up there?

"Seems you are eager to start making a few changes around here." Ma was trying to pry into his business. No doubt about that.

It wouldn't be the first time. He retraced his path to the parlor. "I've heard word that you may have written away for a bride for one of us. Any truth to that?"

"There's nothing for you to worry about." If Ma looked anxious, it was a passing thing. She straightened her shoulders, as if she had made up her mind about something. "Everything works out the way it's meant to anyhow. Is there something you want to tell me?"

"That wasn't an answer, Ma." One thing was clear. He wouldn't allow Clara to get hurt. "There's no one coming for me?"

"I told you not to worry, son." Did Ma look a tad guilty? Maybe it was the light or his imagination because it disappeared as soon as she glanced out the window. "Clara's already outside, waiting for a ride, I suspect. Go on, now. She's a nice girl and could use a little help."

"Thanks, Ma." He tipped his hat in goodbye, ending the conversation, and headed out the door and down the steps. Plans filled his head, ones that were as real as the sludge of snow, rain and mud at his feet, as hopeful as the leaves waving on bared branches. Sparrows and finches winged by as he looked up the walkway, and his emotions rose as easily when he spotted Clara. She stood at the end of the daffodil-lined path near Don Quixote, who was saddled, and Bucky, who was hitched to the buggy. The way she looked held him spellbound.

Gosh, talk about a sight. Clara's yellow-checked dress ruffle swirled and swayed beneath her old coat as she hurried toward him. Her sunshine-gold hair crowned her head in a single braid, and he swore she was twice as beautiful today in the rain as she had been last night, graced by star shine.

When she noticed him waiting for her, she transformed. Happiness put color in her face and magic in her eyes. She swept toward him, bringing the memory of last night with her. His mouth buzzed, remembering the sweet surrender of her kiss. His skin sensitized, and he felt tingling and hot, recalling the amazing thrill of holding her against his chest. Love hit him like a thunderclap and he was helpless to stop it.

"I'm surprised to see you here, stranger." She stopped with a swirl of her skirt, rainwater dancing between them. "Mrs. Baker told me a horse and buggy would be waiting for me, but I didn't imagine you would be harnessing the horse for me."

"Usually that's old Opie's job, but I told him I would do it this once. Remember I wanted to take you on a drive today?"

"How could I forget?" The intimacy from last night stood between them, both exciting and a little awkward. Blushing, she looked away, focusing on the black horse hitched to the fancy, covered buggy. "I don't think I can be responsible for something so fancy. What if something happens?"

"What could happen?"

"Let me think. A landslide. A hungry mountain lion. Something could break on the buggy. The horse might become ill or injured or realize I'm new at driving and run away with me."

"Life is full of risks. Besides, Bucky is twenty-three years old. He's happy enough to take you to town, but trust me. When you turn him toward home, he'll go there on his own. He's of the age where a horse just wants a warm comfortable stall and a bucket of sweet rolled oats. I thought I would escort you today and make sure you know the way."

"That was mighty thoughtful of you, considering the only time I was on the road to town it was blizzarding. All I could see was the snow hitting my face."

"The least I could do. I've been looking forward to this all morning."

"You best be careful, Joseph, or I'm going to start believing you."

"Good. That's exactly what I intend." He held out his hand, both an offer to help her into the buggy and something more.

What did he intend? She was afraid to ask him, afraid to know. Remembering the words he had uttered to her after they had met. *I'm already sweet on you. I know it in my gut. I just know. We are going to be the happiest married couple in these parts.*

Last night had felt like a dream, fondly invading her thoughts all morning. As she went about her work cleaning and dusting, that dream had began to be less real and more fantasy. But now it all came back the moment she accepted his hand. Tendrils of adoration and need twined through her and took hold. She settled on the seat, hardly aware of him climbing in beside her. All she knew was that he was with her, and they were alone together. Just like last night.

Desire she'd never felt before skittered through her veins, and as the clear curtains closed, cutting off the wind and the rain, she was aware of every part of him. His granite thigh pressed against the length of her leg, his unyielding arm against her shoulder. Memories of being held by him and kissed by him left her dizzy.

"Tomorrow is Sunday." He laid his arm across her shoulder and drew her closer. "It's your day off."

"Yes, I'm aware of that."

"Any plans I should be aware of?"

"Why are you asking?" She leaned a little more against him. The way he looked at her, spoke to her, the warm regard in his voice made her feel special again. More like the woman she had always dreamed of being. She no longer felt plain when his gaze roved her face as if he could not get enough of looking at her.

"My family always has a big Sunday dinner," he went on to explain. "It's a bigger event now that my brother is married and Mary Grace was born. Would you like to come?"

"But it's a family dinner."

"Yes, it surely is." Gone were all traces of charm and good humor. Deadly serious, he reined the horse around a grand sweeping corner, bringing a deep forest of nodding, enormous evergreens into sight. The craggy, rugged sides of mountains speared up into the fluffy gray clouds, peaks lost in the rain. "I'm courting you, Clara. It's official."

Her stomach plummeted, as if the buggy had taken to rolling right down one of those mountainsides. It wasn't only a frightening sensation. Delight ribboned through her, brighter than summer sunshine. "You simply decided this on your own?"

"After last night, I figured it was a good step. After all, we shared more than one kiss. You weren't exactly fighting me off."

Heat stained her cheeks, making her skin tight. Was she smiling? She shouldn't be. "Kissing a lady before you are engaged to her is highly improper."

"See? That's why I made the assumption. If you weren't sweet on me, then you never would have kissed me back." His arm around her tightened gently, reminding her of how good it felt to be at his side. Of how very much she wanted to stay with him.

A wise woman would be practical. A man like Joseph could have his pick of women. He might be as serious as stone at the moment, but she well remembered the easygoing charmer who had scooped her onto his horse at the train depot. Fear lashed at her, striking quick and deep.

Lars had been this way. Charming and too serious too fast. Oh, Lars had never been truly interested in her, she could see that now. Not the way Joseph was; he was hewn of something wonderful and masculine she had never seen before.

You're going to get hurt, the voice of experience whispered to her. *He will lose interest and move on, and you will lose your heart. Your whole heart this time, and not just a piece of it.*

True, she realized, but hope grew within her like a young bud ready to open. The hope for this man was something she could not give up on. Even if he broke her entire heart, she wanted more time with Joseph. She had to know what being loved by him would be like.

"But we haven't known each other very long, Joseph, for you to be making assumptions."

"Sure, but the moment you drive through town and every lonely bachelor gets an eyeful of your beauty, sweetheart, you're going to be the most popular person in town. Now, I'm ready to beat every single one of those would-be suitors off to keep you all to myself, but I would rather they kept away because you have vowed to be mine."

"What an imagination you have, Joseph Brooks. I'm just an average girl. The way you go on makes me feel like someone else entirely. Don't get me wrong, I like it, but you're simply being charming again."

"No. In my view, you are the most beautiful woman. I have the suspicion that every day I know you, you will become more cherished to me." He reined the horse to a stop, his gaze colliding with hers, revealing his sincere vulnerability. There was no smile teasing his lips, no jaunty bracket of dimples around his mouth and no shields around his feelings. He was offering her his heart.

His words made her want to blush, but the man seated beside her, honest to the core, humbled her. A tiny voice within her, the one so used to being sensible, whispered to her, *This is too good to be true. Caution!* But as his gloved hand cupped her chin, drawing her into his reverent kiss, love seeped through her, tiny and new at first, like clear sparkling light. She shimmered with it as their lips brushed again. It was as if his love for her wrapped around her like sunshine, enfolding her in a brilliant, protective glow.

"I was fixing to build a house on that south-facing slope there." His words rumbled comfortably through her, his lips brushing her hair, his arm around her shoulder nudging her tight against his side.

"A house?" He overwhelmed her. He was all she could see. What was happening to her? She felt carried away and grounded all in the same moment, joyful and solemn in the same breath. With every passing second, she felt transformed, as if she would never be the same again. The tiny petals of hope opening within her began to bloom like blossoms beneath a summer sky.

I love him. The power of it twisted painfully in her chest and burned in her eyes. She blinked, but her vision remained blurry. There was no hillside and no world beyond the rain-specked curtain. Only Joseph, with love alight on his rugged face—love for her.

"I bought this section of land last year."

"This isn't part of your family's ranch?"

"It borders up against it, but no. I've built my own herd alongside Pa's, and for years I've worked afternoons from fall to spring in my brother Nate's feed store. I saved up and worked hard to make it on my own, not to have my pa hand me what is his."

More love shimmered through her, buoyed by respect for this man. Could he be any more perfect? In the moments of silence, as they peered at the land together, was he imagining the house he would build? The life they would have there?

And yes, she was imagining it, too. Doing her housework with the sun streaming in through wide windows while children played in the fresh mountain grasses. Joseph's warm chuckle and his arms holding her close. Sitting together at night by the fireplace, she with her needlework and he with his newspaper, talking amicably and laughing together over this and that. Putting their children to bed and being alone together.

Her face flamed hot as fire, and she couldn't imagine anything she wanted more than spending the night with Joseph and knowing his lovemaking.

Could this really be happening to a girl like her? She rested her head against his shoulder, basking in a closeness she had never felt before. She didn't have to ask to know that Joseph was pondering these same things. The promise of it was tender on his handsome face.

"I want you to know I have a lot to offer you." He cradled her head, holding her against his chest. "I'm a serious man down deep, Clara. I want to take care of you. I want to spend all of my days with you."

"I believe you, Joseph. I see the man you are." Her old fears told her to move away, to put enough distance between them to keep her safe from disappointment. A new part of her, someone she didn't recognize, did not want to let go of this dream.

"That means a lot to me, sweetheart." Immeasurable love vibrated in those words. "I'll hire a few carpenters in town to help me. We can order lumber from the train yard. Or if you would rather have a log house, we can start cutting timber. You tell me what you want."

She thought of the cozy, wonderful cabin she lived in with the stout walls of honey-gold wood. "A log house. Something with lots of windows."

"As you wish, my lady." His thumb traced the outline of her lips, his eyes hazy with desire, his words rough with devotion. "From this moment on, I live for you."

And I, for you. She lacked the courage to say the words, afraid that his could not be true. She was afraid of so many things, but not this man. He could be her everything, if she let him, the very reason she drew air each day.

Rain tapped at the curtains and drummed overhead, and the hillside was gray with melting snow and puddled water. But in her dreams she envisioned colorful wildflowers, a happy home and a happier life as Joseph's wife.

His thumb traced her bottom lip, sending shocking little bolts of pleasure through her. Apparently he wasn't through romancing her yet, for he caught her in an ardent embrace, sealing his pledge with a flawless kiss.

Yep, things were going pretty well in his view of things. Joseph couldn't say he wasn't proud as he navigated through town. Word must have spread, because everyone who waved from horseback or from boardwalks looked pleased to see a beautiful young lady on the buggy seat beside him. A few folks called out a good day, and more than one married man shook his head as if to say, boy, you don't know the trouble you're getting in to.

Marriage was surely a big step, but by golly, he had wanted to be a married man for some time now. He just never figured he would wind up with such a beautiful and down-to-earth girl. One who could have found herself a husband instead of working hard to make her way on her own. He admired her for that. And after the kisses they shared, he couldn't wait for the wedding night. He'd best get their house built lickety-split.

"That's Poles' Mercantile." He spotted a good-size space along the hitching post and directed Bucky into it. The gelding came to a placid halt and Joseph pulled the brake. "You'll likely find most things on Mrs. Baker's list in there and across the street at the grocery. There's a mail office inside the mercantile. Come on in and I'll introduce you."

"That would be a great help, Joseph." She looked up at him as if he hung the moon, taking his hand to step down from the buggy with grace. Everything about her filled him with pride.

Devotion to her hammered through him, growing with each beat. As he offered his arm to escort her up the steps, he knew it always would. Sure, he may have fallen for Clara at first sight, but the love expanding within his soul was a rare and everlasting thing. He knew it. He would move mountains for her, trade his life for hers, utter his last breath saying her name. The thought of making her his wife caused emotion to lump in his throat, so he didn't talk much as he led the way along the boardwalk.

When he held the door for her and she swished by with a rustle of her skirts and sweetness, he noticed only her. Not the other folks, not the noise and bustle on the street and inside the store. Just Clara Woodrow, daintily tugging off her mittens and cap, looking up at him with love in her gaze.

Love. Yessir, all he could see was his lovely Clara, unbuttoning her coat. His adorable Clara smiling in greeting as Mrs. Pole circled round the counter with her hand extended. The two began to chat, but he still couldn't speak, overwhelmed. Clara was simply his end and his beginning.

"Looks like you've got yourself sweet on your Ma's new maid." Elderly Mr. Pole ambled over, a pipe stuck between his teeth and tugging on his suspender straps. "Which would be all right, if your bride wasn't waiting for you."

"My what?" He couldn't have heard Mr. Pole right. "Clara is my bride."

"No, that would be Miss Pennington. She's the one seated on the bench by the window. I was just about to send the box boy over to the feed store to fetch your brother. She's a real pretty thing, too. A real shame none of your kin thought to pick her up from the train." Mr. Pole winked. "You wouldn't know it to look at me, but I had a way with the ladies back in my day—"

"Wallace, don't you go telling tales," his wife scolded with a shake of her head as she took Clara by the arm. "I'll help Mary's new maid shop for her supplies, if you introduce our young Romeo to his betrothed."

It was all happening too fast, and his brain was like a wagon wheel stuck in the mud. He didn't know any Miss Pennington. Surely there was some confusion. His ma hadn't said a thing about writing away for a bride.

The moment he saw the shock on Clara's face, draining away her joy, leaving her stunned-looking and pale, he realized the truth. His ma *had* been searching for a bride for him. She had simply wanted to keep it a surprise—and she was too late.

"You had best go greet your bride-to-be," Clara said quietly, gently.

He watched her heart break, piece by piece. Amid the

noise and crush of midmorning shoppers, and the street noise as the door opened with a jingling bell, he saw her smile fade and her love close up like a new spring bud against a cruel frost.

"Go to her, Joseph." Clara turned her shoulder to him and walked away with small, dignified steps. She didn't look back, as if she had written him off for good.

Chapter Eight

❧❧❧❧

"Mary Brooks is quite specific when it comes to her teas," kindly Mrs. Pole explained, unaware of the roaring in Clara's ears, making it near to impossible to concentrate on the fact that her every hope was broken.

"Is that right?" she found herself saying as if from a great distance. Although she kept her back firmly turned, she could pick out the confident knell of Joseph's gait amid all the other noises in the mercantile. Her skin tingled with the memory of being in his arms, and pain split through her like lightning hitting a tree, leaving her as if cleaved right down the center. She blinked hard against the pain, determined to give the store owner all her attention. "Mrs. Baker only put tea on the list. Nothing specific."

"That Mrs. Baker knows better. She does this with all the new employees to the Brooks household. She's a queer sort, but a good housekeeper, so I hear. She runs a tight ship. That's why I aim to help you out, dear. You seem like a sweet girl. Here, let's take this basket and get it filled right up for you. Starting with the breakfast tea Mary enjoys in the morning."

"Thank you." Was it her fault her eyes were smarting? She could sense him from two aisles away, and the low murmur of his voice ought to have been indistinguishable in the busy store. But her stubborn ears searched fondly for the sound, taking in his every word.

"Are you looking for the Brooks family?" he asked with a smile in his voice.

Are you looking for the Brooks family? The words echoed in her mind, the same words he had said to her when he'd approached her on the train platform. Her knees weakened, pain slicing through her. Why did it hurt so much?

"Yes, I am," answered a cultured, modulated tone.

A beautiful voice for a beautiful lady, no doubt. Weakness trickled down her limbs, and she hardly was aware of the basket she held or Mrs. Pole placing two different tins of tea into it. One step further brought the newcomer into view. Clara saw a satin skirt trimmed in brushed velvet and the brim of a matching velvet hat. One more step and the delicate lady came into view, more beautiful than a princess, standing tall and slim and regal. Joseph tipped his hat, speaking with the woman, Miss Pennington. They looked good together, her frail good looks and his rugged handsomeness. A good match.

She felt every patch on her faded gingham dress and every scuff on her shoes.

You knew this was going to happen, she scolded herself. Her vision blurred and she blinked stubbornly, determined to focus on her shopping list. People left her. That was simply the truth. She had to be strong and face facts. She had been carried away by his courtship. Down deep she should have known that Joseph Brooks had never been truly going to stay with her.

She wasn't the kind of girl to inspire grand passion in a man, the kind that could bind his love to her for a lifetime.

"I know the list says honey," Mrs. Pole was saying, "but I happen to know Mary prefers sugar with her tea, so let's get both for safety's sake."

"Yes. Thank you." For safety's sake. That was very wise

advice. Clara tried not to sound distracted as she let go of the last of her hopes and dreams. She turned down the next aisle, blotting out the sound of Joseph and Miss Pennington's conversation. She wiped away the imagined faces of her children and erased the image of waking up beside Joseph, of spending the day doing for him and ending it again in his arms.

That life cannot be yours. She followed the store owner along the shelves, adding this and that to her basket, feeling the pain of what she lost. It was a void within her, as if someone had reached in and snatched out every last one of her dreams.

That's what you get for dreaming, she told herself as she set her basket on the counter. The pain she felt was simply the cost of wanting what she could never have.

"I'll just add this to the Brooks' account and you can be on your way. I'll send my husband to check on any mail for you. That will save you a few steps."

"Thank you, Mrs. Pole." As footsteps rang closer she made sure she was facing the other way. She took great care to help Mrs. Pole in tallying the purchases, doing her best to keep her chin set and her tattered heart hidden.

Joseph and his new lady stopped behind her. "Clara? I need to help Miss Pennington with her trunks and get her settled into the hotel. All right?"

She read the apology in his eyes, sincere and forthright, and pure Joseph. He was a good man. This wasn't his fault. Anyone would be dazzled by the lovely lady at his side. It hurt something terrible, but she managed what she hoped was a steady smile. "I'll be fine. Please, get Miss Pennington settled. I know how tired she must be after that long train trip."

"Yes, it was long." Miss Pennington spoke up gently. "I couldn't help overhearing. You must work for the Brooks family. It's so lovely to meet you. My name is Melody."

"It's nice to meet you, too. Where are you from?" She didn't want to like the woman who had come to marry Joseph, but she did. Melody Pennington did not look down on her for being hired help, but offered a friendly smile.

"Boston. To think I had never been far from home until I boarded the train. It has been an adventure, but I am very happy to be here, at my new home. Already it is beyond my expectations." She smiled sweetly up at Joseph.

The man looked uncomfortable, but then, of course he did. He was a good man. She could clearly see how this would go. He would pull her—Clara—aside later and explain things, let her down gently and as carefully as he could. He would do his best not to hurt her, not realizing it was already too late.

Best to make this easy for him. "You two go on. I'm sure I'll see you again, Miss Pennington."

"Melody," she prompted.

Clara nodded. Perhaps the woman didn't understand they were not equals. That for as long as she held a job in the Brooks household, she would have to watch the woman who had taken her place, living the life she wished to have, loving the man Clara wanted with all of her soul.

"When I'm done here, we'll talk," he said. "Will you wait for me?"

"Goodbye, Joseph," she said. His midnight-blue gaze looked nearly black with emotion, and torture hardened the planes of his face. If she felt a swell of love for the man, she ignored it. She spun on her heel, giving Mrs. Pole her entire attention. When the door opened with a chime of a bell and a blast of damp wind, she disregarded it. That was simply Joseph Brooks walking out of her life.

Hers, she had learned the hard way, would go on.

Clara's eyes, full of pain, haunted him as he escorted Miss Pennington into the wind and rain. The brunt of the storm hit him, but he didn't feel it. Clara's heartbreak filled his senses. It echoed in the chambers of his heart and rumbled in his soul.

Sure, he knew what she thought. She feared he would set her aside in favor of the lady from Boston. Clara feared that he was a shallow dandy who charmed every pretty woman that came his way.

Wrong. His boots struck hard on the boards in quick angry beats. Remembering Miss Pennington, he came to a ringing stop and waited for her to catch up. She hurried after him with a hand to keep her hat in place in the brisk winds.

"You seem upset, Joseph." Worry furrowed her ivory brow. "Please, tell me what is wrong? Is it something I have said?"

"No, Miss Pennington. It's hardly your fault." He swept off his hat to rake his fingers through his hair. Torn between wanting to race back into that store and reassure Clara and needing to stay and do the right thing for this woman his mother had promised so much to. "I—"

Before he could say more, Austin Dermot strode to a halt beside him, all smiles. The livery-stable owner looked struck as he gazed upon Miss Pennington's fair features. He cleared his throat. "It's hardly fair, Brooks. I can't find me one beautiful woman to court, and here you've got yourself two to choose from. I'm Austin Dermot, Miss—"

"Pennington." Understanding swept across her face, and sympathy made her blue eyes bluer. "Joseph, you should have told me."

"That's what I was working up to doing." He squared his shoulders, frowning at the way Dermot was staring with unabashed interest at the newcomer. "Austin, why don't you make yourself useful and get a wagon hitched for Miss Pennington."

"I would be glad to." He knuckled back his hat. "Mighty fine to meet you, miss. I'll go fetch the wagon. I reckon you and I will speak again mighty soon."

"Yes, thank you, Mr. Dermot." Miss Pennington bobbed in a polite curtsy. Her fancy frock and finely tailored traveling coat made him think of a tropical bird that had landed here by mistake.

He could do nothing but tell her the truth. This time he kept his gait slow and his pace shorter to match hers. "My ma made you certain promises for coming here, didn't she?"

"You needn't worry about it, Joseph. I took too long making up my mind to come, and now you have fallen in love with someone else." There was no accusation in her words, simply sad understanding. Ma surely had outdone herself finding this upstanding lady.

"How did you know?" He jammed his hands in his pockets.

"I have eyes. It's Clara, isn't it? She is the lucky one to have won your heart."

All Joseph could think about was Clara and the heart-break on her face. Did she think so little of his honor? Or was it simply so hard for her to believe in his love? "I'm the lucky man to have won *hers*."

"You are exactly like your mother's letters." Melody Pennington looked wistful and lost as she led the way down the boardwalk. "I wish you and Clara every happiness, Joseph."

"I wish the same for you." He couldn't help glancing over his shoulder down the length of the block. The mercantile and Clara seemed far away. He longed to run back and comfort her and let her know that everything was going to be all right. His was a forever love, so strong that nothing could break it. But his family had brought Miss Pennington here. He could not very well abandon her to fend for herself on the street. Not with so many anxious bachelors around.

"Goodness, what friendly men there are in this town." The fine lady shook her head, gesturing toward the trio of men across the street in front of the feed store, all tipping their hats and donning their best smiles. Chests puffed out, spines straight and interest sparkling in their eyes all said one thing: the lady from Boston would not be lonely for long.

"I had best send word to my brother. Gabe will help you fend them all off." He would leave Melody in his brother's capable care. Joseph hailed Dermot, who must have rushed to hitch up a team because he was driving fast down the street in a hurry to serve Miss Pennington. "Believe me, you are going to need it."

"So I see." She looked stunned at the attention as the tailor poked his head out of his shop door to tip his hat to her. "I didn't come here to marry just any man, you know."

"I know, but trust me. You never know when love will find you. Let's fetch your trunks from the depot, we'll get you settled in at the hotel. By then my brother ought to be free to help you."

"Thank you kindly, Joseph." There was a note of sadness in her words, and he felt sorry for her. She had likely a story of sorrow, or else why had she come so far to start a new life? Sadness was all he felt for the lady. His heart belonged to Clara one hundred percent, and it always would.

Clara. He hoped Gabe was in his office in town. The faster he could come, the sooner Joseph could get back to his beloved and show her once and for all the way he loved her.

Of course things had to get worse, Clara thought as she sorted through the bundle of mail Mr. Pole had given her. She was merely organizing it according to size to tie it securely so the envelopes and newspapers wouldn't slip all over the buggy seat, when she had spotted four letters addressed to "Mrs. Mary Brooks, Regarding the Maid Position."

She hadn't considered there would be others as hard-pressed as she had been to travel for a good job. Perhaps, once Mrs. Brooks realized the penniless maid had not only fallen in love with her youngest son but had hoped to marry him, she would be fired.

Perhaps that would be for the best. Rain tapped at the curtains as she released the brake. Bucky, his ears swiveled, waiting for her command, jumped eagerly to obey the gentle snap of the reins. The buggy lunged forward into the muddy street, and out of the corner of her eye she caught sight of a familiar set of brawny shoulders and the unyielding line of Joseph's back as he held the hotel's front door for a somber Miss Pennington.

You must stop thinking of him as Joseph, she scolded, the leather reins in hand. *He is the youngest Mr. Brooks.* That was how she must think of him from now on. *If* she thought of him at all. She would be wise to put his kindness to her out of her mind. To forget their moonlight kisses and the wishes shared beneath a snow-filled sky.

The wagon wheels skidded in the mire, and the gelding seemed to throw his weight against the harness. The buggy straightened out, rolling along the last block of the main street. She hardly noticed the people hurrying about their daily activities or the retired men watching from the bakery window.

She especially had to stop thinking of Joseph—the young Mr. Brooks—inside that hotel, seeing to Miss Pennington. Of course the woman ought to have help getting settled; it looked like quite a stack of trunks on the boardwalk in front of the hotel.

He was truly gone. A swift strike of acceptance hit her. She hadn't realized there was a tiny part of her that could still hope. Maybe he was merely being gentlemanly in aiding the woman who had stepped off the train in a strange town, just as she had not long ago, worrying over what could go wrong and if she would be accepted or rejected.

He was right to help Melody Pennington. And as for the tiny hope within her, it was growing weaker, fading with every turn of the buggy wheel. Joseph was not going to put aside such a fine lady as Melody Pennington for her, was he? No. She had to be sensible. She had always been the sensible one in the family, finding work when their shelves were bare; finding more work whenever Ma gambled or drank away their rent money; coming to this town when she had the chance for better employment. The only time she had failed to be practical was when she followed her heart.

If she were smart, she would never follow it again. She was through with love, with trusting men who always left her. The buggy bumped strangely, jostling her in the seat. The road ahead looked soupy, thick with mud and with melting chunks of ice. Bucky did not seem troubled as he forged ahead, drawing her through the worst of the mud. The left side of the buggy lurched again; the rigging rattled; the axle groaned and a bump knocked her onto the floorboards.

Bucky let out a troubled neigh, the sound clear in her head while everything else felt hazy. She'd slid off the seat and onto the floorboards, hardly feeling the fall. That's how upset she was over Joseph. Over the fact that he was going to leave her for another woman, just like last time. Someone who could offer him more, just like Lars had done taking up with the hardware store's daughter whose father was fixing to retire.

But Joseph is not Lars, a small voice of reason whispered. It was hard to hear over the fears and doubts loud within her. Her forehead was sore—perhaps she had hit it on the dashboard. She rubbed her head and climbed to her knees.

"Miss? Are you all right in there?" An older man with a healthy mop of white hair peered in through the rain-streaked curtains at her. "Can you get up?"

"I'm fine. Just shaken." She was surprised when he pulled aside the curtains and caught her by the elbow. He didn't need to help her onto the seat, but he did. A good thing, as it turned out, for she was terribly shaken. "I'm more embarrassed than anything. I'm new at driving."

"I should say so." Kindly, the man gave a single chuckle, looking her over. "You've got a small bump on your forehead, but it doesn't look too serious. Do you hurt anywhere?"

"No, no, but what about the buggy?" It lurched at an odd angle, as if something could very well be broken. How would she ever pay to repair it? This was a very expensive vehicle. She felt ill to her stomach with worry. Remembering the letters that had been on the seat—they were on the floor now—she realized Mrs. Brooks could very easily fire her over this. And how would she explain it? That she had ruined the buggy because she had been ruminating over her employer's son?

"Miss? You don't seem all right. You come out here into the fresh air. Maybe that will clear your senses. Move across the seat, now. Don't worry. I've got you."

"This is unnecessary, but thank you." She scooted toward the door and realized a half-dozen older men in their rain slickers were gathered around the back of the buggy, pondering the problem. She was blocking traffic. She had caused the problem by not paying attention, and yet everyone was so kind. One of the business owners came to the edge of the boardwalk and held a steaming cup. Another had brought a horse and a chain to help extricate the buggy.

"Are you all right?" at least a half-dozen voices asked her as she waded through the mud toward the boardwalk.

This was not the world she was used to, where people were so kind. In the crowded part of the city where she had lived, she would have been yelled at more than once, and being helped was a rare occurrence. But here, a woman placed a bracing cup of coffee in her hands and stood with her beneath the awning. Men exited shops and hopped into the mud to bring their horses to help out. Pleasant conversations rose and fell. One voice rose above the others. A man loped off the boardwalk in front of the hotel and crossed the muddy street, heedless of the rain and the slick mud.

Joseph. Her foolish heart swelled with love and with wishes that had no right coming true. The fault was all hers, she realized. She was too full of fear and doubts to have the right to love a man whose concern was visible two blocks away, though not as obvious as the love in his eyes.

Chapter Nine

"Are you all right?" His hands gripped her forearms, alarm booming in his voice. On the walk over, he had stopped to untie his horse, and even Don Quixote studied her with a look of concern. "You could have been seriously hurt. Why didn't you wait for me, like I asked?"

"You were busy." She felt foolish and ashamed. She couldn't meet his gaze. She didn't deserve a man like him, not really. Her fears and doubts clung to her like rain to her coat, and she felt shabby and unworthy. The regard and respect he showed her was something she had not been able to show him.

"You were upset." He released her, his tone raw with tenderness. "Will you stay here with Mrs. McKaslin while I help with the buggy?"

Her throat closed tight, and she could only nod. She didn't trust her voice. She blinked hard against the stinging heat of unwanted tears. She had thought the worst of Joseph. She had compared him to a much lesser man. Joseph was nothing like Lars. She had known it all along, and the proof of it was striding away from her. Don Quixote blew her a reassuring nicker before he followed his master toward the small knot of men hitching extra horses to the buggy.

Time spent with Joseph had been more fairy tale than what she had known of real life. Times had been hard growing up as she did, in a rough part of town with parents who could not function as adults. The shady and mostly desperate people she had been surrounded with were nothing like these small-town people who gathered around Joseph, listening as he began to speak. Others passing by in wagons or on horseback stopped to lend a hand.

"It will be just fine," the woman beside her said with reassurance. "This happens often this time of year. The men will get the buggy out, and it will be none the worse for wear. You'll see."

"I should have done better." She should have been better. But how did a girl let go of fears that had been with her all her life? How did she learn to stop doubting and start believing?

"Joseph is quite a catch," the lady continued with a maternal smile. "He's from a fine family. He's a good young man. Word has it you came a long way and had a few hard times. What a great gift it must be for you to know a man like Joseph is in love with you."

"Yes." Emotion twisted within her, deep and rich and as everlasting as the earth and sky. A love so bright, she found it hard to see. She turned toward Joseph, and he seemed bigger, greater than ever before. He gestured to a group of men, who braced their arms against the back of the buggy, and others who gathered toward the front.

He held up one hand, stopping to check the harnessing. A truly capable man. One whom a girl could count on to solve any problem the right way. Endless love spiraled through her, taking up all the space within her. Her fears and doubts felt smaller.

"On three!" Joseph's words rose above the noise and commotion and he began to count down. He grabbed hold of the front wheel well and when the men and horses pulled and pushed together, the deep mud relinquished its hold on the buggy. Slowly, painfully, the vehicle lumbered out of the muck and onto solid ground.

"I told you so," the woman at her side said kindly. "Everything will be right as rain. Yes, that surely is a fine young man you have there. I suppose he is fixing to propose soon?"

Tender emotion ached in her throat, making it impossible to answer. Tears swam in her eyes, blurring the man. He raised his hand in thanks to his fellow townsmen and everyone dispersed—the men returning to their wagons, businesses and errands. The only thing she noticed was the impressive man striding toward her. The man too good to be true; but he was.

He was.

"You all right?" He took the cup from her hands, setting it out of sight. "I heard you took a bump to your head."

"I'm fine." Her voice came unnaturally thick and raw. Vulnerable, she hated how she had doubted him. Worst of all, he knew she doubted him. What a failure she was.

"You don't look fine." He caressed away stray curls. His knuckles grazed her skin and stirred up more longing and desire, more love and dreams. All it took was his touch and she was helpless.

"You have a small bump right here." His baritone rumbled intimately, as if they were alone together. He leaned closer and closer still, until his lips grazed her forehead with a gentle, healing kiss. "Maybe that will help."

"Yes." He transfixed her, holding her captive with his tenderness and chasing away every doubt. But it didn't change the truth. "I didn't believe in you, Joseph. I thought—"

"I know." He cut her off, as if to save her from hurting. "You don't have to fear being abandoned. I would never leave you. I love you, Clara. Can you see that?"

"I do." Fear lashed through her, fear of being hurt and left. But they were only that: fears. Hard-won lessons in life, but they did not serve her now. Joseph was her one chance for true love and she did not want to fail him again. "I should have known, Joseph. I still can't believe you chose me."

"Then I will say it again. I love you, Clara." He took her into his arms, the safest place she had ever known. "I will say it as many times as it takes. I love you." He kissed the middle of her forehead. "I love you." He kissed the tip of her nose.

"I love you," she vowed, reaching up to cradle his face with both of her hands. His jaw was slightly rough and as strong as steel. Her heart opened up, and she let go of her fears one by one. His lips brushed hers, sending heated tingles through every part of her.

It was like sitting on the sled on the crest of the hillside, when she had been afraid of crashing, of getting hurt. But that hadn't happened, because Joseph had caught her. And, she knew now, he always would.

"Say that again," he said, breaking their kiss. "I want to hear it over and over."

"I love you, Joseph Brooks." She brushed a kiss to his cheek. "I want to love you forever."

"Golly, am I a lucky man." He chuckled. The warm sound vibrated through her as he hauled her tight against his chest. "Forever sounds just fine with me."

Epilogue

❦

"I'm real nervous about this, and there's no call for it." Joseph leaned against the fence railing and took one long look at the ring sparkling in his hand. Two weeks had passed and each day had been better than the last. He had gone riding with Clara, buggy driving, taking her shopping in town and out to their land for her approval on the house he was building. Warm early-summer sunshine warmed his back and magnified the flawless diamond. This was the ring Clara would wear for the rest of their life together.

Don Quixote arched his neck over the top rail and snorted his opinion.

"Yeah, I know. It's foolish to be nervous." Joseph rubbed his free hand along his best buddy's nose. "She's already told me she loves me. I know she wants to marry me. But it's a daunting thing, asking a woman to be your wife."

The stallion nodded his head vigorously and stomped his right-front hoof. Apparently he had a suggestion on what might make his master forget his jitters and focus on what mattered.

"Whoa, there, fella. That's my future wife you're talking about." Not that he could blame him. The thought of being married to the most beautiful woman in Mountain County and going to bed with her every night sure put a grin on his face. "I had best get to it. I want to make this official."

The stallion nickered, as if wondering what the hesitation was about.

All it took was one glance at Clara and his nerves quieted. His jitters silenced. Happiness lapped through him, and it was his future he saw, with every day happier than the next and every night filled with passion. Not to be disrespectful, but that was sure something he was ready to discover. With any luck, Clara would want a *very* short engagement.

She looked as pretty as a princess, picking rosebuds off the bushes next to the porch. The pink dress she wore, one of the many he'd purchased from the town's seamstress for her, complemented her womanly curves perfectly. She must have sensed him coming because she turned to him, a welcome smile shaping her rosebud mouth—the mouth he hungered to cover with kisses as soon as they were alone together.

"Joseph." His name sounded perfect on her voice, layered with love and happiness. Clara plucked another rose stem. "Did you and Don Quixote have a good talk?"

"As a matter of fact, we did." Mindful of his entire family watching from the porch, he gave Clara only one brief kiss and not the countless hot, lingering kisses he hungered for. "He gave me some good advice."

"Oh? What did he advise?"

"This." He knelt in the grass in front of her and took her left hand in his. That brought his ma to her feet and put a spark in his pa's eyes. Brother Nate grinned widely in approval, seated next to his wife, who held their sleeping baby. Looked like his family approved of Clara, especially Ma, who had tears on her cheeks.

"Clara Woodrow." He said her name with all the love in his heart. "Will you do me the great honor of becoming my wife?"

"Yes. It would be my honor to marry you, Joseph." Joy

transformed her, making her ever more beautiful. She gasped as he slid the ring on her slender finger. "It's breathtaking. Thank you. I'm just—"

"Happy?" he asked, rising to take her in his arms. "A little nervous? It's a big step."

"It's everything. Joseph, you are everything." She laid her hands flat on his chest, the ring sparkling like the most precious vow. "You are my heart's dream."

"And you are mine, my beloved." He kissed her ardently, drawing her tight against him until she blushed. She could feel his arousal, and desire curled through her.

"I love you so much." It was so easy to see their future together. Exchanging vows as man and wife right here in Mary's lovely garden, living together in the cabin until their beautiful home was built and loving each other through the days and nights of their long and happy marriage.

"Looks like we have a wedding to plan!" Mary swiped at her tears, but they kept rolling down her apple cheeks. "Joseph, you have made me very happy."

"Well done, son," Mr. Brooks added pridefully from behind his newspaper. Even Gabe, the oldest Brooks son, who generally disapproved of marriage, offered a smile of congratulations.

"I want a quick wedding," Joseph whispered in her ear, holding her tight enough that she could well feel what was on his mind.

"The sooner the better," she said shyly, hoping he knew what she could not say. She desired him, too, this man who made her feel as cherished as a storybook princess.

As the family gathered round to look at the ring and offer advice on the wedding, Joseph's hand never left hers. Some dreams, she learned, came true. This man's love was the one thing she could always count on.

"How does next month sound?" she offered, already envisioning their wedding with sunshine and sweet mountain breezes and roses. Lots of roses.

"Not soon enough," Joseph quipped. "How about next week?"

"That's not enough time!" Mary protested. "What about a wedding gown? What about the arrangements?"

"Next week sounds perfect to me." She didn't care about having a new dress made. What she cared about was Joseph and starting her life as his wife.

"Yep, absolutely perfect," he agreed with a wink, and she knew that look in his eyes. They laughed together, and she had no doubts. Her life with Joseph would be just like this moment, happy and full of love and laughter.

* * * * *

COURTING MISS PERFECT

Judith Stacy

Dear Reader

I'm often asked where I get the ideas for my books. Though I've written twenty-three romance novels, the seed from which each book grew has been very different.

While I was napping, the vision of a rugged cowboy in a pink ruffled apron led to THE HEART OF A HERO. The title MARRIED BY MIDNIGHT popped into my head during a doctor's visit, and I liked it so much I wrote a book to go with it. THE LAST BRIDE IN TEXAS was inspired by my work as a volunteer tutor for the Los Angeles County Adult Literacy programme.

COURTING MISS PERFECT was much easier. While visiting my sister Martha Cooper, at her home in Virginia, she showed me a set of books she'd acquired from the estate of her late mother-in-law, Latha Cooper. The ten-volume set, *The Mental Efficiency Series*, was published in 1915 and included such titles as *Character: How to Strengthen It; Common Sense: How to Exercise It; Personality: How to Build It.*

Martha told me I should write a story about a young woman travelling the West selling books. That fabulous idea led to COURTING MISS PERFECT.

I hope you enjoy the adventure of Brynn O'Keefe who, with her book *Planning Perfection,* escapes scandal in Virginia, runs foul of the law, finds a lost treasure of jewels, and meets a handsome railroad detective who shows her what 'perfect' really means.

Best wishes

Judith

With much love to David, Stacy, Judy and Seth, and special thanks to Martha Cooper, Latha Cooper, Bonnie Stone, Leighton Stone and Kitty Vollbrecht.

Chapter One

~~~

Texas, 1886

How rude.

Brynn O'Keefe jerked her chin and stared out the window of the passenger car, breaking away from the penetrating gaze of the man seated nearby. He was positively the most ill-mannered man she'd encountered on this trip—or possibly ever.

Seated across the aisle and one row up, the man had inconsiderately stretched his long legs across the seat beside him, barring anyone from using it, and turned sideways so that he faced her. He held up a newspaper, as if he were reading, but they'd been aboard this train for over an hour now and Brynn had yet to see him turn the page. It was merely a ploy to stare at her.

Even though she wore a silk traveling dress, unlike most of the women onboard, who wore gingham or calico, and was considerably younger—only twenty-one years old—she hardly expected to be ogled like a show horse on the auction block. Really, just who did this man think he was?

Brynn clasped her hands together on her lap and reminded

herself this was hardly the worst insult she'd endured these past few weeks. And if it hadn't been for Aunt Sadie allowing her to come along on this trip west, things would have only gotten worse back home in Richmond.

Brynn didn't want to imagine just how much worse.

She fixed her attention out the window at the Texas landscape rolling past beneath the bright midday sun. The journey from Virginia that Brynn and her aunt Sadie had begun several weeks ago had taken them ever westward and, up until this morning, everything had gone smoothly.

Now Aunt Sadie lay ill in their hotel room back in Hayden and Brynn was making this leg of their trip alone. She'd wanted to stay and care for her aunt, but she had insisted Brynn go on without her. Dolly, Sadie's traveling secretary, was there to attend her, and too much was at stake for them to cancel.

Brynn hadn't dared defy her aunt. She was lucky to be here, lucky to get away from Richmond after what had happened—

Good gracious, he was staring at her again!

Brynn pinched her lips together and averted her gaze. How rude could one man possibly be?

Perhaps she was expecting too much, Brynn decided. After all, this stranger was hardly the sort of man she was accustomed to back home in Richmond, where men wore suits, starched shirts and linen cravats. This man had on denim trousers, a pale blue shirt beneath a black vest and a black Stetson pulled low on his forehead.

He looked dangerous.

Brynn stole a quick glance, then averted her gaze. Yes, he looked dangerous, sinister even.

It was his size, she decided. She could see how tall, how muscular he was even seated. Wide shoulders. A broad chest. Probably very strong.

She chanced another look, this time catching a glimpse of his face beneath his wide hat brim. His eyes shifted, moved, so that nothing escaped his attention, and his square jaw was set as if he expected—perhaps even welcomed—trouble.

Definitely not a gentleman.

"Won't be much longer now," the man beside her said.

Brynn turned to him. Now *this* was a gentleman. He wore a nice suit. His shoes shone with fresh polish. She figured him for about the same age as her older brother. He was pleasant looking—certainly not threatening in any way.

She'd met him quite by chance this morning while boarding the train in Hayden. He'd introduced himself as Mr. Hiram Smith and gallantly assisted with her trunks, saving her the expense of tipping the porter. Then he'd requested, quite respectfully, the honor of sitting next to her on their journey. He'd made the perfect traveling companion.

"We'll arrive in Harmony a bit early," Hiram announced as he snapped his pocket watch closed and tucked it away.

A little knot of worry coiled inside Brynn. She hadn't relished the idea of making the journey from Hayden to the town of Harmony alone, without Aunt Sadie. Until they'd embarked on this trip—this "adventure," Aunt Sadie had called it—Brynn had seldom been away from home, and certainly had never traveled alone, unescorted and unchaperoned.

Once more Brynn reminded herself that her life was different now. She had to adjust. And, above all, she couldn't let Aunt Sadie down.

"Is someone meeting you at the station?" Hiram asked.

The ladies of Harmony expected her and would be on hand to welcome her and get her settled, just as the women had done at all the other stops she and Aunt Sadie had made on their tour.

"The mayor's wife," Brynn said.

Mr. Smith's eyes widened. "My, how impressive. That book of your aunt's must be something."

Brynn smiled, genuinely proud of her aunt's accomplishments. Not only had she written a book essential to the well-being of every woman alive, but she'd also arranged this journey to the West, taking her vital message to those who needed it most.

Brynn knew the ladies of Harmony would be disappointed when she stepped off the train alone and explained that Aunt Sadie herself wouldn't be there to discuss and sell her book at the event that was planned. But the ladies would forget soon enough. Brynn had heard her aunt's speeches so many times she could recite them in her sleep.

"How long will you be staying in Harmony?" Brynn asked.

Hiram had mentioned he was a salesman, dispatched from a large textile company in New York.

"Sometimes I stay a day, other times longer. Depends on how sales go." Hiram gave her a conspiratorial smile. "Let's hope the ladies of Harmony are in a generous frame of mind, for both our sakes."

The pitching and rocking of the train slowed and the whistle pierced the air as they pulled into the station. Passengers rustled in their seats, gathering their belongings. Hiram was the first on his feet.

"I'll see to your trunks," he told her, and headed down the aisle.

"Thank you," Brynn said, rising. "That's very—oh!"

Someone brushed past, knocking her back into her seat. Brynn looked up. It was *him*. That awful man who'd been staring at her throughout the entire trip. She watched as he pushed his way down the aisle, jostling the other passengers, and disappeared out the door.

"Of all the nerve…" Brynn mumbled as she straightened her hat.

She gathered her handbag and followed the slow procession of passengers out of the car. She wished she had a few minutes to freshen up before the mayor's wife greeted her. A good first impression was essential.

Around her, travelers crowded the platform craning their necks, searching for friends and family. Shouts rang out as loved ones spotted each other.

Steam hissed from the locomotive. Porters moved trunks out of the baggage car. Freight wagons stood ready, their teams of horses tossing their heads and pawing at the dirt.

So much commotion. She hadn't noticed it before at other train stations, when Aunt Sadie and her secretary had been with her.

Brynn tucked an errant dark curl behind her ear and forced a pleasant, composed expression onto her face. The mayor's wife would be here any second.

And where was Hiram with her trunks?

Brynn rose on her toes, scanning the crowd. No sign of him. But not to worry, she told herself, he'd be along momentarily. The mayor's wife would appear and see that she got to her hotel, and everything would be fine.

Sharp voices drew her attention. She spotted Hiram near the entrance to the station. The conductor was next to him and so was—good gracious, it was that awful man from across the aisle. He towered over Hiram. His expression was grim, his jaw set as he spoke.

Anger flew through Brynn. Was that the way a gentleman was received here in Harmony? She wanted to march over there and give that uncouth heathen a piece of her mind.

But she didn't dare. How would it look if the mayor's wife arrived to find her in the midst of an argument in a public place, with a total stranger?

Heat rushed across Brynn's cheeks. The last thing she wanted was to be the subject of gossip—again.

Determinedly, she turned away. The crowd had thinned a bit. She wished the mayor's wife would hurry up and get there. If the train hadn't arrived early, she would be safely ensconced in her hotel room by now.

The crowd that had gathered at the edge of the platform

parted quickly and a man strode up the stairs from the street. Tall, he wore the same rugged clothing as most of the men she'd seen in Texas. Sunlight flashed against a badge pinned to his chest. She gasped, realizing he was the town sheriff.

He joined the circle of men confronting Hiram.

Another wave of anger surged through Brynn. What had that awful man from the train started? Why had he accosted Hiram, drawing the attention of the train conductor and now the presence of the sheriff? He was a troublemaker, all right, just as she'd thought.

While she watched, words were exchanged, heated at times. Brynn wished she could hear what they were saying. Hiram shook his head repeatedly. Finally, the whole lot of them disappeared into the train station.

Brynn realized then that she and a half-dozen other people were all that remained on the platform. A cold fear gripped her.

Where was the mayor's wife? Wasn't she coming?

Then another fear claimed Brynn. Had she read her aunt's speaking schedule incorrectly? Had she gotten off at the wrong town? Was there a mayor's wife standing at a platform several stops back up the line, waiting for her? Had she inadvertently embarrassed Aunt Sadie?

Humiliation roiled through Brynn. *No, no, no, I couldn't have made a mistake.*

Quickly, she dug into her handbag and found the schedule, then heaved a sigh of relief. She was in the right place, on the right day. Thank goodness, she hadn't made an error.

Several minutes dragged by. The last people on the platform drifted away, and still no sign of the mayor's wife.

Brynn certainly couldn't stand there all day. Somehow she'd have to gather her belongings and find the hotel.

Things were so much easier with Aunt Sadie along.

Brynn plucked up her courage and approached a porter. He fetched her luggage from the baggage car and loaded it into one of the wagons waiting near the platform.

"Are you Miss Davenport?" the driver asked. He wasn't much more than a boy, with a shock of blond hair and an easy smile. "My name's Pete. My ma sent me over from the hotel to fetch you."

"I'm Miss O'Keefe," Brynn told him. "Miss Davenport is my aunt. She's in Hayden, ill."

Pete assisted her onto the wagon seat. He jumped up beside her, flicked the reins and the team of horses lurched forward.

Brynn relaxed a bit. Everything would be fine, she told herself. Of course, it would. After all, in a town named Harmony, how could there be a problem?

Travis Hollister gazed out the window of the station master's office. A wagon with Harmony Hotel painted on the side in red letters rumbled away from the platform. Aboard was the young woman who'd sat next to Hiram Smith during the trip from Hayden.

She was safe, thank goodness. He'd worried over her during the entire journey, watched her like a hawk, afraid of what Smith might do. Travis had been forced to give her the gentlest of shoves when he'd left the train to get ahead of her, keep her from following Smith. He wasn't proud of it, even if it had been for her own good.

"Don't be so hard on yourself, Travis," Sheriff Sutherland said. "I think you're right about Smith."

Travis mumbled a curse under his breath. Even though he and Rafe Sutherland had been friends for years and he respected him as an honest, hardworking lawman, his words brought no comfort.

"All I have to do is prove it," Travis said.

Rafe chuckled. "Shouldn't be too tough, you being a world-famous Pinkerton detective."

Travis smiled at his friend's good-natured ribbing. He'd been an operative for the Pinkerton National Detective Agency for several years now. The agency was the largest—

and most prestigious—private police force in the country, probably the world. Headquarters was in Chicago, but Travis worked out of their Denver office investigating everything from bank robberies, to union uprisings, cattle rustling and theft, for some of the wealthiest clients and biggest businesses in the nation. Now with the booming railroad industry, Travis was assigned to the Texas railway system.

He'd seen Hiram Smith's likeness on a wanted poster and read his description in the bulletin he'd received from the superintendent of the Denver office. The man was reportedly a thief and con artist suspected of stealing a fortune in jewelry from an elderly couple in Houston.

He'd spotted Smith by chance at the train station in Hayden this morning, so he'd boarded the train, grabbed a seat where he could keep an eye on him and made the trip to Harmony.

But when he'd confronted Smith on the platform, the man had denied any involvement in the theft. He'd emptied his pockets and allowed Travis to search his baggage with the sheriff and the station master as witnesses, but no jewelry was discovered. He didn't act like a guilty man. Dressed like an Eastern dandy, Smith looked innocent. Still, Travis's gut told him otherwise.

"I'm not wrong about Smith," he said. "I've seen his kind before, too many times."

"Then where are the stolen jewels?" Rafe asked.

"Good question," Travis admitted. "If they weren't on Smith, then they must have—"

He whirled back toward the window as the Hotel Harmony wagon disappeared down Main Street, a knot of suspicion growing inside him.

Had he looked in the wrong luggage?

He intended to find out.

Chapter Two

Had she said the right thing?

Brynn sank onto the foot of the bed, clutching the strings of her handbag in her fists. Mrs. Millburn, the hotel owner, had met her as Pete pulled the wagon to a stop. Brynn had delivered her carefully prepared greeting and explanation of Aunt Sadie's absence. The woman had seemed properly concerned about her aunt's illness and pleased to see her, but Brynn still worried. It was troubling, thinking she might not have made the sort of impression Aunt Sadie would have wanted.

Everything Brynn did and said in Harmony would be a reflection on her aunt and her aunt's book. How would it look if the niece, traveling companion and substitute lecturer of the author of *Planning Perfection* was anything less than perfect?

Brynn had learned back home in Richmond what would happen if she didn't measure up to everyone's expectations. She couldn't go through that again.

She drew a breath and wandered to the window. From her room on the second floor, the town of Harmony spread out below her. Wooden storefronts, boardwalks, water troughs, hitching posts. Teams of horses pulled freight wagons and carriages. Men wearing guns strapped to their thighs walked the streets alongside women in bonnets, towing little children in their wake. Folks stopped to chat. Not much different from the other towns Brynn and her aunt had visited.

Still, it was unnerving being totally alone, not knowing a single soul.

Better to stay busy, Brynn decided. She opened her valise that Pete had placed on the end of the bed and pulled out her clothing. She frowned, seeing that some of her garments hadn't fared well on the trip. She'd ask Mrs. Millburn about ironing—

A strange case flew out of her valise along with her petticoats, and landed on the bed.

"What on earth?" she mumbled.

She'd never seen the small, red velvet case before, and couldn't imagine where it had come from. She picked it up. It felt heavy, despite its size. She pried open the lid.

Inside was a jumble of jewelry. Rings, necklaces, bracelets. Several large broaches. Sapphires, rubies, emeralds, diamonds and garnets sparkled in the light.

Brynn gasped and her eyes widened. The pieces were gorgeous, absolutely breathtaking and terribly expensive. How had they ended up among her belongings?

She looked at the valise again. It was definitely hers, as were the clothes inside, and she was certain they didn't belong to Aunt Sadie. Somehow, there had been a mix-up.

She could clear this up easily enough. Though she wasn't excited about walking the streets alone, unescorted, she would report this to the stationmaster and let him sort it out.

Brynn tucked the velvet case inside her valise—it hardly seemed a good idea to walk the streets with priceless jewelry tucked into her handbag—then pinned on her hat and headed downstairs. Just as she reached the bottom step, the hotel's front door flew open and a man filled the space. Bright sunlight beamed in around him, shadowing his face, making him a black hulk in the doorway.

Brynn froze in her tracks. Good gracious, he was huge. A wild heat rolled off him, frightening her, but leaving her somehow unable to move.

Then he stepped inside and squared himself in front of her. Brynn's gaze traveled upward and locked on to his face.

It was that awful man from the train.

Irritation, annoyance—something—swept through Brynn. What was he doing here? She couldn't imagine, and she certainly didn't intend to stick around and find out.

Brynn moved to the right, but he stepped in front of her. She dodged left, but he blocked her again.

"Where are you going in such a hurry?" he demanded.

Brynn pulled herself up and looked him straight in the eye. "I hardly see where that's any of your business," she told him. "I'll have to ask you to kindly step aside."

"Like hell," he said.

Brynn gasped. She'd never been spoken to in this fashion before and she should have dissolved into tears. Instead, hearing the challenge in his voice made her want to speak just as harshly to him, as if he'd thrown down a verbal gauntlet that she itched to pick up.

"I insist," she told him, pushing her nose a little higher in the air.

"I'm not going anywhere," he told her, "until I get exactly what I came here for."

"If you don't step aside, I'll be forced to alert the authorities," Brynn informed him.

A crooked smile pulled at one corner of his mouth. "That won't take too long, seeing as I'm a Pinkerton detective."

Brynn's eyes widened. "You're a…a *what?*"

"Travis Hollister," he said, and flashed a badge in her face that he'd pulled from his shirt pocket. "I'm tracking a thief, and I'm convinced you can help me."

Annoyed, she huffed. Why would he think she had any knowledge of a thief?

"I haven't the faintest idea what you're talking about," Brynn said.

Travis drew closer and leaned down, crowding her.

"I believe you know," he said. "I believe you know exactly what I'm talking about. In fact, I think you're an accomplice."

Stunned, Brynn just stared up at him, too overwhelmed to speak.

"What do you know about stolen jewelry?" he demanded.

"Jewelry?" she blurted out. Heat bloomed across her cheeks. Breath went out of her.

"Yeah, jewelry," he said, leaning even closer.

Brynn backed up a step.

"Stolen from a nice old couple in Houston," Travis said.

She bumped into the newel post. Her gaze darted around the hotel lobby, desperate for an escape.

"You're involved with the theft," he said, leaning in. His voice rose. "Admit it."

Brynn's heart raced. What could she tell him? Of course she wasn't involved, but the jewels were, in fact, upstairs hidden in her valise. Wasn't that the exact evidence he needed to prove she was guilty? Would he for one second believe she'd stumbled upon them and was, at this very moment, on her way to alert the stationmaster?

"Well," she said and gulped hard. "I, uh, I—"

"Miss Davenport?" a voice called from the doorway.

At the sound of her aunt's name, Brynn lurched away from Travis and saw four women standing in the lobby, dressed in what had to be their Sunday finest.

"Yes—no—yes," she stammered. "I mean, I'm Miss O'Keefe. Miss Davenport is my aunt."

"Welcome!" A gray-haired woman in a wide-brimmed flowered bonnet stepped toward her, a big smile on her face. "I'm Mrs. Kimball, wife of Mayor Kimball. We're so pleased to meet you."

The three women around her smiled and nodded as Mrs. Kimball made introductions.

Brynn just stared. She couldn't take it all in. Her heart pounded in her chest and she cheeks burned with heat. She couldn't form one single coherent sentence.

Mrs. Kimball and the other ladies stared, waiting, then Brynn blurted out, "This Mr. Hollister thinks I'm some sort of criminal."

The mayor's wife gasped and the ladies turned on him.

"This is preposterous!" Mrs. Kimball declared. "Really, Mr. Hollister, how could you? This young woman is Miss Brynn O'Keefe, in town with her aunt, the renowned author and lecturer Miss Sadie Davenport, invited by special invitation. How dare you!"

"Shameful," one of the other women declared, glaring and shaking her finger at Travis.

"It's an insult," another woman called.

"We've waited weeks to receive this woman!" someone else said.

"Just settle down," Travis said. "I'm investigating a crime."

"We're well aware of who you are, Mr. Hollister," Mrs. Kimball declared, giving her nose a distasteful lift. "But Miss O'Keefe is most certainly *not* a criminal."

Brynn held her breath as Travis studied the group of women. Finally he said, "All right, fine. If that's true, then Miss O'Keefe won't mind me searching her luggage."

Brynn's knees threatened to buckle. She grabbed the newel post to steady herself.

"You'll do no such thing!" Mrs. Kimball declared.

All the women began chattering at once. Travis waved his hands to quiet them.

"All I'm saying is that's the one way to put an end to this, once and for all." He glared down at Brynn. "So how about it?"

"This is an outrage. You will not go through Miss O'Keefe's personal belongings," Mrs. Kimball told her, then pointed toward the door. "I insist you leave this moment, Mr. Hollister. And, rest assured, the mayor will hear about this."

Brynn clutched the newel post to keep herself upright as Travis stared down at her a few more seconds. Then he stepped back, nodded to the ladies and left the hotel. She heaved a sigh of relief as the women crowded around her, offering apologies and encouragement.

"Thank goodness that nasty incident is over and done with," Mrs. Kimball said.

Brynn glanced out the hotel doorway. Across the street, Travis Hollister leaned against the bank building, watching her.

"Good night, Miss O'Keefe," Mrs. Kimball called.

"Thank you for a lovely evening," Brynn said as she stepped into the hotel lobby and waved goodbye to the mayor and his wife, who'd been kind enough to see her safely back to her hotel.

She'd spent the evening at the home of the mayor and Mrs. Kimball. They'd been the perfect hosts, entertaining her with pleasant conversation and good food. Neither had been upset when she'd explained that her aunt Sadie wouldn't be able to present the scheduled lecture to the ladies of Harmony, and that Brynn would do them instead. That was a relief to her.

But Brynn hadn't enjoyed the evening in the least. All she could think about was the stolen jewelry tucked into her valise, and that Pinkerton detective Travis Hollister who seemed determined to pin the crime on her.

Brynn lingered in the hotel lobby for a moment, then stuck her head outside. The town of Harmony was steeped in darkness. Lantern light glowed in the windows of a few shops along Main Street and in the living quarters located above them. A horse and rider plodded past and two men disappeared into an alley down the street.

No sign of Travis Hollister, thank goodness.

Brynn hurried up the stairs. Perhaps he'd been sufficiently dissuaded by the ladies of Harmony this afternoon and had turned his suspicions elsewhere. Perhaps he'd even left town. Dare she hope to believe that he'd forgotten all about her?

Slipping into her hotel room, Brynn quickly locked the door and lit the lantern on the bureau. The flame danced to life, sending shadows into the deep corners of the room.

No, Travis hadn't changed his mind. She knew he hadn't. She'd seen that type of man before, determined and relentless. Tenacious.

Brynn sidled up to the window and peeked out. All was quiet on Main Street.

For a brief moment she considered going to the sheriff. He'd seemed like a nice enough fellow when she'd seen him at the train station this afternoon. He was young, rather pleasant looking. If she took the jewelry to him, explained what happened, wouldn't that convince him that she was innocent?

Or would Travis Hollister claim it was simply a ploy to throw suspicion off her?

Brynn whirled away from the window and hugged her arms to her middle, her thoughts racing.

What if the sheriff didn't believe her? What if Travis convinced him that she was guilty? She'd be arrested. Thrown into jail. Put on trial.

She'd heard about justice in the West. Dreadful prison sentences. Public hangings.

She crossed the room, pacing fitfully.

If she somehow managed to escape prosecution, she'd surely be sent back home in disgrace. She'd been lucky when Aunt Sadie had stepped in and saved her from humiliation in Richmond, but no one else was going to do that. What would her father do this time? Send her to a convent? Marry her off to some distant relative in Maine?

Brynn froze and clasped her palms to her cheeks. She had to leave. Now. Tonight. She had to escape Harmony before

Travis Hollister ruined the one chance Aunt Sadie had given her to salvage her future.

She flung her belongings into her valise, stuffing in everything she could fit. The trunks that had accompanied her from Hayden were filled with her aunt's books; she'd leave them with instructions for Mrs. Millburn to ship them back to Hayden.

Opening the door, Brynn heard voices floating up the stairwell. She ducked back inside and closed the door silently.

She'd have to wait until it was late, very late, and the hotel was quiet. She would hide the jewelry case in the hotel kitchen, then slip through the alleys to the train station. She'd board the next train bound for—well, she didn't care where she went, as long as she got out of Harmony. She'd find her way back to Aunt Sadie somehow.

A feeling of calm swept over Brynn. Her plan was a good one. It would work. She'd be away from this town and, more important, she'd never lay eyes on that terrible Travis Hollister again.

Chapter Three

M̲aybe she wouldn't show.

Travis leaned against the side of Holt's General Store, invisible in the darkness. The alley that ran between the store and the hotel gave him the perfect spot to keep watch. He'd seen no one on Main Street for a while now. Lights in the windows had been extinguished some time ago. He waited with nothing to do but think.

And all he could think about was Brynn O'Keefe. She'd occupied his thoughts since this morning when he'd boarded the train in Hayden, trailing Hiram Smith.

She was pretty. Different from the young women he usually encountered, dressed in fine clothing, with that little hat tipped forward in her dark hair. She'd been easy on the eye as he'd watched her from across the train aisle.

Warmth grew inside Travis as he recalled the curve of her chin and those big blue eyes of hers, which he'd glimpsed when she'd dared to look his way.

Innocent. That's how she looked. Innocent.

Travis shifted and checked the alley in both directions, but saw nothing.

Miss Brynn O'Keefe looked innocent, all right, but did that mean she *was* innocent? She'd had a guilty expression on her

face when he'd said the word *jewelry* to her earlier in the hotel
lobby. He'd seen that look before, many times. He knew what
it meant.

Travis tried to picture her as an accomplice to a jewelry
thief. A possibility, certainly. Maybe that innocent demeanor
of hers was what had won over that old Houston couple.

He'd know soon enough.

Hiram Smith had taken a room at Fletcher's Boarding
House. Travis had given her son two bits, and the boy had
promised to come find him if Smith left the place. Travis had
decided to watch the hotel himself. If Brynn or Smith made
a move to leave town tonight, he'd know whether they were
innocent or not.

So all he had to do was wait.

His thoughts drifted back to earlier when he'd confronted
Brynn in the hotel lobby. He'd been harsh with her, but he'd
found that was the easiest and quickest way to get a confession out of a criminal. She'd surprised him by speaking just
as harshly to him. Her cheeks had turned pink and her eyes
had sparked, causing something to flash inside him, too.

He fought off the feeling that claimed him again and forced
his thoughts back to tonight's task.

Dread pooled in the center of his belly. He didn't want
Brynn to show up tonight. He didn't want her to be guilty of
stealing those jewels, and he especially didn't want her to be
involved with Hiram Smith. What he really wanted was—

Movement off to his left drew his attention. A figure dashed
across the alley and disappeared behind the general store.

"Damn," Travis muttered.

There was no mistaking that shape, silhouetted in the
moonlight. Short, curvy, a bouncing bustle weighed down by
a heavy valise.

Heaviness pressed down on Travis. Brynn O'Keefe was
heading toward the train station. That could mean only one
thing: she was guilty.

* * *

Brynn dashed across the rear of the general store, staying in the shadows. She was almost there. She hadn't paid much attention when Pete had driven her to the hotel earlier, but she was certain the train station was just a little farther, and once there she'd—

A man stepped out in front of her. Brynn screamed. He lurched toward her. She swung her valise. He ducked but she caught the side of his head. His hat flew off.

"Damn!" he swore.

Brynn took off running. She'd only gone a few steps when a strong arm looped around her waist, lifted her off her feet and pressed her against the side of the building.

"Settle down," he commanded.

Her heart raced. That voice. It was familiar. She'd heard it before.

Brynn leaned her head back, looking up. Gracious, he was tall. And wide. Huge. Towering over her, blocking her escape by his mere presence.

His face materialized out of the darkness. She gasped as she recognized Travis Hollister.

Of all people to run into! How dare he jump out at her, frighten her so!

Why on earth was he lurking in the alley in the middle of the night?

Anger boiled inside Brynn, and she was about to demand an explanation when reality hit her like a pail of cold water.

Wouldn't he ask the same question of her?

Brynn's heart thundered harder now. She couldn't let him know what she was up to. How would she explain her presence?

"Oh, Mr. Hollister," she said, forcing a calm, conversational tone into her voice. "This is a…surprise."

"Yeah, I'll bet it is." He glared down at her, his gaze harsh and unforgiving.

Brynn eased her valise behind her.

"I was just…just going for a…a stroll," she said.

He didn't say anything, just kept staring.

Brynn drew in a deep breath. "Just taking in the air."

"Carrying your valise?" Travis asked. He scrubbed the tip of his fingers against his forehead where she'd hit him. "What have you got in that thing, anyway?"

Brynn didn't answer, but he didn't give her a chance. He fetched his hat from the ground and clamped it on, then planted himself in front of her again.

"You're heading for the train station," he said.

She couldn't deny it, especially after he'd seen her valise. But she still didn't want to tell him the truth. Her mind raced. She had to come up with something believable.

"Actually, you see, despite the warm welcome I've received from the ladies in town…" Brynn gulped. "Well, the truth is, I'm frightened here in Harmony."

"Of what?" he demanded.

"For one thing," she said and gave him a pointed look, "a strange man jumping out of the shadows and scaring me half to death."

Travis gave her a rueful look. "So let me get this straight," he said. "You're so frightened about staying here in Harmony, you slipped out of your hotel in the dead of night and headed for the train station *alone?*"

She knew her explanation sounded ridiculous, but she couldn't reverse herself now.

"I didn't want to offend the ladies of Harmony," she said, lifting her chin in a way she hoped presented an air of authority. "The mayor's wife has been very warm and welcoming, and I couldn't possibly insult her. It simply isn't done. "

Travis kept glaring. "You're telling me that it's better to slip away in the middle of the night, with no explanation to anyone, than to just tell Mrs. Kimball that you're leaving?"

Obviously, he didn't believe a word she was saying. She tried another tactic.

"And you, I suppose, are an expert on manners?" Brynn challenged.

"I'm an expert on criminals," Travis told her. "And I know you're up to something."

"I'm not a criminal," she told him. "I'm here as an invited guest to deliver lectures on the perfect way to run one's home and conduct oneself."

Travis rolled his eyes. "I've heard some tall tales in my time, Miss O'Keefe, but that's about the biggest one I've come across."

"I'll prove it to you." Brynn yanked open her valise and pulled out her aunt's book. "See? It's all right here."

Travis took the book and stared at the cover. *"Planning. Perfection?"*

"Page thirty-two," Brynn said, wagging her finger at the book. "'Upon entering a room, a woman should walk with moderate steps, head up, and a composed expression on her face.'"

Travis stared at her for a few seconds, then tilted the book to catch the moonlight and flipped the pages. His frown deepened.

"That's what it says," he conceded. "But it doesn't mean anything. You could have memorized that passage."

"'Chapter Four—Setting the Perfect Table,'" Brynn told him, then quoted from memory when he'd found the correct page. "'A table set to receive guests should reflect the personality, taste and mood of the evening perfectly. The perfect hostess should take care to select the perfect china and silver pattern. Complementing the table linens is a must and will ensure a perfect foundation for the occasion.'"

Travis looked up from the book, a deep groove between his eyebrows.

"That's what it says," he admitted. "But it doesn't prove—"

"'Chapter Nine—Selecting the Perfect Stationery,'" she said. "'Quality stationery is the perfect way for a woman to convey her station in life through correspondence.'"

Travis flipped the page, but she rushed on. "'Chapter Thirteen—Selecting Perfect Attire. Dressing to perfection is a must for every woman. There's no excuse not to look perfect, no matter the circumstances.'"

He turned more pages.

"'Chapter Twelve—Planning the Perfect Outing—'"

"Enough," he told her, and snapped the book shut.

"I can go on," she told him.

"Don't," he said.

"Surely that proves that I'm telling you the truth about who I am and why I'm here," Brynn said. "Isn't it perfectly clear?"

He pushed the book back at her. "Let me make something *perfectly* clear, Miss O'Keefe. When I questioned you about a jewel theft, you refused to cooperate. Then, at the first possible moment, you tried to sneak out of town. I might not know how to set a perfect table, but I do know when someone looks perfectly guilty."

A knot hardened in Brynn's stomach. She had to admit he was right, she did *look* guilty.

Travis glanced up and down the alley, then huffed irritably.

"There's only one thing I can do about this tonight," he told her.

Brynn gasped. "You're not taking me to…to jail, are you?"

He gestured to the book. "Is there a chapter that covers selecting the perfect cell?"

Her eyes widened. "You can't possibly— You wouldn't really— You—"

"I'm taking you back to the hotel," he said, and picked up her valise.

Brynn nearly collapsed from relief and she was about to thank him, but his expression was harsh, and somehow she couldn't bring herself to say the words.

He leaned down until his face was even with hers. His scent washed over her, soap and cotton. She saw the dark shadow around his chin, a day's growth of whiskers.

An odd desire claimed her, held her in place. For a moment she thought he would kiss her.

Kiss her? Brynn gave herself a mental shake. Why on earth would she have thought such a thing?

Travis didn't seem to notice, thank goodness, because he said, "You'd better stay at the hotel tonight. Don't even think about running again. I've been with Pinkerton a long time. I've worked the railroads for years. I know every stationmaster, every lawman up and down the line. I can find you in a matter of hours, and you won't like it when I do."

What she didn't like was being threatened, but thought it wiser to keep her mouth shut. Travis Hollister did, in fact, seem capable of keeping that promise.

He caught her arm, his fingers loose around her elbow. Warmth spread up her arm. Brynn jerked away, but she wasn't sure if it was because she didn't like being led as if she really was a criminal or because of the odd feeling his touch brought.

They followed the alley and entered the hotel through the rear door. In the kitchen, Brynn willed herself not to look at the shelves where she'd hidden the jewelry. They passed through the dining room. In the lobby, wall lanterns burned low. They stopped at the foot of the stairs.

"Which room are you in?" Travis whispered.

"I'll see myself upstairs," she told him. "I'll not have my reputation ruined by being seen with a man outside my door."

He seemed to accept her concern, though she could tell by his expression it didn't suit him. He handed her the valise.

Brynn hesitated, somehow reluctant to leave. Something about this man pulled at her. Something she didn't understand.

"I want your word you won't leave this hotel tonight," he said.

His voice was soft, not demanding as it had been. His expression had softened as well.

"It's not safe," he said.

"You needn't worry," she told him, surprised to hear her own voice had softened, also.

"Promise me." He caught her chin and turned her face up to his.

The depth of his eyes drew her in. She couldn't turn away—she wasn't even sure she wanted to. He seemed to hold some power over her.

Travis eased closer. His scent washed over her. Brynn's heart rate picked up.

"Promise me," he said again, his warm breath brushing over her lips.

Before she could say a word he kissed her. His lips covered hers gently but with a heat she'd never experienced. Slowly he moved his mouth over hers. His arm circled her shoulders and drew her closer. He deepened their kiss.

Brynn melted against him. She couldn't stop herself. His hard chest sank into her softness, sending her thoughts reeling.

Then, too quickly, he pulled away. Travis gazed down at her for a long moment and stepped back.

He shifted uncomfortably and cleared his throat, as if giving himself a mental shake. He nodded toward the stairs.

"You'd better go," he said.

Heat bloomed in Brynn's cheeks. "But—"

"You'd better go," he said, a little more forcefully this time.

She headed up the stairs, her feet heavy and her mind racing. She hardly knew what to make of this. First, he accused her of being a criminal, then he kissed her.

She turned back. Travis waited at the foot of the stairs staring up at her.

"So you believe me now?" she asked. "You know I had nothing to do with stealing those jewels."

He bristled. "Nothing's changed. As far as I'm concerned, you're still a prime suspect."

Chapter Four

"**Y**ou're acting like a half-starved dog chasing after a dry bone," Rafe said as Travis took a seat across the desk from him in the sheriff's office. "Let it be."

Travis sat back in the chair and shook his head. He'd come by Rafe's office to talk over a few things. The office was quiet this morning, no sound of prisoners in the cells at the rear of the building. The room was sparsely furnished with a desk, a couple of chairs and racks of rifles on the wall alongside a dozen wanted posters. The place smelled of gun oil and coffee from the pot simmering on the stove in the corner.

"Miss O'Keefe is involved, somehow," Travis said.

Rafe gave him a hard look. "You'd better come up with some proof."

"If I could have searched her luggage at the hotel yesterday, I'd have all the proof I need."

"Not your best move," Rafe told him. "I've had the mayor's wife and nearly every woman in town in my office, complaining about you."

Travis was ready to tell Rafe how unconcerned he was about upsetting the ladies of Harmony when the door swung open and Pete Millburn hurried inside. He helped out with the hotel his mother ran and did odd jobs all over town, including the express office.

"Morning, Sheriff," he said, holding out a large envelope. "Packet just came for you."

"Thanks," he said, taking it from him.

"And this telegram came for you, Travis." He fished a small white envelope from the stack of mail he carried, and handed it to him.

Travis shoved it into his shirt pocket without opening it. Most of his instructions from the Pinkerton headquarters arrived by telegraph. If he was being given another assignment, he didn't want to know about it yet, not until he had a handle on the jewel-theft case.

"If you don't mind me saying so, Travis," Pete said, "you might want to avoid Holt's General Store today. Place is full of ladies and, judging from what I overhead a little while ago, they're none too happy with you."

Travis nodded his thanks and Pete left the sheriff's office. Rafe shot him an I-told-you-so look across the desk.

"She's up to something," Travis insisted. "One mention of the word *jewelry* and she nearly fainted. Looked guilty as sin."

Rafe pulled a knife from his desk drawer and sliced open the envelope.

"That's not proof," he said.

Travis hesitated a moment. He knew he had to tell Rafe everything if he expected his help, but he wasn't that anxious to mention last night in the alley. Because what followed in the hotel lobby made him feel guilty as sin.

He'd kissed her. He'd not even known he was going to do it—though he'd thought about it since he'd first laid eyes on her on the train that morning. He'd looked at her in the golden glow of the lantern light and couldn't help himself. Her cheeks were flushed and a few tendrils of her dark hair had curled around her face. And those lips. Beautiful lips that begged to be taken.

The urgent craving that had claimed him last night presented itself once more. Travis shifted uncomfortably, forcing his thoughts back to the moment.

"She tried to sneak out of town," he said.

Rafe looked up from the wanted posters he'd dumped out of the packet. His brows drew together.

"Damn," Rafe muttered.

They sat in silence for a few moments, and Travis figured Rafe had come up with the same question that he had. When he spoke, he knew he was right.

"Do you think Miss O'Keefe is really who she says she is?" Rafe asked. "Really here to give lectures on—hell, whatever it is she's here to give lectures on?"

Travis shrugged. "She can quote her aunt's book chapter and verse. But maybe that's just her cover. She and Smith might go town to town, conning all sorts of people that way."

"You think that aunt of hers is in on it, too?" Rafe asked.

"Seems like a stretch," Travis admitted.

"Miss O'Keefe's behavior is suspicious," Rafe pointed out. He sat back in his chair and thought for a moment. "Why would she try to sneak out of town if she's really innocent?

Rafe's words seemed to slap Travis upside the head, jogging his memory.

"I've got to check on something," he said, and left the sheriff's office.

He strode down the boardwalk, for once not paying much attention to the people around him. His mind was back to the morning when he'd spotted Hiram Smith on the train platform in Hayden. Travis had recognized him and started to approach when Smith had struck up a conversation with Brynn standing nearby. While Travis watched they'd chatted, then Smith had carried Brynn's belongings to the baggage car.

"Damn," Travis muttered under his breath as he entered the Whites' Rooming House.

He took the steps two at a time up to his room on the

second floor. He always stayed at Mrs. White's place when in Harmony, and he insisted on the room facing the street.

Morning light filtered in through the white lace curtains as Travis threw open his satchel and sorted through the bulletins, reports and wanted posters he'd accumulated. He found the information on Hiram Smith sent to him by the Denver office. When he'd received it several weeks ago, he'd skimmed the facts and committed Smith's image to memory. Now he read it in detail.

This time the report caused his breathing to slow, as if a heavy weight was suddenly pressing against his chest.

Not only was Hiram Smith a suspected jewel thief and con man, he was a murderer. He'd served time in Pennsylvania a couple of years ago for shooting a merchant during a robbery attempt.

The image of Brynn bloomed in Travis's head. Sweet, beautiful Brynn. He couldn't bear the thought that something might happen to her. Anger gripped him, stronger than he'd experienced in a long, long time. As a lawman, it didn't pay to get mad. Keeping a clear head served him better. But this time, thinking of Brynn and the possibility that Smith might hurt her fired his temper.

Sitting in the sheriff's office a few minutes ago, Rafe had wondered aloud why Brynn would try to sneak out of town if she was, in fact, innocent of the crime Travis had accused her of. He'd wondered the same. Then suddenly it hit him.

Brynn was afraid of him.

The anger that had claimed him a moment ago wound down to something different. Sadness.

He couldn't blame her, though, after the way he'd treated her on the train, then again in the hotel lobby. But, still, it troubled him. And the fact that he was simply doing his job brought him no pleasure.

Brynn was guilty of nothing more than allowing a well-dressed gentleman to assist her with her baggage at the train station. Perhaps Smith had spotted Travis, recognized him as a Pinkerton detective. Desperate to rid himself of the stolen jewels he carried, Smith had seen Brynn—a young pretty woman traveling alone—and targeted her. He'd put her luggage in the baggage car and slipped the stolen jewelry inside.

It was just the sort of thing a con man like Smith would do. And his plan had worked, too. He'd seemed innocent as a newborn babe when Travis had confronted him at the Harmony train station.

Travis shoved the reports back into the satchel and left the room. He headed back to the jailhouse and found Rafe still seated behind his desk.

"Brynn is innocent," Travis announced, striding toward him.

Rafe's eyes widened. "A while ago, you said she was guilty."

Travis fumed silently for a moment. He didn't like being wrong. He didn't like being made a fool of. But more than that, he didn't like innocent people getting hurt.

"Smith hid the jewels in Brynn's luggage," he said.

Rafe got to his feet. "You know that for a fact?"

"It's the only thing that makes sense. He hid them, then she discovered them when she unpacked at the hotel. And she might have turned them in right away—"

"If you hadn't barged in, thrown your weight around and threatened her," Rafe said.

Travis wasn't proud of what he'd done, but he didn't disagree.

"Smith's done time for murder," he said.

Rafe frowned. "I don't like the way this is shaping up. He'll get that jewelry back from her, one way or the other."

"She's innocent," Travis said, "but that just puts her in more danger…thanks to me."

"Then you'd better find a way to make it right," Rafe said.

"I intend to," Travis told him.

Both men were quiet for a moment, thinking.

"Chances are, Smith won't try anything here in town," Rafe said. "He knows you're onto him. Most likely, he'll wait until she leaves town. He'll find a way to get on the same train as her, then he'll—"

"I'll talk to her."

"That won't do a lick of good," Rafe told him. "She's denied involvement all along. She won't change her story now."

Travis knew he was right. Brynn would never admit to having the jewelry. She had no reason to trust him.

He didn't like the feeling.

"If she stays in Harmony, I can keep Smith away from her, keep her safe until I can find the evidence I need to arrest him," Travis said. "All I have to do is make sure she doesn't leave town."

Rafe shook his head. "How are you doing to do that?"

"I'll figure out something."

He kissed her—and he *still* thought she was a jewel thief.

Brynn fumed silently as she stood in front of the mirror above her bureau. She pushed a pin into the back of her hair. It took some doing to tame her hair, and this morning her tresses seemed to behave worse than usual.

Maybe that was because her own bad behavior was on her mind.

Her thoughts drifted back to last night. She'd let Travis kiss her. *Kiss her.* She'd stood alone in the dark hotel lobby with him, unchaperoned, and let him kiss her. Not only that, but she'd kissed him back.

At least no one had seen her.

Brynn cringed at the thought of Aunt Sadie finding out how she'd conducted herself. She'd probably ship her back to Richmond on the next train. And how would Brynn explain that to her father and brothers?

Since her mother had died several years ago, Brynn had

kept herself busy with church and charity work, and taking care of the family home. She'd had a few suitors, but none was good enough for her father. He ran a mercantile and had a particular sort of husband in mind for Brynn. A wealthy one, with social connections in the city. Her father was determined to raise the O'Keefe standing in Richmond and he intended to do it by marrying Brynn off to the right sort of family.

That had almost happened.

Determinedly, Brynn placed her hat on her head and shoved in two pins. She didn't like to remember how she'd humiliated not only herself but her entire family, how she'd destroyed her father's dreams—and left tongues wagging all over the city in the process.

She gazed at her reflection, turning her head left, then right, checking for errant strands of hair, and decided that she'd better see to her problems here in Harmony for the present.

Travis floated into her mind once more. She'd lain awake half the night thinking of him, tasting his kiss on her lips, feeling his strong arm around her, his thick chest against her.

Brynn flushed at the memory, and turned away from the mirror. Travis Hollister was no gentleman. She'd been right about him from the very first moment she'd seen him on the train when he'd blatantly ogled her. Why, a gentleman would never kiss a lady the way he'd kissed her. She'd been kissed before—once—and it was nothing like the kiss Travis had given her. Of course, that first kiss she'd received back home in Richmond had rather reminded her of the fish she'd prepared for supper that night, but still, a lady shouldn't be kissed the way Travis had done it.

Maybe she'd ask her aunt to include a chapter in her upcoming book on the perfect kiss.

Brynn felt her cheeks flush once more. Good gracious, how had she become so consumed with *kissing?*

She snatched up her handbag and left her room, annoyed

that Travis had occupied most of her thoughts since yesterday. Plus, he'd kissed her and he still thought she was a jewel thief.

She had to put an end to this. Just before dawn she'd considered allowing Travis to search her room and her belongings to prove her innocence, though the idea of him touching her personal things sent a hot rush through her, for some reason. But the search would be pointless now. Travis would only claim that she'd hidden the jewelry elsewhere, thus proving nothing. She'd even considered turning in the jewelry, explaining things, and hoping for the best. But the image of her father flashed in her mind and she couldn't bear the thought of disappointing him yet again.

At the top of the stairs, Brynn paused and drew a deep breath. She would find Travis this morning and try, yet again, to convince him of her innocence before this situation got any further out of control. What else could she do?

When she reached the lobby Brynn spotted a young woman seated on the gold velvet settee near the registration desk. Young, pretty—probably no older than herself—she had on a vibrant green dress that set off her blond hair and huge blue eyes.

"Miss O'Keefe?"

She rose from the settee and approached Brynn. "I'm sorry to disturb you first thing in the morning, but I just have to talk with you right away. Please allow me to introduce myself. I'm Olivia Asher. My mother is on the committee who invited your aunt here."

Brynn remembered seeing the woman's name mentioned in the correspondence she'd helped Aunt Sadie with. She couldn't help smiling at Olivia's warm greeting.

"Please call me Brynn," she said. "What can I help you with?"

"I'm getting married," Olivia said.

She smiled and her whole face lit up. Brynn couldn't hold back a smile of her own.

"Congratulations," she said.

"I'm just so excited. He's a wonderful man. I love him to pieces," Olivia declared. "And I want our wedding to be perfect."

"Every bride does," Brynn agreed.

Olivia glanced back and forth, then leaned in a little and lowered her voice.

"That's why I'm here," she said. "I absolutely must have a copy of your aunt's book, and I'm scared silly that you'll sell them all at the lecture tonight before I can get one. So can I please, *please,* buy one from you now?"

At that instant Brynn wished with all her heart that Aunt Sadie could be here. She'd poured hours of work into writing her book for women just like Olivia, and she'd have been gratified at seeing her enthusiasm.

"Of course," Brynn told her. "I'll run upstairs and get one."

She dashed up the stairs, got a book from the trunk and returned to the lobby. Olivia passed her the money, took the volume in both hands and hugged it to her chest.

"I can't wait for my mama to read this," Olivia said. "Would you like to meet her? She owns the dress shop just down the street."

Brynn decided that confronting Travis could wait a few minutes. After all, what kind of problems could he cause for her in so short a time?

"I'd love to," she said, and they left the hotel together.

The town was busy at the early hour. Teams of horses and mules pulled wagons and carriages through the streets. Merchants swept the walkway in front of their stores and set crates of goods out for display. Men and women crowded the boardwalk.

"Tell me about your wedding plans," Brynn said.

Olivia launched into a detailed explanation of everything she and her mother had planned, what they intended to do, what they hoped they'd be able to do. Brynn got caught up in her excitement.

"Are you planning to—"

Brynn stopped midsentence when she spotted Travis on the boardwalk ahead of them, headed their way. Her stomach did an odd little flip, then lurched when she saw who was walking beside him.

The sheriff.

"Let's take a look at the mercantile across the street," Brynn said suddenly.

Olivia seemed not to notice her distress as Brynn hurried across the street, dodging a freight wagon. On the boardwalk on the other side, Brynn glanced back.

She gasped softly. Travis and the sheriff had crossed the street, too, and they were headed directly for her.

Maybe it was coincidence, Brynn told herself, as Olivia described the flowers she'd selected for her wedding. She took a cursory glance at the fabrics displayed in the window of the mercantile and said, "Let's cross again."

Olivia followed obediently as Brynn led the way to the opposite boardwalk. She glanced back. Travis and the sheriff made their way across the street, also.

He was going to arrest her. Brynn fought off her rising panic. Travis had somehow convinced the sheriff that she was involved in the jewel theft, and he intended to cart her off to jail.

What would her father do? What would the ladies back in Richmond say when word eventually reached them? Would Aunt Sadie ever speak to her again?

"Let's...let's go inside," Brynn said, casting her gaze toward the shops, desperate for an escape. She couldn't just stand there and be captured.

"Sure. You'll love the fabric in— Oh, look who's coming," Olivia said.

To Brynn's horror, she waved to Travis and the sheriff. The men picked up their pace and strode purposefully toward them.

Chapter Five

"Brynn, have you met Rafe Sutherland?" Olivia asked. Her cheeks turned a soft shade of pink. "Rafe is my intended."

Olivia went on with the introductions, but Brynn didn't hear a word she said. Rafe Sutherland, the town sheriff, was engaged to Olivia?

Relief flooded Brynn as she mechanically made small talk with Olivia and the sheriff. Thank goodness. He wasn't coming to arrest her. He'd simply seen the woman he loved on the street and come over to visit.

Of course, that didn't explain why Travis was with him—and the man hadn't offered an explanation. In fact, he'd done little more than utter a greeting and stare at her.

"Would you like to see the new fabric Mama just got in?" Olivia asked Rafe.

He smiled, as if seeing fabric were the most wonderful thing in the world. The two of them said goodbye and headed down the boardwalk together.

As Brynn watched them go, an odd knot coiled insider her. It took a moment to realize it was envy. They made an attractive couple, and their feelings for each other were obvious.

An unwelcome memory floated through Brynn's mind.

She might be planning her own wedding now in Richmond, if it hadn't been for her blunder.

"They look happy together," Brynn murmured.

"They do," Travis agreed.

She turned at the sound of his voice. For once it wasn't demanding. He gazed down the boardwalk after them, as if he, too, felt the connection Olivia and Rafe had left in their wake.

"When I saw you walking with the sheriff, I thought you were coming to arrest me," Brynn said.

"I'm not arresting you. Not yet, anyway," Travis said.

He studied her for a moment, as if attempting to see deep inside of her, search her soul for something. Brynn felt herself flush under his close scrutiny.

"I've been thinking about your situation," Travis said. "I've decided to give you a chance to clear your name, once and for all."

Brynn drew back a little, suspicious of this sudden turn of events.

"What did you have in mind?" she asked.

"Plead your innocence to the judge," Travis told her. "If he believes you, you're free to go."

Her spirits soared. Could it really be that easy?

"That's it? That's all I have to do?" she asked, suddenly impatient to get on with it. "I'll go now. This minute. Where can I find him?"

"Slow down," Travis said, and waved his hands. "The judge rides the circuit. You'll have to wait until he gets here."

"Will that be by tomorrow?" she asked, looking around as if the judge might materialize right before her eyes.

Travis shook his head. "More like a week—"

"A *week?*"

"—or two."

"Two weeks!" she exclaimed.

"If you're lucky," Travis added.

"I'm supposed to meet my aunt. We have to continue her tour. I can't stay in this town for two weeks," Brynn insisted.

Twin frown lines formed in his forehead.

"Is that your way of saying that you're afraid to face the judge?" he asked.

"No, of course not. It's just that—"

"Seems to me a person would be happy to plead their innocence directly to a judge." Travis drew a little closer. "An *innocent* person, that is."

"I am innocent," she told him.

He shrugged. "Then convincing the judge won't be a problem."

"What am I supposed to do about expenses?" Brynn asked, hoping this last protest might earn her a reprieve.

"The agency will pick up the tab," Travis told her.

Brynn pressed her lips together to keep from protesting further. The very last thing she wanted was to stay in this town a minute longer than necessary. There had to be a way to get out of this.

But to do that, it would seem she first had to get around Travis.

Applause rose from the crowd seated in the church's fellowship hall. Brynn had just delivered her lecture on setting the perfect table, and every woman in the place had listened attentively. Throughout her talk, she'd seen women whispering to each other, nodding their approval. Satisfaction grew inside Brynn. Aunt Sadie had been right in taking this tour west. The women here desperately wanted this information.

Brynn was careful to keep a pleasant but humble expression on her face, as she'd seen Aunt Sadie do after each lecture, when the women left their seats and crowded around. Olivia had agreed to sell *Planning Perfection* at a table nearby, the duty Brynn usually performed at her aunt's lectures.

"I'm purchasing new china," Nan Prescott said to Brynn.

"Could you please help me with the selection? I have a catalog from a wonderful company in New York City."

"You have a catalog from New York City?" the woman next to her asked. "I'd love to see it."

"And I could use your help with some new linens," Effie Stanton said.

Ruth Asher, Olivia's mother, spoke up. "I'm anxious to read your aunt's book, but I just know I'll still have questions about the wedding."

As she'd seen Aunt Sadie do, Brynn referred them to the appropriate chapter in the book or answered their questions outright. Still, it didn't seem to be enough for the women of Harmony.

"You simply must give another talk," Ada Holt declared. Around her, heads bobbed and a chorus of *yes*es rose from the women. "Violet?" she called to the mayor's wife. "Please. You have to convince Miss O'Keefe to continue her lectures here."

Mrs. Kimball elbowed her way into the group surrounding Brynn.

"Would you?" she asked.

Dozens of eager faces watched her. The women all cared about their homes and wanted to make them perfect. More than any of them, Brynn knew how important it was to conduct oneself in a perfect manner. It warmed her heart to know she could help them.

But that didn't change the fact that she was supposed to return to Hayden and continue with the tour, as soon as her aunt was up to it. Brynn didn't know when Aunt Sadie's health would allow it. And, of course, she still had to figure out what to do about Travis's insistence that she remain in town until the circuit judge arrived.

"I'd love to stay, but I'll have to check my schedule," Brynn said, thinking that covered most everything.

Mrs. Kimball shook off Brynn's concerns and announced to the women, "I'll let you all know the details."

The ladies smiled and called their thanks as they slowly left the fellowship hall. Olivia gave Brynn the money she'd collected for the books.

"I heard Mama ask if you'd help with my wedding," she said. "Would you really do that?"

Brynn couldn't refuse. "I'll help any way I can."

She left the fellowship hall with Olivia and her mother, anxious for a little peace and quiet after the long evening of delivering the lecture and answering so many questions. Outside in the churchyard, the sheriff waited.

"Just in time to walk you ladies home," Rafe said, smiling at Olivia.

Even in the darkness, Brynn could see Olivia's face light up.

"We don't usually get walked home by the sheriff and a Pinkerton detective. Are you expecting trouble?" Ruth asked in a lighthearted fashion.

Brynn's heart lurched as Travis stepped out of the shadows.

"I'm always expecting trouble," he said.

"Causing trouble, more likely," Olivia said, and everyone laughed.

Everyone but Brynn.

Rafe headed across the churchyard with Olivia on one side, her mother on the other. Brynn held back.

"You'd better not be here to arrest me," she told him, pushing out hcr chin as if to dare him to do just that.

"You don't need to worry as long as you agree to talk to the judge." Travis angled closer. "Do I have your word on it?"

Brynn fumed silently. She didn't want to agree to anything this man said, but didn't see any alternative…that didn't land her in jail, anyway.

"Fine. I'll speak to the judge." She gave him an impatient huff and stomped away.

Travis was in front of her in two long strides, stopping her in place.

"You'll agree to stay in town?" He asked, but the words sounded more like a demand to Brynn.

She put her nose in the air, hoping it indicated that speaking to him further on the subject didn't suit her.

"Yes, I'll stay."

She tried to leave again, but Travis blocked her. He was a formidable wall in front of her.

"Promise me," he said.

His voice sounded softer, the words a plea rather than a command. Something in his tone touched her.

"I promise," she said.

He studied her for a long moment, as if judging whether to believe her. Finally he nodded toward the fellowship hall.

"Sounds as if the ladies of Harmony want you around for a while, anyway," he said.

"You heard my lecture?" she asked, genuinely surprised.

"In my line of work, you never know when you might need to set a perfect table," he said, and grinned.

Brynn grinned, too. She couldn't help it, seeing the comical expression on his face. It changed him. In a flash the tough Pinkerton detective disappeared and a handsome man appeared.

Handsome? The notion took Brynn by surprise. She'd been so worried over what Travis might do, what problems he might cause her, she hadn't looked at him closely enough to realize that he was, in fact, quite handsome.

"Do you really believe all that stuff you were telling the ladies?" he asked, as they crossed the churchyard. Ahead of them, lights from the windows along Main Street glowed, drawing them back to town.

"Certainly," Brynn insisted.

"Perfection," Travis said. "That's a tall order."

"Striving for perfection is the only way to run one's life," Brynn told him. "Don't you want to be perfect in your work?"

"Never occurred to me to try," he said. "Do you expect to be perfect all of the time?"

"I expect I'd better be perfect when I talk to the judge," Brynn said.

Though they'd discussed the situation earlier and she'd agreed to it, she decided it wouldn't hurt to revisit it.

"Isn't there some other way to handle this situation? My aunt expects me back in Hayden in a few days, and we have to continue on the tour. I can't stay in Harmony for weeks."

Travis stopped suddenly and looked down at her, his expression hard.

"You promised me you'd stay."

"Yes, I did. And I'll stay, just like I promised," Brynn said. She sighed heavily. "But it puts me in a very difficult position."

"It doesn't exactly suit me, either," Travis said. They started walking again, and stepped up onto the boardwalk at the edge of town. "With you staying here, that means I have to stay here, too."

A jolt rippled through Brynn. She hadn't considered that Travis would have to stay in town, also. And she didn't understand why the idea left her with such an odd feeling.

"I don't like being tied down," Travis told her. "I stay on the move."

She stopped on the boardwalk and looked up at him. Richmond suddenly seemed very dear to her. The house she'd been raised in, her friends, her brothers, her papa—even though he was terribly upset with her.

"You don't have a home?" she asked. "Anywhere?"

Travis shrugged as if the notion were no big deal. "I don't need one and I don't want one."

"What about your family?"

"My ma died when I was young, so my aunt raised me. My pa was a lawman, gone most of the time."

A vision of Travis as a boy sprang into Brynn's mind.

"And every time he visited, you wanted to leave with him," she said.

He blanched, somehow startled by her words, then said, "He taught me right from wrong. He dedicated his life to the law. It was important work."

Travis started walking again, as if he'd said too much, or perhaps was afraid she'd ask another question. Brynn walked with him.

"So believe me," Travis said, "I'm no more anxious to stay here in Harmony than you are. That judge can't get here fast enough to suit me."

They entered the Harmony Hotel. The lobby was empty, the dining room closed for the evening.

The night before flashed into Brynn's mind. His kiss. Their kiss. The feel of him, the scent, the taste. Everything came rushing back.

Would he kiss her again?

He didn't. An odd disappointment settled over Brynn as she realized that not only did Travis *not* intend to kiss her, he seemed set on keeping his distance. Purposely, it appeared, he stood at least a yard away from her.

"Good night," she said.

"Good night," he replied.

She hesitated a moment, then turned and headed up the stairs. She'd only gone a short way when she heard his heavy footfalls on the risers behind her.

Brynn stopped and turned back to find him a few steps below her. The height difference put them on eye level; it was nice not having to look up at him for once.

"Stop following me," she told him.

"I'm not following you," he said.

Her back stiffened. "Of course you are."

"No, I'm not," he said.

"Shh!" She glanced up the stairs, then back at him. "You're going to wake everyone in the place."

"You're the one raising such a ruckus," he pointed out. His brows drew together. "You're a suspect in a crime, don't forget."

"Do you kiss all your suspects?" she asked.

"Only the ones who need kissing," Travis said.

With one giant step he was on the riser with her, looking into her eyes, the wild heat she'd felt from him once more covering her. Brynn's heart rate picked up. Her knees trembled.

"I won't have my reputation called into question by your presence upstairs," she said. Heat filled her cheeks, hearing her words spoken in a breathy sigh.

Travis angled closer. "I'm just doing my duty. You're in my custody."

"What?" Her eyes widened, the warmth he'd created in her suddenly turning cool.

"I'm duty bound to make sure you're here when the judge arrives," Travis told her.

She took a step back. "I told you I'd stay. You have no right—"

"Need I remind you that I caught you trying to sneak out of town?" he asked.

There wasn't much she could say to that, which didn't suit her in the least. Still, she couldn't let him have his way.

"Nonetheless, I insist you stop following me," she said.

"I told you, I'm not following you. I'm going up to my room."

Breath went out of her. "Your room?"

Travis motioned toward the second floor. "Top of the stairs, on the left."

"But…but that's where my room is," she exclaimed.

He gave her a slight smile. "And mine is right next to yours."

Chapter Six

Would she find Travis in the hotel dining room this morning?

The idea popped into Brynn's head as she left her room and hurried down the stairs. At the entrance to the dining room she paused. Bright morning sunlight beamed through the white curtains, making the pale blue linens sparkle. Several tables were occupied, some with businessmen, others with families dressed in traveling clothes. The low hum of conversation and clinking silverware filled the area.

No sign of Travis.

Good, she told herself, as she took a seat at a table beside the window. He'd occupied too much of her thoughts already, especially when she had a much more important issue to contemplate.

Her freedom.

The serving girl stopped at her table and filled her coffee cup.

"I was at your lecture last night," she said, and her eyes took on a dreamy look. "I can't wait to read your aunt's book."

"She'll be pleased to hear that," Brynn said, and asked for the morning breakfast special detailed on the chalkboard at the entrance of the dining room.

"Coming right up," the young girl said, and hurried away.

When she disappeared through the swinging door to the kitchen, Brynn caught a glimpse of the shelves of canisters near the stove. She said a silent prayer that the cook wouldn't need cornmeal anytime soon, since that's where she'd hidden the jewelry.

She sipped her coffee thinking of the old Houston couple Travis had told her about. The jewelry had probably been in their family for years. They must have been heartsick when they'd realized it had been stolen.

Obviously, the real thief had planted the jewelry in her luggage at some point. At the hotel in Hayden or during the ride to the train station, perhaps. Maybe in the baggage car once the train got underway, or after it arrived in Harmony. Lots of people had access to the baggage and that certainly included a thief looking for a place to hide stolen property.

Brynn glanced out the window. She half expected to see Travis striding down the boardwalk toward her, but didn't. She turned back to her coffee.

She wished she could return the jewelry to its rightful owner, but she didn't dare. Not yet, anyway. Once she'd spoken to the judge, cleared her name and secured her freedom, she'd give it to the sheriff in secret. Or maybe she'd take it back to the Houston couple herself, somehow.

The serving girl brought her breakfast. Brynn gazed out the window as she ate. Many of the faces looked familiar to her now. She and her aunt had traveled extensively these past weeks. Communities and towns had rolled past, oftentimes unnoticed. Brynn took comfort in recognizing so many of Harmony's citizens.

Through the window, she caught sight of Mrs. Kimball on the boardwalk heading toward the hotel. The woman nodded when she spotted Brynn, and a few seconds later she appeared at her table.

"I'm glad I found you," Mrs. Kimball said, after accepting Brynn's invitation to join her. "I wanted to be the first to speak with you."

Worry settled over Brynn. Had the mayor's wife somehow found out that Travis, a Pinkerton detective, considered her a criminal?

Mrs. Kimball didn't give her a chance to ask.

"For some time now, I've sensed that the ladies of Harmony needed more help, and last night your lecture proved it," she said. "I've spoken with many of them, and the mayor, of course, and decided that the time to act is now. What we need is a ladies' social club. A place where women can meet, share problems and exchange ideas."

Brynn smiled. "That's a wonderful idea."

"Yes," Mrs. Kimball agreed. "Ada Holt has agreed to donate an unused portion of her building for a meeting place. Once we've given it a good cleaning, a fresh coat of paint and proper furnishings, it will make an excellent meeting location."

"Sounds like a worthwhile project," Brynn said. "And fixing it up will be a joy."

"I'm glad you agree," Mrs. Kimball said, "because I'd like you to head up the project."

"Me?" Brynn asked, surprised.

"Of course. You're perfect for the job. And since you're staying in Harmony for the next few weeks, you'll have plenty of time to see it through."

"Staying in Harmony?" Brynn asked. "Where did you hear that?"

"Why, my dear, it's all over town."

"You look like hell," Rafe said.

Travis didn't argue. Not after the night he'd had.

He paused on the boardwalk where Rafe stood outside Holt's General Store. The streets of Harmony were busy this morning, with lots of people going about their business—

which was exactly what Travis would have been doing, if he hadn't overslept.

He'd been awake most of the night. How could he sleep with Brynn in the next room? Nothing but a thin wall separated them, and though he couldn't see through it, he may as well have, thanks to his imagination.

Brynn, undressing. Layers and layers of soft clothing stripping away. Brynn standing in front of the mirror, pulling pins from her hair until it cascaded down her back in heavy waves. Slipping into a thin nightgown, the hem brushing her calves. Sliding between the crisp sheets—

"Anything new on Smith?" Rafe asked, bringing Travis back to reality.

He shook his head. "I sent a telegram to the Denver office asking for more information. Haven't heard anything yet."

"I've seen Smith around town, visiting stores, calling on shop owners, peddling that fabric of his." Rafe shrugged. "He's acting like a salesman, not a jewel thief."

"The bastard is a con man. He knows how to keep up appearances," Travis said.

"I heard you're bunking over at the hotel now," Rafe said, then scowled. "Look, Travis, I agreed to go along with keeping Miss O'Keefe in town to protect her, but I won't be a party to you sullying her reputation."

Travis just stared at him. Many a criminal—and most honest men—would be frightened into silence by the look Travis gave him, but not Rafe. They'd been friends too long.

"Makes me wonder where your interest in this case stops and your interest in Brynn begins," Rafe told him.

Travis formulated a response—a denial—but the words would not come out.

"I've seen how you look at her. She's a good-looking woman, but it's something more than that," Rafe said. "What's going on?"

Once again, Travis tried to muster a rebuttal but failed.

Truth was he'd spent more time worrying about Brynn than investigating Hiram Smith.

And thoughts of Smith certainly hadn't kept him up all night.

"It's natural," Rafe said, and shrugged. "A man gets to the point where he wants to settle down."

"Just because you're getting hitched, doesn't mean everybody else wants to," Travis told him.

"Hell, Travis, you've been at loose ends most of your life," Rafe said. "Nothing wrong with wanting a home and a family."

"I like my life the way it is," Travis said.

Rafe nodded down the boardwalk and grinned. "We'll see how much you like your life in about one minute."

Travis looked up. His heart lurched at the sight of Brynn making her way through the crowd of morning shoppers. He could pick her out easily in that little hat she always wore tipped forward in her thick dark hair, and her pink lips that seemed to turn up in a natural smile, her smooth, even gait that made her appear to be floating rather than walking—

His heart lurched another time, but for an entirely different reason. Brynn wasn't floating, she was marching, and those pink lips were drawn in a tight line, and she seemed to be heading straight for…him.

"Looks as if your suspect might want to have a word with you," Rafe said, and chuckled. He slapped Travis's shoulder and hurried away.

She was a pretty little thing. Travis couldn't take his eyes off her. She came toward him all puffed up with anger, cheeks pink, mouth set, eyes narrowed. Yet somehow she still looked composed, dignified.

Suddenly Travis wanted to kiss her. The feeling nearly overwhelmed him. He wanted to take her in his arms, bury his face in her neck, cover her lips with his.

"You low-down snake," Brynn hissed as she stopped in front of him.

And, for some reason, that made him want her more.

"If I hadn't gotten into so much trouble over outbursts such as this," Brynn said, "I'd tell you exactly what's on my mind right now, Mr. Hollister, and you wouldn't like it."

Travis came to his senses.

"Let's go over here and talk," he said. He caught her elbow and led her toward the alley.

"Have you no shame?" Brynn demanded. She dug in her heels and pulled away from him. "I'm not going to be seen slipping into an alley with you."

Travis jerked his chin toward the crowded boardwalk. "I don't think your aunt's book suggests a public street as the perfect place for such a discussion."

"Of course not."

Travis shrugged. "So take your pick."

There was no place they could go for a private conversation, no respectable place, anyway. It didn't suit Brynn, but she put her nose in the air and huffed to the corner of the general store, then took a step into the alley. Travis followed.

Brynn pushed her chin out and rose on her toes, stretching up to her greatest height.

"Why is it that everyone in this town believes I intend to stay here?" she wanted to know.

"I—"

"My reputation is at stake here," she told him.

"I understand—"

"What have you told people?" she demanded. "That I'm some sort of criminal?"

"I knew you'd—"

"Or that I'm suspected of breaking the law?" she asked.

"I can explain—"

"About to be hauled off to jail?"

"If you'd just let me—"

"I realize you don't think it necessary to conduct yourself in anything approaching perfection," she said, fighting to keep some sort of hold on her anger. "But how could you be so thoughtless?"

Brynn stared up at him, waiting for an answer. Travis just looked at her, not angry, not upset or offended by her outburst. In fact, it almost appeared that he was struggling not to smile.

"So this sort of thing has gotten you into trouble before?" he asked. "Not what the good folks back in Richmond consider *perfect* behavior, is it?"

Embarrassment heated Brynn's cheeks. He knew her greatest secret—because she'd just blurted it out.

"That's quite a temper you have," Travis said.

Brynn couldn't keep up pretenses any longer. Her shoulders slumped in surrender.

"My worst fault," she admitted. "And it has gotten me into all sorts of trouble."

"A little trouble now and again isn't so bad," Travis said.

"That's quite a statement, coming from a lawman," she said.

He eased closer. "Your kind of trouble, I can handle."

Heat sprang from him, covering her with intense warmth. It coiled inside her, making her aware of everything about herself. The color of her dress. The tendril of her hair that had come loose. Her bodice that seemed a bit too small suddenly.

Everything about Travis seemed more intense, also. His smooth jaw and chin, freshly shaved. The curly dark hair that sprang from the opening at the top of his shirt. What did it feel like? Was it soft? Coarse? What would he think if she ventured a touch?

His gaze caught hers and held it. Brynn broke away, fearing he could somehow read her thoughts.

"I'd like to know—" Her voice shook. She drew herself up and tried again. "I'd like to know why everyone in this town thinks I'm going to stay here. Did you tell them that?"

He nodded. "I did. And don't go thinking I let it be known that you were a suspect, waiting to talk to the judge. I said nothing of the kind."

"Good," Brynn said, breathing a little easier. "So what reason did you give for my staying in town?"

"I told everybody that I'm courting you."

Chapter Seven

"**P**ink," Mrs. Kimball declared, then turned to Brynn. "Don't you agree?"

Brynn glanced around the vast room that was to be the Ladies' Social Club. Ada Holt had purchased the building that adjoined her general store, intending to expand her business, but hadn't yet felt the time was right to begin the renovations. She'd gladly donated the space to the ladies' club. Mrs. Kimball headed up the committee to turn the empty room into a fashionable gathering place and, in turn, she'd asked Brynn for suggestions.

But not without sharing a few ideas of her own.

Pink walls? Brynn managed to keep her lips from turning down in a distasteful frown, and contemplated the room.

It was in dreadful condition. According to Ada, the place had been empty for several months prior to her purchasing it. Now a thick layer of dust lay on everything. The windows were smudged; two of the panes were broken. Spiderwebs clung to the corners.

On the plus side, the building had housed a bakery, so it had a kitchen in the back. The front door opened directly onto Main Street, allowing easy access for the women, and the big windows allowed for lots of sunlight.

In Brynn's mind she saw the place in its finished condition. Comfortable chairs arranged in a cozy group, tables for dining, a small area near the back of the room where children could play while their mothers visited. A perfect place for women to meet.

"Perhaps a creamy butter color for the walls," Brynn suggested. "We'll do pink table linens and accessories. Lots of pastels will give the place a light, airy appearance."

While Mrs. Kimball squinted into the dim recesses, contemplating the paint color, Brynn wandered through the doorway at the rear of the room and into the kitchen. This area of the building had fared no better than the rest of it, thanks to months of abandonment. A cookstove remained, along with a large sideboard and cupboards, but they were nearly unrecognizable, thanks to the dirt, dust and grime. Whoever took on the task of cleaning this place would certainly have a tough job.

As she left the kitchen, Brynn saw that Effie Stanton, the wife of Harmony's bank manager, and Nan Prescott had joined Mrs. Kimball in what was to be the social club's meeting room.

"We're all in complete agreement," the mayor's wife called. "Buttery yellow walls, as you suggested."

The women craned their necks, taking in the dank, dirty room; all of them, most likely, having the same thought.

"Yellow will certainly brighten up the place," Mrs. Stanton ventured.

"I didn't realize the room would need so much work," Mrs. Prescott said, shaking her head. "Where will we get the money for the renovations?"

"And who will do the cleaning?" Mrs. Stanton wondered.

"Details can be worked out," Mrs. Kimball said.

No one had a suggestion on just what those details may be, or where the money would come from, however.

Mrs. Stanton turned to Brynn. "I believe you're needed next door," she said, and nodded toward Holt's General Store.

Mrs. Prescott's face suddenly blossomed with a knowing smile. "Oh, yes. You should go. Right away."

Brynn had no idea why Ada Holt would want her, but felt there was nothing more to be accomplished here, under the circumstances.

As the other women continued to talk and pace around the meeting room, Brynn walked next door. Holt's General Store was among the best in Harmony, always immaculate, with good quality merchandise filling the shelves. She'd heard that the Holt family had been merchants back east for generations before venturing west. Someone mentioned that Ada's younger brother Tyler had struck out for California some months back in hopes of establishing another store out there.

Clutching a broom in her hand, Ada paused when Brynn walked through the door.

"What can I help you with?" Brynn asked.

The woman tilted her head and smiled. "I'm supposed to ask you that question."

Brynn smiled in return and nodded next door. "Mrs. Stanton said I was needed here."

Ada frowned as if trying to figure out why Effie Stanton would have sent her to the store, then nodded her head in understanding.

"I believe Effie thought you'd want to help this customer," she said, and pointed the broom handle toward the back of the store.

Brynn walked down the aisle, copper pots on her left, woolen blankets on her right, expecting to find one of Harmony's young women in a dither over what to buy. She'd become the fashion consultant to nearly everyone in town since the night of her lecture at the church social hall.

But she didn't find a young woman struggling over color or pattern selection. Instead, she saw a man standing over a table display of shirts.

Brynn stopped in her tracks. Travis.

She knew him in an instant, even though his back was turned. Tall, terribly tall, with those unmistakable wide shoulders. Long legs. A gun belt slung low on his hips.

He whipped around, as if sensing her—or someone—behind him. Brynn started at his quickness. His hand went for his gun and his eyes narrowed.

Then, just as quickly, he recognized her and his expression transformed once again. He turned to face her, shoulders relaxed, a half grin pulling at his lips.

Her heart warmed a bit, realizing he was glad to see her. Then her spirits plummeted. It was just an act meant to bolster the story he'd concocted about courting her.

When she'd confronted him on the street several days ago and he'd admitted to it, she'd been so stunned she couldn't speak. She'd just walked away.

"Mrs. Stanton sent me here," Brynn said, maintaining a discreet distance from him. "I suppose she thought I'd want to help you shop, thanks to that lie you've spread all over town."

"Good," he replied. "The story's working."

Brynn eased a little closer and lowered her voice. "I can't believe you have the gall to tell such an outlandish tale. The townspeople are supposed to be your friends. How can you deceive them this way?"

"It's a perfect cover story—and you like things that are perfect," he said, and his grin widened.

"Nowhere in my aunt's book is there any mention of telling the perfect lie," Brynn told him.

Travis shrugged. "Nobody in town is suspicious. Nobody thinks you're in custody, awaiting a hearing with the judge. Way I see it, you ought to be grateful that I came up with such a convincing story."

Her temper flared. "You expect me to *thank* you for all these problems you've caused—"

"Shh," he said, glancing over her head. "You don't want to jeopardize our cover story, do you?"

Brynn pressed her lips together, holding in her words. The last thing she wanted was to be talked about—more than she already was.

"Why would those women send you over here?" he asked, sorting through the stacks of folded shirts. "I can pick out my own clothes just fine."

She looked at his shirt. "I don't know about that."

He glanced down at himself. "There's nothing wrong with this shirt."

"It's awfully drab," she said, sorting through the items on the display table.

She'd never shopped for a man before, except for her brothers, of course, and her father. But this was hardly the same. Shopping for clothing for Travis seemed terribly personal.

Still, he needed some guidance.

She picked up a red shirt. "This would look nice on you."

"And make me a big target for every outlaw gunning for me," he said.

"How about this one?" she asked, holding up a yellow one.

"That one will make it real easy for some gunslinger to pick me off in a crowd," he grumbled.

"How about this baby blue one?" she suggested.

"No lawman can ever be taken seriously wearing a baby blue shirt," he said. He raised an eyebrow. "Are you trying to get rid of me?"

"Yes, but not by seeing you killed."

"That's no way to treat the man who's courting you," he pointed out, rifling through the shirts again.

She huffed irritably. "If you're insistent on keeping up this courtship ruse, you could at least act the part," she told him.

He eased closer. "And you know what it's like to be courted?"

"As a matter of fact, I do," she told him, and lifted her chin a little.

She thought he'd chuckle at her comment, but instead his brows drew together in a deep scowl.

"By who?" he asked, the words coming out in a command.

At once, Brynn regretted bringing up the subject of previous courtships. She certainly didn't want to get into what had happened back in Richmond.

"Is this man the reason you left home with your aunt?" Travis asked.

She was surprised he'd figured it out. But maybe she should have known better. After all, he was a detective with the largest, most prestigious private law enforcement agency in the country. Investigating and putting together pieces of a puzzle were what he did for a living.

"It's not something I wish to discuss," Brynn said. She'd intended the words to come out in a sharp rebuke, but they sounded soft and gentle instead.

Travis watched her as if his stare might cause her to tell him more, but she determinedly glared right back until he finally turned away.

"I'll take this one," he said, picking up a black shirt.

"You already have one like it," she said.

"You noticed?" he asked, and seemed to enjoy knowing that little fact.

"It's so dreadful, how could I not?" she countered.

Brynn sorted through the shirts and selected a deep green one. "Buy this one," she told him. "It will bring out your eyes."

"Just what every lawman wants," he grumbled.

"It looks perfect." She held it up to his chest. Her fingers brushed him.

Travis inhaled sharply and drew himself up straighter, as if some unseen current had suddenly raced through him. He leaned down, his gaze smoldering.

"Was that man back in Richmond perfect?" he asked in a low voice. "Did he give you a perfect kiss?"

His breath fanned her cheeks and he moved closer until his

lips touched hers. A little groan rattled in his throat. Brynn gasped and leaned in.

He moved his mouth over hers, blending them together. Heat rushed from him to her, taking her breath away.

He broke off their kiss. Brynn's eyes fluttered open. A few seconds passed before she realized what had happened—and where she was.

Good gracious, she'd let Travis kiss her in public. And she'd enjoyed it. Her cheeks flamed anew. How humiliating.

Was this part of the ruse he'd come up with? Or was he sincere?

Either way, it didn't matter. She certainly wasn't going to allow him to take advantage of the situation—or her.

She whipped around and left the store. On the boardwalk she pretended to look in the shop window, letting the breeze cool her cheeks. Voices from behind drew her attention. She glanced back to see Mrs. Kimball, Effie Stanton and Nan Prescott heading toward her.

At that moment Travis stepped out of Holt's General Store carrying a bundle wrapped in brown paper. Brynn couldn't read the expression on his face, couldn't imagine where his thoughts might lie. All she knew was that she'd had quite enough of him manipulating her life, dictating where she could go. True, the plan he'd come up with left no one in Harmony to speculate that she was actually in custody, under the watchful eye of a Pinkerton detective, and perhaps she should have been grateful. But she wasn't. She'd had quite enough of Travis having his way on things.

The women walked over, their gazes darting from Brynn to Travis and back again. She could only imagine what they were thinking: how good the two of them looked together; what a perfect couple they made; when the wedding would be.

"We've come to a decision," Mrs. Kimball announced as the women stopped in front of Brynn and Travis. "We're going to have a bake sale after church services on Sunday to raise money for the Ladies' Social Club."

"Reverend Harrison has to agree to it, of course," Mrs. Stanton pointed out.

"But we're certain he will," Mrs. Prescott added. "I'm going to talk to the reverend this afternoon."

"And I'm going to head up the fund-raising," Mrs. Stanton said.

"We'd like you to be in charge of decorating the social club," Mrs. Kimball said.

"We loved your idea about the wall colors," Mrs. Prescott told her, nodding wisely.

"You're the best suited for the job," Mrs. Stanton said. "After all, you have extensive knowledge of the very latest in home decorating tips from your aunt's book."

"You simply must do this," Mrs. Kimball told her.

Brynn was flattered by the offer. No one had ever asked her to take on such a big project. Her mind raced with all sorts of ideas for filling the meeting room with everything necessary for a warm, welcoming spot.

Then another idea came to her. If she was busy with the social club, she could more easily avoid Travis—and the temptation of kissing him in public buildings.

"I'd be delighted to head up the project," Brynn told them.

All the women smiled and nodded their approval.

"Excellent," Mrs. Kimball declared. "We'll go over all the details after the fund-raiser on Sunday."

"In the meantime, go ahead and get started," Mrs. Stanton said.

"No need in waiting," Mrs. Prescott agreed.

"Get started?" Brynn asked. "How? If there's no funds yet—"

"With the cleaning," Mrs. Prescott said.

Brynn's eyes widened. "You mean that I should clean that entire building…myself?"

Mrs. Kimball chuckled gently. "No, of course not. We'll find you some help. There are lots of strong men in Harmony who'll gladly help out with such a good cause."

"No need for that," Travis said. "I'll get some men together and get that building cleaned up myself, as long as Miss O'Keefe is there to make sure it's all done perfectly."

"Wonderful!" Mrs. Kimball declared.

Chapter Eight

Brynn read her aunt's letter once again, hoping, for some silly reason, that the words might somehow change. They didn't.

Pete had delivered the letter to her this morning while she ate breakfast in the hotel dining room. Getting a letter from Aunt Sadie felt odd. So much had happened here in Harmony, Brynn felt very disconnected from her aunt.

Aunt Sadie didn't feel the same, however. In her letter, which had been penned by her secretary, she instructed Brynn to return to Hayden immediately. Aunt Sadie was worried over her, concerned that her trip to Harmony had taken longer than expected. Even though Brynn had telegrammed her right away, notifying her of the delay—no mention that she was awaiting a hearing before the circuit judge, of course—her aunt was concerned about her. Now she insisted that Brynn take the next train back to Hayden.

The other troubling news Aunt Sadie had shared was that she still wasn't well enough to continue the tour. Brynn knew that her aunt occasionally suffered from crippling headaches, with effects that sometimes lingered for weeks. This one seemed worse than usual. Aunt Sadie's secretary had written to the towns where she was scheduled to speak and explained the situation. Everyone understood, she reported.

Brynn paused outside the express office, staring at the gold letters painted on the window. She had to tell her aunt something—other than the truth, of course. The only thing worse than being a suspected jewel thief was having her family find out about it.

So there was nothing to do but lie.

Travis popped into Brynn's head as she recalled his suggestion that Aunt Sadie include a chapter in an upcoming book on telling the perfect lie. Maybe it wasn't such a bad idea.

Brynn pulled her shoulders up straighter. There was nothing left to do but go inside and send Aunt Sadie a telegram telling her how desperately she was needed here in Harmony. Of course, it wouldn't be a complete lie, Brynn told herself. After all, she was heading up the Ladies' Social Club project. Still, it brought little comfort to Brynn, especially since she had Aunt Sadie to thank for getting her away from Richmond.

"Good afternoon, Miss O'Keefe," a man said.

She turned and saw Hiram Smith on the boardwalk. He smiled pleasantly and tipped his hat.

"Good afternoon to you." She smiled in return, genuinely pleased to see him. He looked like a gentleman, just as he had on the train ride from Hayden, well turned out in a fine-looking suit and carefully knotted cravat. She'd seen no one in Harmony who looked so nice.

"May I say, Miss O'Keefe, that you are a welcome sight in this town," Hiram said, his smile widening a bit.

"Why, thank you, Mr. Smith," she said. "It's more than kind of you to say so."

"May I inquire about your aunt?" Hiram asked. "I hope her health has improved."

Brynn had explained to Hiram on the train from Hayden

that Aunt Sadie was too ill to continue her tour. She was surprised that he'd remembered, and pleased that he'd asked.

"She's still not well," Brynn said.

"And unable to continue her tour?" he asked, then shook his head. "That puts you in quite a predicament, I'd say, having to forge ahead with the lectures on your own."

"Actually, I'll be staying here in Harmony for a while longer. The ladies in town have all been very kind," Brynn reported.

"Your lecture was well received, I understand. I wish I'd known the time and date earlier. I'd have attended."

"I'm afraid you'd have been quite bored," Brynn said.

"I doubt that. I've heard ladies mention it all over town as I've called on them," he said, nodding to the sample case he carried.

"I certainly hope you and your fabrics are being well received, also," she said.

"I believe I have you to thank for that, Miss O'Keefe. Every woman in town is anxious to present a perfect home," Hiram said. He paused for a moment, then said, "Perhaps you'll allow me the honor of calling on you? I assume you're staying at the Harmony Hotel?"

"Yes, I'm at the hotel," she said, but wasn't sure how to answer his other question.

How nice to be called on by a gentleman—or at least someone who didn't suspect her of a crime. But thanks to Travis's announcement that he was courting her, being seen with Hiram might start tongues wagging, and that was the very last thing she wanted.

"Please think it over," Hiram said, and she was pleased he hadn't pushed her for an answer.

"Good day, Miss O'Keefe." He tipped his hat respectfully, as a gentleman would, and walked away.

Brynn watched him for a moment, then warmth rippled up her neck. She turned and saw Travis across the street watching her.

* * *

"Everything's set," Olivia said to Brynn in a low voice. "Looks as if we'll have a good turnout."

Around them the church was nearly full, as the townsfolk settled into the pews, awaiting the start of the Sunday service. Today was the fund-raiser for the Ladies' Social Club and, from the looks of things, the women of Harmony had done a good job getting the word out.

Olivia and Rafe had stopped by the Harmony Hotel this morning and asked Brynn to walk to the service with them. She appreciated seeing their friendly faces.

Olivia leaned forward, gazing at the people seated in their pew.

"I don't see Mrs. Stanton, do you?" she asked.

Brynn looked around the room but didn't see her, either. She was more surprised that she hadn't spotted Travis among the congregation. Nor had he been outside her hotel this morning, or on her walk to the church. He'd accompanied her through the streets of Harmony or watched her from nearby every time she'd set foot out of her hotel.

"No, I don't see her," Brynn whispered back. "Wait. That might be her seated—"

"Oh, I see her," Olivia said.

"Shh," Rafe said softly, and nodded toward the front of the church where the service was beginning.

Miss Marshall seated herself at the piano and began playing "Amazing Grace" as Reverend Harrison stepped through the doorway near the altar, clutching his Bible. The choir filed in after him, the congregation came to its feet and everyone began to sing.

Where was Travis? Brynn wondered as she sang along with everyone else. Why hadn't she seen him this morning?

Her spirits lifted a little as it occurred to her that perhaps he'd left town, called away to investigate something more important than her. Did that mean she could leave Harmony?

Then, just as quickly, her thoughts shifted and a wave of dread pressed down on her. What if Travis was investigating another case? Could he possibly be in danger? Had something happened to him? Had he been shot, injured—or worse?

A thousand thoughts jetted through Brynn's mind, all of them alarming. What if something dreadful happened to Travis? What if she never saw him again?

She would ask Rafe, as soon as the service was over. He was the town sheriff, plus Travis's friend. He'd know, surely.

Brynn said a silent prayer for his safety and turned her attention to the hymn, then gasped as she spotted Travis singing in the choir. She blinked, thinking her worry over him had played a trick with her mind, then looked again. But no. It was Travis.

He stood with the choir of four men and six women, easy to spot, since he was so tall. Dressed in a white shirt and wearing a string tie, he held the hymnal and raised his voice in song along with everyone else.

Stunned, Brynn could only stare. She'd known Travis as a Pinkerton detective, a strong, decisive man upholding the law, sometimes on his own terms. She hadn't expected this side of him existed.

The service passed in a blur for Brynn, and when the reverend gave the closing prayer and urged the congregation to attend the fund-raiser to take place at the adjoining fellowship hall, she moved out of the church along with everyone else.

While children played on the lawn and men gathered to talk, the women went inside the fellowship hall to prepare the food. Later, desserts would be sold and the mayor would address the townsfolk, asking for donations for the social club.

Brynn watched with a stab of envy as Olivia and Rafe parted company at the steps to the fellowship hall. They lingered for a moment just looking deeply into each other's eyes, before Olivia went inside. Brynn's heart ached a little, seeing the two of them so much in love.

Then Travis caught her eye and that little ache disappeared. In its place was—well, she didn't know just what it was but it wrapped around her like two warm arms.

She smiled and walked toward him, unable to stop herself.

"You surprised me," she said, gazing up at him. "I had no idea you sang in the choir."

"Whenever I'm in town," he told her, as if it were the most ordinary of things, the answer he gave anyone who asked. But then he paused, as if he saw her in a different light, and said, "Advice from my pa."

"He was a lawman, too," she said, remembering.

Travis nodded. "He told me that dealing with outlaws and criminals all the time could affect a man. He didn't let that happen to him and he didn't want it to happen to me. He said I should go to church every Sunday so I wouldn't forget there are good people in the world."

"What wonderful advice," Brynn said. "I'm sure I'd enjoy meeting your father."

"He'd get a kick out of you," Travis said.

They stood at the steps for a moment, just looked at each other, then both seemed to realize what they were doing.

"I'd better get inside," Brynn said.

Travis nodded. She expected him to move on but he didn't. He stood at the bottom of the stairs watching her until she was safely inside the fellowship hall. But instead of finding his gesture annoying, as she might have before, it pleased her.

"Get the biscuits, would you?" Olivia asked, breezing past her and handing her an apron.

"Certainly," Brynn called, looping it over her head.

Around her the women of Harmony moved quickly and efficiently, getting the tables prepared and the food ready to serve. They talked and laughed. A hum of excitement filled the room, quickly enveloping Brynn, making her feel as if she were a part of it all.

Tying the apron strings behind her, Brynn stole another

look outside. Travis stood with a group of men, talking. Yet he wasn't still. His head moved from side to side, his gaze darted relentlessly, taking in everything and everyone around him. He missed nothing. Travis would never be caught unprepared, Brynn knew.

Just as she turned back inside, Hiram Smith bounced up the steps and stopped in front of her, giving her a start.

"Good afternoon, Miss O'Keefe," he said.

He wore a fine suit, well turned out as a gentleman should be, and tipped his hat.

She touched her hand to her chest and drew in a quick breath. "Good gracious, you startled me."

"My sincere apology," he said, and offered a slight bow. "Might I have a word with you?"

Brynn glanced back at the other women who were hard at work, expecting her to join them, when Hiram spoke again.

"It concerns the fund-raiser," he said. "I'd like to make a donation."

"How kind of you—"

He pressed his finger to his lips, silencing her.

"I'd like to keep this between the two of us," he said, lowering his voice. He eased a little closer. "You see, Miss O'Keefe, I don't want the good folks of Harmony to get the idea that, with my donation, I expect anyone to buy my fabrics in return. As a salesman and a representative of my company, I wouldn't want it to appear that I'm attempting to ingratiate myself with anyone or take advantage of a worthy cause."

"I doubt anyone would think that," she said. "I'm sure they would appreciate your generosity."

Hiram shook his head. "My experience has been otherwise, and I don't dare take a chance."

Brynn considered his words for a moment. A man whose livelihood depended on public perception had to be careful what he did. Hadn't she learned that herself the hard way back in Richmond?

"I'll fetch Mrs. Kimball," Brynn said. "She'll be happy to accept your donation."

"I'd rather give it to you personally," he said and smiled. "You understand my situation more than anyone here. Perhaps we could arrange a time when I could meet with you? Would tomorrow morning be convenient?"

"I'll be at the Ladies' Social Club meeting room all day. We're starting on the renovations," she said. "I doubt I'll be finished until suppertime."

"Sounds like an ambitious day," Hiram said with a hint of admiration in his voice.

"I'm sure I'll be exhausted by then," Brynn agreed.

"I'll come by the social club just before suppertime," Hiram said. "You'll wait there for me, won't you?"

"Of course I will," she said and smiled. "The project desperately needs your donation."

He smiled politely, tipped his hat and blended into the crowd in the churchyard.

Brynn watched him go, thinking how different he was from the other men in Harmony, in manners as well as dress. She'd known from that first day on the train that he was quite a gentleman. Now she knew he was generous to a fault, also.

Her home in Richmond flashed in her mind. Papa had expected her to marry a gentleman—one he'd selected himself. Brynn had been in agreement and, if not for her blunder, might have expected a marriage proposal in a few months.

Her gaze wandered to Travis.

Richmond seemed so far away, her life there such a long time ago.

Travis kept to the shadows. He'd been a lawman too long to advertise his position late at night. He didn't expect trouble, but old habits died hard, even on the rear balcony of the Harmony Hotel.

The town had quieted for the night. Travis had sat in the

hotel lobby until all the guests had retired to their rooms for the evening, and he'd made sure one particular guest was among them. Brynn.

It was hard seeing her disappear up the stairs and into her room, especially after the day they'd shared at church. Brynn had made herself a part of the community with an ease he hadn't expected from a woman raised in the East who lectured on the importance of achieving perfection in all phases of one's life. He'd listened to the reading she'd done from her aunt's book on the church lawn this afternoon. Her voice was soft and sweet, tantalizing. He imagined having her all to himself, her whispering to him, her breath caressing his ear, in the most private of moments.

They'd eaten together, seated side by side at the trestle table, surrounded by friends. Everyone had accepted his story that he was courting her so no one questioned his attentiveness. It was a ploy he found easier and easier to pull off. Especially when he was close to her, taking in her scent, watching her delicate movements and imagining so much more.

So, of course, he couldn't sleep knowing she lay in bed in the room next to his. The balcony above the alley behind the hotel proved the perfect spot to take refuge. No one used it much; most everyone preferred sitting on the front balcony that overlooked Main Street.

Travis gazed up and down the alley, restless but unwilling to leave the hotel. He had to stay on guard. He'd seen Smith approach Brynn twice now, once outside the express office and again today at church. He was up to something. Travis knew it.

His gut knotted thinking what Smith might do to Brynn. If what he suspected was true and Smith had hidden the jewelry in Brynn's belongings, the man would stop at nothing to get it back. Nothing.

With a heavy sigh, Travis made up his mind. He'd have to talk to Brynn, try to get her to tell him the truth. Maybe she trusted him enough now, but even if she didn't, he had to warn her about Smith.

Telling her about his suspicions might tip his hand, if she really was Smith's accomplice, but Travis knew she wasn't. He'd told her she must face the circuit judge to clear her name when, all along, he'd wanted to keep her in town, make sure she was safe.

Yes, he'd wanted to keep her safe. At least, that's the way it had started out. But now…

Rafe and Olivia floated through Travis's mind. They were happy. Any fool could see it. They both had family close by, they'd live in Harmony for a long time. They understood each other, wanted the same things. They'd have a good marriage.

Being married under those circumstances wouldn't be so bad, Travis thought. Having a wife, a home to return to at the end of each day could be the best thing a man might have.

But only if the wife wanted to be there. And only if the husband wanted to come home to the same place night after night.

Travis shook off the thoughts. He had more important things to deal with right now.

He had to talk to Brynn, tell her his suspicions about Smith, warn her that she was in danger. Urgency overwhelmed him. He had to tell her now, tonight. Waiting until tomorrow seemed intolerable, despite the late hours and the eyebrows it would raise if he were seen.

Travis headed back into the hotel.

Chapter Nine

A knock sounded on Brynn's door, jarring her from her thoughts. She glanced at the clock on the bureau. Late. Too late for callers. But would that stop the ladies of Harmony if they had a question about something in her aunt's book?

Today at the church fund-raiser, while children played games and men pitched horseshoes, she'd done a reading from *Planning Perfection*. Mrs. Kimball had asked her to do it. Dozens of ladies had gathered around listening intently to Aunt Sadie's advice on the perfect way to decorate a parlor. Questions and comments had followed, one after another. As Aunt Sadie had predicted, the thirst for knowledge among the women of the West was great.

Brynn abandoned her journal entry and rose from the little writing desk in the corner. She pulled on her wrapper. She'd readied herself for bed and was hardly presentable for company. But if some young woman had a burning question that simply could not wait until tomorrow, she'd just have to put up with Brynn in her nightgown with her hair down and her feet bare.

Silently, so as not to disturb any of the other hotel guests, Brynn opened her door a crack and peeked out. Through the tiny slice between the door and its frame, she spotted Travis.

Her heart thumped into her throat and hung there.

Before she could react, he pushed his way inside and closed the door. Brynn fell back a step, too stunned to speak.

Not that he gave her a chance, anyway.

"What are you doing opening your door at this time of night?" he demanded. "*Anybody* could have been waiting in the hallway."

He seemed to fill the entire room. In the dim light he looked taller, his shoulders wider. His presence seemed to rob the room of air.

Travis appeared to have some trouble breathing himself. His gaze dropped to her bare feet, rose over her hips and her waist where she'd cinched her wrapper, then lingered on her bosom for a second, then took in her hair loose about her shoulders before finally landing on her face.

Heat ignited within Brynn. Her only clear thought was that she should have been outraged at his boldness, but she wasn't.

Finally she found her voice.

"What are you doing here?" she asked, and managed to sound a little indignant.

"You might be in danger," Travis told her.

"Of what? Someone barging into my room in the middle of the night?" she demanded. "You have to go. I can't have my reputation compromised like this. I can't have people talking about me again."

"Nobody saw me," Travis said. He touched her shoulder, and somehow it calmed her. "I wouldn't put you in a bad position. I swear. I was careful. Nobody saw me."

She believed him. Something in his tone, his expression, assured her she needn't worry.

Travis pulled his hand from her shoulder and drew himself up. "I saw you talking to Hiram Smith today at church, and the other morning outside the express office. I'm afraid he means you harm."

"Mr. Smith is a gentleman," Brynn insisted.

"I believe he's a jewel thief."

"Oh, those jewels again," she complained.

Brynn whipped around and stalked to the other side of the room, more to hide her guilty reaction to the mention of the word *jewels* than because she was tired of hearing about them and Travis's suspicions.

His footsteps thudded behind her and she sensed his presence at her back.

"I need to ask you again if you know anything about stolen jewelry," he said quietly.

For an instant she was tempted to tell him the truth. Then she could take him down to the kitchen, dig through the crock of cornmeal, hand the things over and be done with them. How glad she'd be to have the whole incident off her back.

But would doing so prove her innocence, or make him more angry? Was he using some supposed concern for her safety as a ploy, hoping she would confess? And if she did, would he only be angrier at her for not telling him the truth in the first place?

As before, Brynn felt she didn't dare risk it. She turned to face him.

"I did not steal jewelry from those people in Houston—or anyone else," she said, which came out sounding sincere because she was, in fact, innocent. "And I intend to plead my case to the circuit judge to prove it. You know that. Why are you here?"

"Because I believe Hiram Smith is the thief. I believe he hid the jewelry in your baggage," Travis said. "And if I'm right, I'm afraid he might hurt you to get it back."

Brynn gasped. It never occurred to her that Hiram Smith could be a criminal of any sort, or that he'd planted the jewelry in her luggage. He was a perfect gentleman, the one person she'd encountered on her trip to Harmony who she'd reckoned was the least likely to do such a thing. And she'd never once considered that the person who'd planted the jewelry might put her in danger.

Now more than ever she wished she could tell Travis. Those wide shoulders of his had never looked sturdier. What a welcome relief it would be to explain what had happened, let him handle it, take the burden—and the threat—onto himself.

But she didn't dare. She'd gone too far proclaiming her innocence to back up now.

"If you really think I could be in jeopardy, why are you keeping me here?" she asked. "Why not let me leave?"

"I can protect you here."

"You can use me as bait, more likely," Brynn realized.

To her surprise he didn't deny her words. He didn't become angry at her accusation. Instead he looked hurt.

Travis glanced away. "I supposed I deserved that," he said quietly. Then he lifted his gaze and Brynn saw an intensity burning in his eyes. "Stay away from Smith. He's dangerous."

"I don't believe you," she said. After all, Hiram had been kind and considerate. Why would she think the worst of him?

"I'm asking you to trust me," Travis said. "Please. I don't want you to get hurt, Brynn."

They gazed at each other, a long lingering look. Finally Travis left the room and slipped silently into the hallway.

"Fabulous!" Mrs. Kimball declared.

Brynn looked up from scrubbing the sideboard to find the mayor's wife standing in the kitchen doorway. Beyond her in the meeting room, the half-dozen or so volunteers still on the job were busy cleaning, scrubbing and making repairs.

They'd been at it all day. Brynn had borrowed a simple dress from Olivia, rolled up her sleeves, tied a scarf around her hair and set to work early this morning. Townsfolk had come and gone all day doing what they could before returning to family and jobs. Some had worked, others had brought food, others suggestions and ideas. Everyone had worked hard.

Including Travis. He'd been there all day working harder than anyone.

"Looks as if we'll be ready for paint tomorrow," Mrs. Kimball predicted as she scanned the kitchen.

Travis paused in the repairs he was making to the back door and gestured with the hammer in his hand.

"Just a few more things and we'll be finished," he agreed. "We'll start painting at first light."

Mrs. Kimball nodded her approval. "As soon as you're finished here tonight, come to my place. I'm making supper for all the volunteers."

"That sounds heavenly," Brynn said and truly meant it. She was tired, bone weary, and a good meal with friends seemed the perfect way to end the day.

"Come as you are," Mrs. Kimball insisted. She smiled kindly. "I doubt even your aunt would frown on us not looking perfect at supper, under the circumstances."

Brynn gave her a grateful smile in return. "I agree completely."

Mrs. Kimball departed and Brynn began scrubbing the sideboard once again. Travis was next to her, nailing wooden strips around the door to trim it properly. The work was hard and, really, Brynn had seldom done this kind of scrubbing and cleaning. Thanks to her father's successful business, their family had always employed a maid.

But, oddly enough, Brynn found that she didn't mind any of the chores she'd performed today. It felt good to have a purpose, to work toward a goal, to see the results of her efforts.

Her home back in Richmond floated through her mind. She'd never do anything like this if she still lived there. What would she be doing at this very moment, she wondered, if she hadn't come west?

The answer came to her in a flash and she cringed.

"Are you sick?" Travis asked.

She realized that he'd been watching and saw her shudder.

"Just thinking about home," she told him.

He turned to her, the hammer dangling from his hand.

"You must be anxious to get your aunt's tour wrapped up and get back to Richmond," he said.

Brynn cringed again. If she hadn't been so tired she may have been able to keep up pretenses, but the hard day's work had made her too weary.

"I'm not at all anxious to get back home," she told him, dipping the scrub brush into the water bucket.

"Don't you miss your family?"

"Some," she allowed. "But, well, let's just say that the longer I stay away, the better."

His brows pulled together and the tiniest grin touched his lips.

"What did you do?" he asked.

"Nothing," she blurted out.

"I know a guilty face when I see one. You did something. You might as well tell me because I'm imagining all sorts of things."

She drew herself up. "I'm not telling you anything."

"Okay, then, I'll guess." Travis thought for a second. "Let me see. You got caught in a, shall we say, *romantic* moment with the preacher."

"No!"

"Your best friend's husband?"

"Of course not!"

"Okay, then it must have been—"

"I didn't get caught with anyone!" she exclaimed. "I called the grande dame of Richmond society a name."

Travis reeled back. By the stunned expression on his face, she could see that even he knew the problems that created.

"What did you call her?" he asked.

Brynn's anger grew, remembering. "I told her she had the taste level of a sow and, until she learned how to decorate her own home, she should keep her pig-snout nose out of everyone else's business."

"Damn…"

"She was insufferable!" Brynn declared, flinging the soapy scrub brush out and gesturing eastward. "A young woman—

a perfectly delightful woman—moved to Richmond as a new wife and invited everyone in our circle over for tea. And that horrible know-it-all woman had the gall—*the gall*—to insult her parlor furnishings in her own home!"

"Well, hell," Travis said. "I think she ought to be shot."

"I blasted her, all right," Brynn said, "with words."

"I guess that caused a pretty big stink," he said.

Brynn rolled her eyes. "The story was told and retold. Absolutely everyone heard it and repeated it. And, of course, I became the villain for causing a scene. Young women simply don't do things like that. It's a mark of poor manners and ill breeding. My father…"

Suddenly exhausted, Brynn dropped the scrub brush into the bucket of water. For weeks now she'd managed to push the details of everything that had happened into the far recesses of her mind. Now they all came back.

"My father expected me to marry well, to improve our family's social position." Brynn sighed heavily. "It was the only thing I could do to help, to please him. And I failed completely—after he'd selected the perfect husband for me."

"Husband?"

Brynn nodded. "His family owned a number of businesses in Richmond. They were very well thought of, well respected. The connection would have elevated Papa's position in the community and vastly improved his own business."

"Your pa was mad at you?" Travis asked.

"Luckily, Aunt Sadie took me on her tour with her. Papa hoped things would settle down while I was away, but no one will forget what happened," Brynn said. "I'll be expected to apologize for the things I said, which I suppose I should."

"Even if what you said was true?"

Brynn nodded.

"Can't say I'd be too happy about going home, either, under those conditions," Travis told her.

The day had finally taken its toll on Brynn. The work, the

long hours and, finally, sharing her disgrace in Richmond had worn her down.

She wiped her hands on her apron. "I think we've done enough for today."

Travis pounded the final nail into place and put his hammer in the toolbox.

"I hope Mrs. Kimball's got a big meal laid out," he said, "because I'm hungry."

They washed up at the sink, then walked through the meeting room and saw that the few remaining volunteers were also finishing up their work. Everyone left together.

Brynn locked the door and turned to find Travis standing close, watching her. His expression held a mix of pride and intensity.

"I say, good for you for telling that old heifer what you thought," Travis said. "If I'd been there, I'd have applauded."

His words touched her heart as no one else's had. Absolutely no one in Richmond had defended her. They'd all been shocked by her behavior. Some had quit socializing with her. Her family had been angry and disappointed.

Tears seeped into her eyes as she gazed up at Travis.

"Thank you," she whispered.

He touched his thumb to her tears, wiping them away, then splayed his fingers over her cheek. Brynn leaned into his palm, soaking up this warmth, his strength. For once, thinking about what happened back home didn't seem so bad.

"We'd better go," she said, though she didn't really want to. Standing here with Travis next to her seemed so right.

"I guess we'd better," he agreed, though his words didn't carry much conviction.

They headed down the boardwalk together. The sun had dropped to the horizon, casting the town in dim shadows. The streets were nearly empty.

"I promised the reverend's wife I'd lend her my aunt's book," Brynn said. "I need to stop by the hotel and pick it up."

They went inside the hotel. Brynn was halfway up the staircase when a task she'd forgotten caused her to stop and turn back. Travis stood in the lobby, leaning his shoulder against the door casing, looking up at her.

"I just remembered," she said, feeling foolish. "I was supposed to wait at the social club. Mr. Smith was coming by with a donation."

Travis pushed himself upright. "Hiram Smith?"

"I know you have your suspicions about him," Brynn said. "But he insisted I meet him this evening to accept his donation."

"Smith expected you to be at the social club? Not here?"

"Yes. And I think his generosity should prove to you, once and for all, that he's not—"

"You're not going anywhere."

Travis bounded up the steps, caught her arm and hustled her into the lobby.

"What on earth has gotten into you?" Brynn asked.

He grasped her arms and leaned down.

"Smith expects you to be waiting for him at the social club," he said. "I'm going to check your room. Give me your key."

Brynn rolled her eyes. "This is silly. Mr. Smith—"

"Give me your key," he said again.

She dug into her skirt pocket and handed him the room key.

"Stay here," Travis told her. "Don't come upstairs. No matter what, don't come upstairs."

Brynn watched as Travis took the steps two at a time, quickly and silently. Surprising for a man his size. He disappeared down the hallway.

Several minutes dragged by. Brynn watched the top of the stairs, expecting to see Travis. She was tired and hungry, and she wanted to wash up and get to supper at Mrs. Kimball's.

"This is silly," she murmured, and headed up the steps.

Chapter Ten

The door to her room stood open a few inches but that didn't surprise Brynn. Travis was still inside, presumably. Another hunger pain gnawed at her belly reminding her of the hot meal awaiting them at Mrs. Kimball's home, making her more anxious to get the book she'd promised the reverend's wife and leave. She walked closer, intending to insist that they leave right away, but stopped at the sight of her room.

Through the slice of open doorway Brynn saw the covers stripped from her bed and flung onto the floor. Her bureau drawers stood open, her clothing spilling out.

Stunned, she pushed the door open and rushed inside. From the corner of her eye she glimpsed Travis across the room. The barrel of his pistol glimmered in the fading light. He saw her, shouted, but his words were lost as someone grabbed her from behind.

Brynn screamed but an arm closed around her neck, choking off her words. A hand pressed against the side of her head.

"Back off!" the man threatened. "I'll break her neck!"

In the mirror she saw that it was Hiram Smith, still dressed in his suit, holding her captive. She grasped his arm, trying to push him away. He was too strong.

"Stay back!" he shouted, dragging her toward the door. "I'll kill her. I swear I'll kill her."

"Take it easy," Travis said.

Her gaze met his. He looked calm, almost serene, and he communicated that to her with his eyes. She stopped struggling.

"Put the gun down," Hiram said.

Travis hesitated, taking in the dynamics of the situation, weighing his possibilities. Finally he tossed his pistol onto the bed.

"Just tell me where they are," Hiram said to Brynn. He gave her a shake. "Tell me where you put the jewels!"

She gasped. Hiram Smith had put the jewelry in her bags. He'd stolen them in Houston. Travis had been right all along.

"Let her go, Smith," Travis said, taking a menacing step closer. "If you hurt her, I swear, I'll kill you."

"Tell me!" Hiram shook her again, harder this time.

Brynn struggled to draw a breath. His arms pressed painfully around her throat. He sounded desperate.

She reached up and raked her nails down the side of Hiram's face. He cursed and loosed his grip. Brynn threw herself away from him. Her feet tangled in the bed covers piled on the floor and she fell into them.

Travis lurched forward and picked up his gun. He pointed it at Hiram.

"Put your hands up," he commanded.

Hiram froze. His gaze darted to the open door.

Travis leveled his pistol at him. "You can run if you want, but you'll only die tired."

Hiram didn't move.

"Put your hands up!" Travis shouted that with such command, Brynn jumped.

Hiram lifted his hands above his head. Travis turned him around and slammed his face into the wall, then kicked his feet out from under him and pinned him to the floor.

"Give me your scarf," he said to Brynn.

Stunned, she just stared.

"Brynn, I need your scarf," he said, with such gentleness it jarred her into action.

She unwound her scarf from her hair, as Travis holstered his pistol. He wrapped it around Hiram's hands, securing them at his back.

"Are you all right?" he asked her.

She managed to nod.

Travis jerked Hiram to his feet and stepped out into the hallway.

"Pete! Pete, get up here!" he shouted.

Brynn sat on the floor, unable to get up. She couldn't quite take in what had just happened. Her mind couldn't seem to process it.

Then she heard footsteps running up the steps, Travis's voice, then footsteps again. He stepped into the room again, dragging Hiram with him.

"I'm taking Smith to the jail," Travis said. "Pete's getting his ma. She'll stay with you until I get back."

Brynn didn't want Travis to leave, but knew he had to go. She tried to tell him just that, but her throat seemed frozen. All she could manage was a quick nod.

A few seconds later Mrs. Millburn rushed through the doorway, Pete on her heels, and gathered Brynn into her arms.

"Oh, you poor dear," she said. "What you've been through!"

Brynn tried once more to speak, but no words came out. Mrs. Millburn didn't seem to notice as she rattled off rapid-fire instructions to Pete who rushed out of the room. Travis disappeared with Hiram Smith.

"Let's get you downstairs," Mrs. Millburn cooed. "A nice cup of tea will help considerably."

Brynn wanted to protest, but didn't seem to have the strength. Mrs. Millburn took her down the back stairway to the kitchen and assisted her into a chair at the table. The room was warm and smelled of apple pie. Just as a hot cup of tea appeared in front of her, the back door opened and in marched a dozen women, Mrs. Kimball leading the way.

"You dear, sweet girl," Mrs. Kimball declared. "Pete brought us the news. You can relax now. We're here to take care of you."

The women swarmed around Brynn. Someone put a shawl around her shoulders, someone else lifted her feet onto a stool. Her teacup was topped off. Everyone offered a hug, a gentle pat on the back or a hand squeeze, along with words of comfort. The room buzzed with concern. Brynn had never felt more cared for in her life.

"Thank goodness Travis was there," Mrs. Prescott declared.

All the ladies agreed.

"I shudder to think what might have happened," Mrs. Stanton added.

Mrs. Kimball pushed her way closer to Brynn.

"Please, Brynn, promise me that you won't let the actions of that despicable Hiram Smith drive you out of Harmony," she said.

"You've brought so much to our town," Ada Holt agreed. "We couldn't bear it if you left—"

Travis marched into the room, his mere presence silencing the ladies for a moment. Brynn's heart lurched at the sight of him. Never had he looked taller, stronger, sturdier. More than anything, she wanted him to hold her in his protective arms.

"Thank you, ladies, for taking care of her," Travis said, nodding respectfully to the women. His tone was tight, worried, bringing a new wave of emotion to Brynn.

"And thank you, Mr. Hollister, for getting that criminal off our streets," Mrs. Kimball declared, as the women nodded their agreement.

Travis seemed not to notice their words. All of his attention was focused on Brynn.

"I'd like to get her upstairs now," he said.

The women moved back, allowing Travis to take Brynn by the hand. They called their good wishes as the two of them left the kitchen and headed up the stairs.

Back in Richmond, this would never have been allowed, and Brynn was glad the women of Harmony didn't protest. They knew Travis was courting her and understood his concern.

He guided Brynn into her bedroom and pushed the door closed, then made quick work of spreading the covers on the bed again. Gently, he seated her on the edge of the mattress.

"Are you all right?" he asked, kneeling down in front of her.

"Yes, I'm fine," she said. A knot rose in her throat but she gulped it down. "Really, I'm just…"

She burst out crying. Travis pulled her into his arms, hugged her to his chest and held her. She sobbed and clung to him, soaking up his strength until she couldn't shed another tear.

Brynn eased away from him. He pulled out his handkerchief and wiped her tears.

"You were right," she said and sniffed. "Hiram was a criminal, all along. I didn't believe you and—and—"

"It's okay," Travis said, and hugged her to him again. "You need to forget about the whole thing."

She shook her head frantically and felt tears threaten again. "I can't forget. I don't think I'll ever be able to forget what just happened. We could have both been killed."

He smiled gently. "You need to think about life, not death."

Travis kissed her gently on the mouth. Brynn braced her arms against his chest, then curled her fingers into his shirt. He groaned softly, causing her to gasp. Then he lowered his head until his lips brushed against her cheek, fluttering kisses across her soft skin.

Tightening his grip on her, Travis pulled her full against him.

"What about the cover story you told everyone in town about us courting?" she asked. "Is this real, or just part of your ruse?"

"I never thought I'd care for any woman the way I care about you," he whispered. He sank his fingers into the thick hair at her nape.

Brynn knew she should pull away. She knew where this would end. The young women in her social circle back in Richmond were innocent, but not uninformed.

But after what had just happened with Hiram Smith, she didn't want to think about what was right, only about what was real. And Travis and this moment were real.

Travis deepened their kiss, coaxing her with his lips. He slid his hand down her spine, then brought it forward to cup her breast. She moaned softly and relaxed in his arms.

Travis scrambled to his feet and lifted her onto the bed. She gazed up at him, saw the passion in his eyes.

"If you don't want this," he said, "just say so."

She clung to him, her arms tight around his neck.

"I don't want to stop," she told him. "Please, don't stop."

Travis stretched out beside her, kissing her, touching her as no man had ever done before. Brynn returned his kisses as he worked his way through her layers of clothing, then pulled off his own. A groan rumbled in his chest as he rose above her. He lifted her to him.

All conscious thought left Brynn, leaving nothing but swirling feelings and emotions. The incredible heat and power of his body overwhelmed her as he slid inside her.

She locked her arms around his neck, lost in his kisses. He pressed deeper. Desire pounded inside her. Urgency claimed her, stole her breath. His movements mesmerized her, grew more frantic, rose to a pitch until great waves of pleasure broke in her. She called his name and grabbed a handful of his hair. Travis shuddered, then collapsed on the mattress beside her, spent.

"I'm hungry," Travis said. "How about you?"

"Starved."

Brynn lay in the crook of his arm, the two of them cuddled on the bed together. Moonlight streamed through the window, giving the room an ethereal aura. She guessed that it was well after midnight, but didn't know for sure. Locked in Travis's arms, time seemed to stand still.

"I'll go down to the kitchen," he said, "bring us back something to eat."

She touched her palm to his bare chest, amazed that he gave off such incredible heat. With him at her side, she'd never suffer through another cold winter.

"Don't leave," Brynn said. "I'll go with you."

He grinned, seemingly pleased that she wanted them to remain together.

He rose and sorted through their tangle of clothing. Brynn marveled at the sight of him.

"I should have trusted you," she said softly.

Travis looked back at her as he pulled on his trousers.

"I gave you no reason to trust me," he said. "Besides, I didn't trust you either, at first."

"And now?"

"Smith made it clear that you weren't involved in the jewel theft. He told Rafe at the jail the same thing," Travis said. He sat down beside her on the bed and took her hands. "The truth is I suspected you of being his accomplice. But it didn't take long for me to figure out what really happened."

"I found the jewelry in my valise the day I got here," Brynn admitted. "I was afraid to tell you, afraid of what you might do."

He leaned in and kissed her cheek. "And how about now?"

She blushed and whispered, "I like the things you do now."

Travis took her lips with his, kissing her deeply. Then he pulled away and drew a heavy breath.

"We'd better go get something to eat now, or it'll be a while before we leave this room again," he said.

They dressed and crept silently out of the room so as not to disturb the other guests. Slipping down the back stairway, they went to the kitchen. Travis lit the lantern and searched the cupboards.

"You'd enjoy something made with cornmeal tonight," Brynn predicted.

He looked back and frowned. "Not really."

"Yes, you would," she told him and pointed to the crock on the top shelf of the sideboard.

Travis lifted it down. Brynn removed the lid and pulled out the case of jewels.

"You'll see that they get back to that Houston couple, won't you?" she asked.

Before Travis could answer, voices floated in from the lobby. Brynn's eyes widened. She certainly didn't want to get caught in the kitchen with Travis in the middle of the night, her hair down, clothing slightly disheveled. While she didn't regret what they'd done, neither did she want to advertise it.

Travis crept to the kitchen door. Brynn followed. He slid his arm around her shoulder and held her close as they both peeked out.

Mrs. Millburn, dressed in a wrapper, stood at the registration desk across from a white-haired gentleman. Beside him was a battered leather valise. They chatted easily as he signed the register.

"A late guest?" Brynn whispered.

Travis didn't answer. She looked up and saw the tight lines in his face.

"Who is it?" she asked.

"The circuit judge," he finally said.

The realization finally hit Brynn. She was free to leave Harmony. She wasn't a suspect. Hiram Smith was in custody, so she no longer needed the protection Travis had given her by keeping her in town. She could go back to Hayden, back to her aunt's tour—anywhere.

"You're free to go," Travis said, as if reading her thoughts. "You can head back to Richmond now."

Richmond?

Everything in Brynn rebelled at the thought. In that instant she knew exactly what she wanted. She'd never been more sure of anything in her entire life.

"I don't want to go back to Richmond," she whispered.

Travis glared down at her, his jaw set. He took her hand and led her to the other side of the kitchen where their voices wouldn't be heard by Mrs. Millburn or the judge in the lobby.

"Richmond is your home. Your family is there," Travis said. "Folks have probably already forgotten about what happened."

"It's not that." Brynn shook her head. "I do owe that woman an apology for the names I called her, and I don't mind giving her what's due. But that's not the reason I don't want to go home."

"Then what is it?"

She drew a breath, glad to say aloud the realization that had finally come to her, the reason she'd not wanted to return to her home since setting out on Aunt Sadie's tour.

"If I go back, Papa will find me a husband," she said. "And I don't want that sort of husband. I don't want that kind of life."

Travis shook his head. "That's a big decision. Are you sure?"

"I've never been more sure of anything in my life," she said.

He studied her for a moment, then said, "Maybe I do need to take you before the judge, after all," he said.

Chapter Eleven

"Take me before the judge?" Brynn demanded. "Whatever for? You told me you believed me, that I wasn't involved in that jewel theft, and now—"

"I still believe you," Travis said, and took her hands in his. A soft smile pulled at his lips. "I want to ask him to marry us."

"Marry us?" she gasped. *"Marry us?"*

"I love you, Brynn. But until just now, when you said you didn't want to return to Richmond, I never expected you could be happy in a place like Harmony with someone like me," Travis said.

"But what about your job? You told me yourself that you always wanted to move around," she said.

"I could stay in one place if I had a good reason to stay," Travis said. He looped his arms around her and drew her close. "And I can't think of a better reason to stay than having you as my wife."

She shook her head. "You'll come to dislike me, if you have to change your life that much."

"I'm ready for a change. Being here in Harmony, getting closer to the townsfolk, seeing their lives day to day made me realize that I wanted something more than moving around all the time," Travis said.

She'd felt the same closeness with the people in Harmony. She understood why he would feel that way.

"Only thing is," Travis said, "you'll have to realize life here won't be like in your aunt's book. I can't make things perfect for you, much as I'd like to."

"We have a few things to work on," Brynn agreed. "Like learning to trust each other more."

"So you'll marry me?" he asked.

She wanted to say yes and rush upstairs to the judge's room and have him perform the ceremony tonight. But she knew it wasn't the right time.

"Yes, I'll marry you, but not now," she said. "We need to get to know each other better."

"My feelings for you aren't going to change," Travis said. "But if you want to wait, we'll wait. How about spring? How does that sound?"

Brynn smiled. "Perfect."

* * * * *

COURTED BY THE COWBOY

Stacey Kayne

Dear Reader

The characters of this story have been with me for as long as I've been writing. When I sat down to write my first book I was inspired by two young boys eager to mend their father's broken heart, likely influenced by my own sons, who were six and seven years old at the time. Kyle and Jake Darby stole the show...likely why their father's story never quite made it to completion. But the Darby family wasn't left out in the cold: they made their first published appearance in their uncle's book, the first book of my *Bride Series*, BRIDE OF SHADOW CANYON. Kyle played a larger role in THE GUNSLINGER'S UNTAMED BRIDE as a US marshal ready to help his cousin bring the bad guys to justice. Up to his old antics of stealing the spotlight, Kyle reminded me I had promised him a story of his own.

Long before I wrote BRIDE OF SHADOW CANYON and THE GUNSLINGER'S UNTAMED BRIDE, I had started to develop Kyle's journey to finding love. His heroine, Constance Pauley, was inspired by a true story told to me by my stepmother about a young lady living in Montana in the early 1900s. She'd been burned in a boarding house fire and was sent by train to San Francisco to be treated for her burns. She later became a schoolteacher and found her way to our California valley, where she married a local farmer. I am forever inspired by such tales of misfortune, fortitude and triumph.

I hope you will enjoy Kyle and Constance's journey as they struggle to overcome hardships and finally open their hearts to love.

Special thanks to my editor Lucy Gilmour, for her faith and enthusiasm for this story.

Stacey

> *Dedicated to the hero of my heart~*
> *my husband of twenty years.*

Chapter One

⁓⦿⦿⦿⁓

Montana Territory, 1883

Thick clouds of gun smoke swirled up on the cold morning breeze. U.S. Marshal Kyle Darby eased out from his position behind an upturned wagon, his gaze honed in on white curtains flapping from a second-story window.

"Come on out, Chandler! We've got you outgunned and there's nowhere to run." Eight of his men and four local lawmen surrounded the run-down house serving as a hotel on the far edge of this rural township, each positioned behind bullet-riddled barrels and wagons they had pushed into position.

"Goddamn traitor!" Chandler shouted. "You shot two of my best men!"

Kyle grinned and reached into his coat pocket for a smoke. *All in all, not a bad morning.*

Infiltrating dens of criminals was all part of a bounty hunter's profession. The fact that he now wore a star didn't change his line of work. Same job. Less pay. He'd hunt down the likes of Ned Chandler for no pay at all.

As he pulled his cigar case from his pocket, a slender gold

ring caught on his little finger. The fat diamond winked at him in the sunlight, souring the start of his good mood. Shifting his silver case of smokes to his other hand, he stroked his thumb over the smooth gold band, a token to remind him how foolish a man could be.

John Logan, a fellow U.S. Marshal, crouched beside him. His dark eyebrows rose beneath the brim of his black hat. "You planning to propose to Chandler to get him and his gang out of there?"

"Whatever it takes to get 'em to the gallows," Kyle said, ignoring the question in Logan's gaze as he tucked the useless trinket back into his coat pocket. He'd rather deal with bloodthirsty outlaws than the marital bargaining methods of gold-digging women. Unlike women, outlaws he understood. Chandler was stalling. He hoped to sneak out under the cloak of nightfall after reaping his fill from poor unsuspecting fools.

Perhaps not so different from women after all.

Kyle struck a match and held the flame against the tightly packed tobacco of his cheroot. The tip crackled as his gaze trailed down the front of the run-down house. The flimsy structure was more grass than wood, rotted siding filled with sod patches to keep out the critters and the elements. Touch of a flame, and the place would go up like a shooting match.

"I put a deputy on each side of the house," said the local sheriff, a stout man with a wide mustache who'd annoyed Kyle last night with his hesitation and constant complaints. Wasn't their fault the band of outlaws chose this town to rendezvous with their gang leader. He'd been waiting a long time to meet up with Ned Chandler and would have been willing for the sheriff and his deputies to stay locked up in the sheriff's office this morning.

"Did all our shooting wake you?" Logan asked.

Kyle suppressed a grin. He'd been working with Logan for six months, and had liked the seasoned marshal instantly.

The sheriff scowled. "You said sunup."

"We said daybreak," Kyle corrected. His men had sneaked into the house before sunrise and cleared out all the rooms not occupied by an outlaw. "Did you find the proprietor?"

"Mrs. Farrell said all her other tenants are out and accounted for."

"Awful quiet," said Logan. "It's makin' my back itch."

"They're saving the rest of their bullets for an ambush." It was past time to put an end to Chandler's business of killing, robbing and raping.

"This is your last chance to surrender!" Kyle shouted to his captives.

"Or *what?*" Chandler called back. Coarse laughter filtered through the upper open windows and a bedroom on the lower left.

Chandler clearly underestimated Kyle's talents of persuasion. He clamped his cheroot in his teeth. Lifting his rifle, he took aim at a kerosene lamp on a table inside the front window and fired. The glass globe shattered.

"Fine idea," said Logan, nodding with approval.

"What are you doing?" asked the sheriff.

"What I do best. Give me cover fire," he said to his men.

Logan straightened and raised his rifle. Two other marshals followed suit, cracking off shots.

Kyle stepped a few paces beyond the wagon, took a last drag from his cheroot and tossed the lit cigar through the open window of the front room. Glowing embers sparked across the kerosene and burst into an orange glow. A blanket of fire coated the table and caught the draperies. Within seconds, heat rolled out of the window like a breath from hell, flames licking out and up the walls. The breeze swirled ribbons of fire across the wood front.

"You set Mrs. Ferrell's house afire!" shouted the sheriff.

Kyle moved past him. "The government will pay for a new one." He turned his attention to the half-dozen lawmen spaced across this side of the house. "They'll come out shooting. *Be ready.*"

"He's burning us out!" voices shouted from inside. Flames were quickly swallowing the house. Certain Chandler would send most of his men out the front while he tried to escape through the back, Kyle worked his way around the barricade. At the side of the house where there were no windows, he ran across the yard. Gunfire erupted in the front yard followed by shouts and another barrage of gunfire.

Smoke swirled around him, stinging his lungs as he made his way toward the back door. Just as he eased into position, the door burst open. Smoke rolled out, followed by a dense figure covered in a dark shroud. Chandler straightened, shrugging off a wet blanket, two revolvers in his hands. Kyle was already on him, pressing his Colt to the middle of Chandler's back.

"Drop 'em."

Chandler stiffened, his guns falling to the ground as he raised his hands. "You sneaky bastard."

Kyle raised his gun to the man's temple and dragged him toward the waiting lawmen. "Come on out, boys," he shouted toward the house.

Men spilled out of the smoky doorway, coughing and choking, their hands raised in the air. Marshals swarmed in on them.

Kyle clapped a set of handcuffs onto Chandler good and tight. The outlaw swung around, his narrowed dark eyes widening at the sight of him.

"Darby?"

The flash of surprise gave Kyle a slight stroke of satisfaction. "Hello, Ned."

"Didn't we get enough of playing cowboys and robbers as kids?"

"As I recollect, keeping you Chandler boys from stealing our stock wasn't a game."

"Sure it was, but then, you never were quick to catch on. You still pining over my sister?"

Chandler's sneer resurrected six years' worth of suppressed rage, tempting him to forget about the star pinned to his chest and the dozens of witnesses milling around them.

"I can see you're still miffed over Victoria's little deception."

Convincing a man that he'd found a woman worth loving and then wiping out his safe while he waited in a packed church for his bride's arrival wasn't what he'd call "a little deception." He'd been young, blind and painfully foolish.

"That courtship might have cost you a bundle, but you did get to dabble beneath her skirts."

Kyle fisted the front of his shirt. "Mind your filthy tongue," he growled.

Chandler's grin widened. "We sure had a time spending your money."

"That money and your ignorance is what got her killed." By the time he'd caught up with her in Nevada, she had stepped in front of a bullet meant for Ned. Her dear brothers had left her behind to die alone in the street.

"Must smart to know she chose the grave over you."

"I find comfort in knowing she's not alone. I've already sent five of you Chandlers on to keep her company."

All traces of humor fled from Chandler's eyes as anger darkened his expression.

"Oh, yeah, that was me. I've been riding with your boys for a while now. Got your message about the job your brother Billy has lined up in the Redwoods. Once I hand you over to an executioner I'll be heading on to California to make sure the rest of your kin get a proper send-off."

"Don't start counting chickens, *Marshal Darby*. Chandler men aren't so slow as the womenfolk."

Disgusted by his lack of respect for the sister who'd died trying to defend his rotten hide, he shoved him toward one of the deputies. "Take him to the jailhouse. And make sure—"

A woman's shrill scream pierced the brisk air, raising the fine hair across Kyle's skin. The men fell silent as all gazes turned to the house now engulfed by flames. Another scream split the silence.

"Mrs. Farrell!" The feminine voice rang clear.

"Son of a bitch," Kyle breathed. They'd left a lady inside.

Chandler's low chuckle drew his gaze. "What's the matter, Marshal Darby? You only like to burn outlaws?"

"That's my maid!" A woman broke away from the crowd gathering to watch at a distance. She clutched a shawl around her nightdress, her long gray hair loose against her shoulders. "That's Connie!"

"You said all were accounted for," shouted Logan, rushing to stop the woman from moving closer.

Flames reflected in the woman's tear-glazed eyes. *"My house."*

Kyle gripped Chandler's shirt, lifting the outlaw to the tips of his boots. *"Where is she?"*

"Right where I left her, I suppose. She's a spirited little filly. Must have worked off the gag."

Smoke billowed out from the open door. Bright-orange flames curled up from the top-story windows and twisted across the roof. "Get them to the jailhouse," he shouted to his men. He shrugged off his coat, tossing it to the ground as he ran toward the growing inferno. He grabbed the wet blanket Chandler had used to run from the burning house.

"Let 'er go, Darby," Chandler called after him. "Ain't a woman been born worth dyin' over!"

He would not be responsible for burning a poor woman alive. He pressed his hat down tight, dragged the damp blanket over his head and charged against the waves of heat pouring out of the open door. Instantly drenched in sweat, he ducked low, trying to see through the thick smoke stinging his eyes and nose. Bursts of orange and yellow flared on either side of the narrow hall and glimmered overhead like lightning in a storm cloud. Another scream sounded from up ahead. Thankful she was on the lower floor, he hurried through the first open doorway.

A young woman stood beside a bed engulfed by fire, the massive flames reaching high where a portion of ceiling had fallen through. Armed with a bed linen, she swatted at the fire leaping from the mattress, her expression ferocious as she fought the bright glow racing up her skirt.

Spotting a full laundry basin a few feet inside the door, Kyle picked up the tub as the linen in her hands caught fire. He doused her.

Fire hissed and sizzled as she staggered back, coughing and sputtering. Flames continued to blaze from the mattress. She screamed and yanked at the wrist tied to the bedpost. Kyle drew his knife, cutting her free as he wrapped the damp blanket around her and lifted her into his arms. She struggled against his hold, her fists pummeling his chest with painful force.

"I want to help you!" he shouted over the roar of the fire raging around them.

Coughing from the smoke, she strained to peer up at him. Tears streamed from golden eyes bright with determination. "The others," she cried as he carried her into the hall. "You have to get them."

She didn't know the others had made a safe evacuation, leaving her behind.

"Everyone's out!" He felt her relax against him even as she coughed from the thick billowing clouds choking the both of them. Tightening his hold, he ducked low to avoid the wave of flames rolling over the ceiling. The dim light at the end of the burning hall looked miles away as he raced beneath falling embers.

The moment he leaped into cool morning air, the woman tensed in his arms. Her scream popped his eardrums. Moving beyond the blinding haze of smoke, he saw her blistered hands for the first time. The lower portion of her skirt had been burned away. The sight of charred broken flesh above the singed laces on her boots took the breath from his aching lungs.

"Connie!" The proprietor ran toward them, forcing Kyle to angle Connie's injured legs away from her.

"Lady, get back! She's hurt."

"Over here," shouted Logan.

Kyle spotted him standing beside a waiting wagon. The marshal rushed toward them. His eyes flinched at the sight of the girl's legs. He wrapped a side of the blanket over her exposed skin and draped Kyle's coat over the girl's shoulders, covering her to her thighs as he ushered them toward the wagon. "This man will take her to the town doc."

Kyle jumped onto the flat trailer, cradling Connie against his chest. "Go!"

A whip cracked as he sat down. Connie pressed her face to his shirt, coughing in between her jagged breaths.

"Hold on, darlin'. You're gonna be all right."

She continued to cough, her wheezing gasps shorter with each breath.

"Try to relax, honey. It's just a few blocks."

She sucked in a hard gasp then went limp in his arms.

"Connie?" He pressed his fingers to her slender neck. Her pulse beat strong. He brushed dark curls away from her soot-smudged face, thankful her long black hair hadn't taken to a flame.

How could he have known Chandler had a hostage—how long had he held her captive? She'd been fully dressed at the break of dawn. He hoped she'd merely been an early riser and discovered during the ambush.

The wagon slowed. A short while later Connie was lying on the doctoring table. Kyle stayed at her side. A large nurse stood beside him, ready to administer chloroform should she rouse while the local doctor worked on her legs. A balding man in his fifties, Doc Mason had already bandaged her hands and set to work on her blistered shins. Her leather boots had protected her ankles and feet.

Kyle kept his gaze on the delicate features of Connie's face. In his mind he kept seeing the moment his cigar touched down on that kerosene-coated table, the spray of sparks, burst of fire—her determination as she fought those flames.

"Ms. Winslow," Doc Mason said to his nurse, "I'll apply the tourniquets. Bring in the large instruments."

The hefty woman turned away.

"You may want to step out for this," the doc lamented, using the back of his wrist to push his spectacles back up to the bridge of his nose. "Such a shame. Sweet girl. Orphan as I understand. 'Round eighteen. Ain't a man gonna want her now."

Kyle refused to believe a man would be put off by a bit of scarring to her legs and hands. The few moments he'd stared into her honey-shade eyes he saw a strong will, a bright spirit not easily dimmed.

"She'll have suitors," he said. "Stockings will cover any scarring."

"She won't have much use for stockings once we amputate from the knees down."

"Amputate?"

A box clanked onto the far end of the table and Kyle realized "large instruments" included a saw. His gaze shot to her legs. The doc was belting leather straps at the base of her slender thighs. The sight of the charred and broken flesh below turned his stomach.

"It's just *burns*."

"Infection will kill her." The doc reached for a scalpel and Kyle reached for his gun.

"Wait a damn minute!" He leaned over the girl, aiming the barrel of his Colt at Doc Mason's head. The doc's eyes widened behind his round spectacles.

"Hellnation, boy! I ain't the one who burned her."

Rage coiled as guilt stabbed at his conscience. "You're the

one trying to cripple her! Amputation is awful drastic for blistered skin."

"Take a good look at that charred flesh, son. Those burns go too deep. Her hands might heal, but her shins…" He shook his head. "Infection will set in and kill her for sure."

There had to be another way. His cousin was a doctor. They'd had some horrible fires in 'Frisco and Daniel had treated severe burn victims. "I have a cousin in San Francisco. He's treated serious burns without the loss of limbs."

"This ain't 'Frisco, Marshal. In these parts, what ya can't heal, ya cut off 'fore it kills you."

"Not today," he said, his gun still trained on the older man. "I'm going to send a wire to my cousin. You touch that saw before I get back and I swear I'll put a bullet through your bald head."

The doc took a step back and raised his hands.

Through the heavy darkness of her mind, Constance Pauley tried to make out the gruff voices talking around her. Pain throbbed through her legs, distracting from the sting in her fingers. Men continued to talk around her.

Where am I? Visions swirled in her mind, frightening faces, cold laughter, the sound of gunfire as flames lashed, biting at her flesh.

The fire!

Her eyes flew open, widening as a dizzying blur of faces wavered before her. She lunged up, but a sturdy hand on her shoulder prevented her attempt to sit.

"Easy now, Connie. Try to lie still."

Her gaze snapped up to the flushed, round face of Doc Mason. Light reflecting off his spectacles increased the kaleidoscope effect of her vision.

"My legs hurt," she whispered. Her voice didn't sound at all like her own. "My head feels…strange."

"It's the laudanum. Lie still, now. You've suffered serious

burns. We've found a doctor who can help you. Nurse Winslow will accompany you and continue to administer the laudanum."

A pinch-faced woman appeared before her with a brown bottle and a spoon. Doc Mason continued to talk as the woman shoved the spoon into her mouth, banging her teeth. Constance winced as the liquid clawed its way down her tender throat.

"When you arrive in California—"

"California?" she croaked. She sat up in a rush, looking wildly at the faces around her. She couldn't be shipped away, not again. She'd finally found a job, a life of her own. "I didn't start the fire!"

"You're not in trouble, child." Doc Mason smiled warmly. He eased her down and tucked the blanket over her shoulders. "We found a doctor who can treat your burns."

Burns? She knocked the blanket back again and stared in horror at her bandaged hands. She'd been burned. How could she find work?

"We're ready, Doc," another voice shouted.

Ready? *Ready for what?*

"Very good," Doc Mason called back. "Everyone grab ahold."

Constance screamed as she was hoisted up, realizing only then that she was lying on a stretcher.

"Don't be alarmed," Doc Mason said, staying beside her as the men carried her outside. Sunlight blinded her. A whistle pierced the air.

They were at the train station. They were putting her on a train!

"No," she pleaded, the weeks she'd spent on an orphan train still fresh in her mind.

"They'll take good care of you in San Francisco. Don't be frightened, Connie."

Don't be frightened? She'd finally found her own life and they were sending her away! She knew what the train brought…more strangers, new hardships, another place to feel unwanted.

Darkness swirled around her, easing her fright, drawing her away from the noise, commotion and chaos.

Please, let this be a bad dream.

Hours later, pain pulsed through her shins with each beat of her heart. The train trundled along, rattling her head against her makeshift bed. The standard car offered no sleeping compartments. A board had been placed between two bench seats, the hard surface unforgiving, emphasizing every grain of sand on the track. Curls continually bobbled across her face, adding irritation to torture.

"Are we in California yet?"

"Barely a quarter of the way." Nurse Winslow, sitting on a bench in front of her, peered over her shoulder. "Don't bother asking for more medicine. You need to wait at least another hour, and I won't be swayed by your impertinence."

Since when was openly praying for mercy and deliverance considered impertinent? Her teeth rattled and the back of her head felt as though it was being repeatedly struck.

"Damnation, but the wheels of this train must be square."

"Mind your tongue," snipped Nurse Winslow.

She couldn't think beyond the pain Nurse Winslow refused to dull. She lifted narrowed eyes, meeting the woman's stern gaze. "I'm cold."

"Doc said burns like yours are inclined to give shivers and you already have two blankets."

Perspiration dripped from her temples, yet still she shivered. Never had she hurt so. "Dear God," she whispered, "please help me." Anything to ease this pain.

Brakes squealed as the train jerked forward. *Thank you, Lord.* The rattling in her head would stop, if only temporarily.

When the train finally stilled, Constance let out a long sigh of utter relief.

"Twenty-minute stop," a porter called from out on the platform.

"Sweet mercy," exclaimed Nurse Winslow, in the brightest voice Constance had heard out of the stingy old bag. She stood and scuttled out of view.

"You don't know the meaning of the word," she muttered to herself.

A soft rumble of laughter suggested her whispered words had been overheard. A lash of fear tensed her aching body. She hadn't been aware of anyone else in the car. Of course, she couldn't hear anything over the rattling of her skull.

"Nurse Joy could use schooling on that term," agreed a sonorous voice.

His voice. The man who'd rescued her, saving her from the fire.

Fear squeezed her chest as she listened to his approaching footsteps. The fire hadn't burned away the memory of being pinned to the bed, a rope burning across her wrists as those horrible men told her all the vile things they intended to do. Had gunfire not erupted, she held no doubt they'd have followed through with their threats.

Warm blue eyes came into view; indigo eyes, which happened to be set in a quite handsome face.

"Good afternoon." His lips eased into a slight smile.

"Not really," she replied in her scratchy voice.

His eyes widened. "Those yahoos didn't even put a blanket under you?"

She gasped as his large hands moved to the sides of her head.

"Don't be frightened," he said in his smooth, hypnotic tone. "I'm putting my coat under your head."

Relief eased her tension as he lifted her head from the hard wood then gently eased her upon a soft cushion. She turned to peer at the fluffy lamb's-wool lining of his heavy coat.

"It may not be too clean, but it's soft. I hope you won't be offended by unpleasant odors."

It did smell—like a cowboy. Closing her eyes, she breathed in the masculine scent. *Sunshine, tobacco and horses.*

A tender touch trailed across her forehead, forcing her eyes open. He brushed her unruly curls away from her face, his smile compassionate as he sat next to her feet on the small portion of bench not covered by the board.

He looks like a cowboy, she thought as she stared up at his tanned face. Dark stubble shadowed his sharp jawline. Straight brown hair, tucked behind his ears, rested against the ivory cotton covering his broad shoulders.

"You saved me from the fire."

"I'm sorry I didn't get to you sooner."

"I'm grateful."

"If there's anything else I can do to ease your discomfort, say the word."

Knowing she shouldn't, unable to resist the chance to dull the sharp pain ravaging her body, she said, "If there's a black bag—"

"Have it," he said, reaching over the bench and lifting the medical bag. He pulled out the brown bottle. "A spoonful?"

"Posh on the spoon. Pull out the cork and pour it into my mouth."

He smiled and warmth spread through her like a soothing balm, easing the throbbing ache of her burns. *Glory be.* She'd never seen such a handsome face. *Such nice teeth,* she thought, certain she'd never seen such straight, white teeth. He pulled the cork out, his long arm easily reaching her as he set the glass rim against her lips.

"Just a sip," he said as he tilted the bottle. "I don't want to overdose you on the stuff."

Anxious for the relief of sleep, she swallowed deeply. As he drew the bottle away, she sought the warmth of his gaze, the comfort in his smile.

"Are all cowboys angels in disguise?" she whispered.

"Believe me, I'm no angel."

"You're very kind."

"Not usually. I have a soft spot for pretty girls with honey-colored eyes and dark curls."

His tender tone and gentle gaze caressed her senses, dissolving her fear and pain for the longest, sweetest moments.

"Rest," he said at last. "I'll watch over you." His fingers brushed across her forehead and her eyes drifted shut. "Keep your spirit bright. You're going to be just fine."

She wanted to thank him for easing her pain, to ask his name, but found she could no more lift her eyelids than she could force her lips to form a single word. As a peaceful darkness settled over her, she thought of her cowboy sitting nearby, his velvety voice and tender touch...

Chapter Two

California, 1885

For two years he'd dwelled in her thoughts and her dreams: the man who'd come to her rescue, a cowboy with warm indigo eyes and a gentle smile. Had it not been for the coat he'd left behind, Constance would have thought him to be a laudanum-induced dream.

Again, she lifted her hand toward the window, angling her wrist until a stream of sunlight transformed the clear stone into a splintering array of brightness—her own personal star. Such treasures she'd found hidden in the pockets of her cowboy's coat. She often wondered what type of woman would inspire a man to buy such a precious and expensive ring. She must be beautiful, this bride of her cowboy.

Beyond the window an expanse of green and gold rolled by as the train rattled along the tracks. Grass-covered hills rippled toward the tall peaks of the Sierra Mountains. Constance sucked in another deep breath, trying to quell the excitement building inside her. Soon she'd begin her new life as the schoolteacher of Pine Ridge. Finally, she'd been given a chance to start fresh with a new life in a new town where no one knew of her past or her burns.

A couple shuffled past in the narrow aisle. She smiled at their perplexed expressions. She didn't care if she looked odd. She liked the feel of the oversize work coat. The weight of the heavy leather and sheep's wool felt like a warm embrace reaching from her chin to her knees. Dipping her hand into the breast pocket, she pulled out the silver cigar case. She ran her fingers across the letters engraved on top. *K.D.*

The initials of my cowboy. She pressed the small button on the end, letting the rectangular lid pop up. Smiling at the thin brown rolls, she inhaled the calming scent of stale tobacco. His warm smile flashed in her mind. He was her last memory before waking in San Francisco with Dr. Norwood's narrow face leaning over her. Her cowboy had departed sometime before, or so Nurse Winslow had stated as she ranted about the beastly treatment she received by the ruffian who had muscled her out of the way as he sat beside her patient, administering laudanum whenever she roused.

He had protected her while she slept, keeping the pain at bay.

The very thought always moved Constance to tears. Her cowboy's forgotten jacket had been her only source of comfort and courage during those long, painful months of treatment. Doctors had scraped, poked and prodded at her burns until she thought the painful torture would never end. After several agonizing months she had been dumped off at the nearest mission where the nuns had tended the rest of her recovery, a debt she had repaid by working in their school.

A whistle sounded as the train rocked forward. Clusters of buildings came into view. By this evening she'd be in the mountain town of Pine Ridge.

Passengers gathered belongings as Constance slipped the cigar case back into the leather pocket. She shrugged off her coat and safely tucked the ring into the deep pocket of her skirt. She opened the carpetbag on the seat beside her to retrieve her white gloves and quickly pulled them on, covering patches of shiny pink skin. While the others bustled past she made her way down the center aisle. She brushed the heavy wrinkles from her faded floral skirt. A hideous pattern of brown and orange flowers, the dress was the nicest of the three Sister Agnes had given her. By the end of the month she would be able to buy clothes of her own.

No longer the clumsy orphan, she was a *schoolteacher.*

The platform had nearly cleared by the time she emerged from the car. She hadn't been told who would be greeting her to take her up to Pine Ridge. She'd only been told to arrive on the morning train. Nearing the station house, a young lady in a lavender dress caught her attention. Tall and slender and strikingly pretty, she drew many gazes. Constance couldn't help but notice the fine cut of her dress. Her bonnet of lavender and white matched the fancy outfit perfectly. Tiny golden ringlets lined her naturally rosy cheeks. Her blue eyes searched the departing passengers. Catching her gaze, a smile brightened the young lady's face.

"Miss Pauley?"

Oh, dear. "Yes."

"I'm Stella Darby," she said, rushing forward. "I'm so happy to meet you. I'm to be your assistant at the school."

Her assistant? "How wonderful."

"Kyle intended to be here, but he's been detained in the stockyards. He said to give his apologies."

"Kyle Darby," she said, realizing this must be his pretty young wife. "I didn't realize he'd be meeting me here in the valley."

"We've actually been here for a few days. Your arrival coincided with my family's spring drive. They had trouble in the stockyard this morning, but he'll be along shortly. Should we get one of the porters to unload your luggage?"

Heat crept into her cheeks as she glanced at her carpetbag. "This is all I have."

"Oh." To Stella Darby's credit a smile quickly replaced her surprise. "Of course. Can I carry your belongings?"

Constance tightened her hold on her coat. "*No*. Thank you. I don't mind carrying them."

"Then we'd best get you to the wagon. We have a long ride ahead of us, which will give me time to tell you about the school."

Following her pleasant hostess through the station house, she felt tattered and underdressed. Nothing new there, she'd never been otherwise.

Confident and capable, she reminded herself. This was her fresh start.

"The community has been anxious for your arrival," Stella said as they reached the boardwalk outside. "So far we have eighteen students, many who've never had the opportunity to attend a school."

"The schoolhouse is new?"

"Yes, ma'am. Pine Ridge is newly founded, not quite two years ago. Kyle has been overseeing much of the construction. My mother and I spent weeks organizing the classroom, but you're welcome to change anything you like."

A brand-new school all her own. What a wonderful surprise.

As they followed a line of fencing to the next boardwalk, hoots and hollers of male voices grew louder. Dust clouded the air above a maze of fencing. Men on horseback were scattered throughout the large stockyard. Others straddled fences around the many holding pens.

Something clanked against her boot. Constance glanced down at her cigar case lying in the dirt. She set her carpetbag down and quickly picked up the silver box. She brushed off the dust before tucking it into her skirt pocket.

"*Runaways!*" someone shouted—just as the ground beneath her feet began to tremble. "*Clear the road!*" A rush of profanities followed the coarse shout.

Standing in the center of the heavily rutted road, her gaze

locked on a steer barreling down on her. A herd of the giant horned beasts charged in a cloud of dust and thunder. Frozen by fear, she faintly heard Stella call her name. Someone grabbed her from behind and hoisted her up. Her back slammed against a hard surface, knocking her breath from her lungs. She glimpsed a blue shirt before he pressed against her with crushing force, shielding her.

Shouts and rumbling moved past and she tried to catch her breath. She opened her eyes and was partially blinded by her fallen hair. A man held her imprisoned between his hard body and the fence. Her feet dangled aimlessly above the ground. She instantly struggled against his hold on her waist.

"Sir," she called in a weak breath, and batted at the loose curls dangling in her face.

He set her onto her feet, easing back enough for her to see a firm wall of brown leather and blue cotton, but he didn't release her. He held her pinned to the fence, *trapped.*

"Let me go!" she shouted, shoving at his chest.

"Connie?" whispered the rich voice from her dreams.

Constance peered up through her tangled hair. Wide indigo eyes stared down at her. She wondered if she'd actually been trampled and knocked unconscious. "It's you. *My cowboy.*"

His gaping expression eased into a slanted grin.

"I mean, *no,*" she shouted, realizing what she had said to a man of true flesh and bone, and muscle. "Not *mine,*" she corrected. "The— *A. A cowboy.*"

His smile widened and a blush sizzled into her cheeks.

"My name is Kyle."

It hadn't been the laudanum. He was truly handsome. His height and powerful shoulders completely shadowed her from the mid-morning sun.

"Kyle Darby," he said, pulling off his brown hat to shove his hand through fallen strands of straight dark hair before tugging the hat back on. "That was a close shave. Are you okay?"

Kyle Darby? The name she had been reading and rereading on her acceptance letter for the past month was the name of *her cowboy?*

The initials on the cigar case, *K.D....Kyle Darby.* Her new employer?

"Connie?" His brow creased in concern. "Are you hurt?"

"*You* are Kyle Darby?"

"My whole life," he said with a wink and a nod, and there it was: the easy charm that had captivated her on the train.

"Kyle!" Stella ran across the wide, dusty road. "Is she all right? I am so sorry, Miss Pauley! I thought you were right beside me."

"Miss Pauley?" Her cowboy's handsome face transfixed with shock. "*You're* Constance Pauley?"

Her gaze moved between Stella and her cowboy. Just as she'd always suspected, her cowboy's bride was...*perfect.* Just like her cowboy. Kyle Darby...*her new employer.* As that truth sank in, her chest burned and the world began to tilt.

"Connie!"

His powerful hands engulfed her waist.

"I'm all right," she assured him, trying to combat her dizziness and the hands sending shivers clear to her toes. She gasped as the earth was again swept out from under her feet.

"I won't drop you," he whispered near her ear. "If you don't get into some shade, you're gonna faint for sure."

"Hey, Kyle," called another masculine voice. "What you got there?"

"Schoolteacher," Kyle shouted back as he carried her into the shade of a tree and set her onto something solid.

Constance released the breath she'd been holding since his arms had surrounded her, only to suck in another sharp gasp as his large palm slid across her back. A calming gesture, one completely lost on her.

"She had a good scare with your runaway steers," he said, his gaze taking in her gloved hands and drifting to her skirt as though trying to see the scarred skin beneath the layers of fabric and black stockings.

"No fooling?" called the approaching voice. Two men on horseback reined in beside them.

"She's the young lady from Montana, Jake," Stella informed them as one of the men swung down from his saddle.

The young lady from Montana? Her spirits plummeted. He'd told them. The approaching man's compassionate gaze went straight to her skirt, dashing all her hopes of making a fresh start in a new town where no one knew of her past.

"You knew?" Kyle said to Stella.

"Well…yes. I thought I'd surprise you." His wife cringed beneath his angry gaze.

"Miss Pauley," he said, "are you feeling better now?"

Better? She felt betrayed. *Cheated!* She eased away from his large palm. "Yes. Thank you, Mr. Darby." She started to rise. His hand covered her shoulder, holding her in place.

"You might want to rest a spell. The heat in this valley can take the breath right out of you."

The heat bursting through her had nothing to do with the climate and everything to do with his hand on her person. Looking away from him, she met the brown eyes of the other man.

"Jacob Darby, ma'am," he said, removing his hat, revealing dark, curly hair. "Please accept my sincere apologies. I hope you weren't hurt."

"No. Thanks to Mr. Darby. I appreciate your concern, Mr. Darby."

"Save the formal title for my big brother," he said, grinning as he slapped Kyle on the back. "Call me Jake. I see you've met our sister, Stella."

Sister? Not his wife. Her gaze moved from Jake to Kyle to Stella, noting their resemblances, and the pity buried beneath their gentle smiles. Anger nettled at her temper. She never would have taken the job had she realized it was another form of charity. Then again…how often had she prayed to discover the identity of her cowboy? Of all the inopportune situations in which to have her prayers answered. When would she learn all train excursions resulted in disappointment? She would be using her first paycheck to buy a stagecoach ticket out of here. She wasn't about to stay in the company of folks who looked at her as if she were some wounded puppy.

"Con— I mean, Miss Pauley," Kyle corrected. "Are you sure you're not hurt? Did I knock your head when I pinned you against the fence?"

"I'm *fine.*" Her bitter tone brought a flare of surprise into his eyes. "Thank you," she added, forcing a polite smile.

"Ma'am?" An older cowboy nudged his way between Kyle and Jake. "Jed Doulan," he said, touching his fingers to the brim of his black hat. "Are these your belongings?" he asked in a low voice. "Our steers did them some damage." He held out a tangle of dirt-coated dresses and undergarments.

Saints and sinners! Constance leaped off the crate and grabbed her clothing from the man's hands. "Thank you," she said, trying to quickly bury her undergarments inside the coat draped over her arm. Her cheeks blazed with renewed heat.

"We'll gladly replace all you lost."

"I'm sure they'll be fine, Mr. Doulan."

"Daddy, I found another one." A young girl in cowboy attire rode alongside Mr. Doulan.

"Hand it to the young lady."

She jumped down from her saddle and ran toward her, discreetly passing her a pair of trampled drawers.

"Uncle Jed and April," said Kyle. "This is Miss Constance Pauley. The new schoolteacher for Pine Ridge."

"Nice to meet you, Miss Pauley." April gave a slight curtsy in her denim britches and leather chaps, then spun with her auburn braids flinging behind her as she hurried back to her horse.

"A pleasure," Constance lied, while wondering how she would ever live down such embarrassment. "Please excuse me." She turned and hurried toward the train depot, wishing she had enough money for the next westbound train and willing to ride in a freight car.

Realizing she was being followed, she risked a side glance.

Stella offered an encouraging smile and gently looped an arm in hers. "We'll walk around to the wagon," she said, guiding Constance toward a side street. "There's a burlap sack in the back we can use for your clothes."

Kyle Darby's sister was clearly as infuriatingly kind as her brother. Reaching the wagon, Stella retrieved the promised sack and held it open. Constance stuffed in the torn and dirty clothing. As she shoved in another faded dress, she noticed Stella's sympathetic gaze.

"I intended to buy nicer clothing."

"Oh, no, I—" Stella's eyes widened as she pressed a hand to her chest. "Miss Pauley, I didn't—"

"It's all right," Constance insisted. "The nuns at the mission gave me those dresses. As soon as I have my teaching wages—"

"You won't have to wait that long," Kyle said from directly behind her.

Constance spun around, shocked by his sudden intrusion.

"Stella will take you to the dress shop to be fitted right now."

"She can't. I don't have any money." If she had, she'd already be clutching a ticket for the first ride to anywhere but here.

"Those clothes were torn to shreds by Darby and Doulan cattle. The Double D Ranch will replace them."

"Yes, ma'am." Jake stepped beside his brother. "You purchase anything you need and—"

"You're most kind, but I couldn't."

"It's settled." Kyle plucked his coat from her grasp and

tossed it into the wagon. "Stella will go with you. Make sure she buys a few dresses," he said to his sister.

"I only had two in my bag," she protested.

"Two, then." He took her by the elbow and led her toward the boardwalk.

"Mr. Darby, you really don't need—"

"Call me Kyle." She gasped as his arm slid around her waist. "Watch your step, now."

Her boot bumped against the raised walk, causing her to stumble.

Good gracious! If he'd stop touching her and smiling at her and befuddling her mind, she might be able to stay on her feet! The man was married or at least engaged—he shouldn't be handling her with such familiarity.

The ring. She stopped, breaking away from his hold. "I have something of yours."

Dark eyebrows shot up beneath the brim of his hat as she reached into her pocket. She opened her hand, holding the ring out in her gloved palm.

Stella gasped. Kyle stared at the glimmering stone, his face void of expression. Judging by Stella's gaping mouth, Constance assumed she'd made another blunder. Intense silence stretched. Kyle took her hand in his and closed her fingers over the ring.

"Finders keepers."

He resumed his hold on her elbow and practically dragged her another ten feet up the walk before stopping abruptly. He opened a door and pushed her inside a shop filled with fabrics before the bell had finished its jingle. She whirled around.

Stella stood in his place.

"I take it this ring is connected to unpleasant memories?"

Stella nodded. "Broken engagement and I imagine wounded pride. She left him waiting at the altar," she said softly.

Constance cringed. Heaven help her, she was not getting off to a good start with her new employer.

Chapter Three

Someone had followed him into this valley.

Kyle walked toward the stockyard, irritation and caution riding his spine as his gaze paused on every face, searching amid the cattle for crew from the Double D and other ranches. Last week a mutilated horse at his place and now steers busting out of every pen? He'd been in the direct path of two breakouts since sunrise, the second stampede damn near injuring Connie. He would have merely hopped the fence if he hadn't seen her standing farther down the road, her arms clutching his old coat. For a split second he'd thought he must have been about to die and she was a figment of his imagination. Not until he'd had her in his hands did he believe she was really there.

As if having his eighteen-year-old sister living under his roof wasn't worry enough with some vengeance-seeking lunatic on the loose, now he'd have Connie to worry about. *Constance,* he silently corrected. *Constance Pauley.*

The reminder tightened the strained muscles across his shoulders. When he got Stella alone, he was going to wring her little neck.

"Hey, Kyle!"

His cousin hopped a fence and strode toward him. The

founder and ex-sheriff of Pine Ridge, Juniper Barns understood his concerns about this morning's mishaps being connected to the trouble on his ranch.

"Find anything?"

Juniper held out his palm, revealing a pile of bent nails. "Someone pried these out of the fencing."

"I knew it."

"Don't go jumping to conclusions."

"I don't have to jump far. Our family has been loading cattle in this stockyard for years. I ride along and suddenly they've got steers running to hell and back."

"It happens."

Kyle leveled his gaze on Juniper's pale blue eyes.

Juniper turned toward the cattle crowding into the narrow channel as they were herded toward a loading ramp.

"Exactly. This was deliberate."

"We don't know if it's connected to the vandalism on your place."

That *vandalism* had left him with an orphaned foal. He'd be a long time forgetting the sight of Blaze, his favorite mare, slashed and on the ground, her young foal lying in the pool of blood surrounding her.

"The local lawmen are looking into it and Günter is watching your house while you're here. We'll send a few men from the Double D to ride up the mountain with you. How's the schoolteacher?"

"*Not who she's supposed to be,* but otherwise unharmed."

A grin tipped Juniper's mouth. "Rumor has it she's the wildflower you brought home from Montana."

Dread pooled in his gut. "I didn't bring her *home!* I took her to Daniel for doctoring. Were you and Lily in on this?"

"Hell, no. We arrived from San Francisco yesterday. Lily has her hands full running her office and tending to Rosemary. You're the town overseer. You gave Stella and her mother rein over the teacher applicants."

He'd read every application—what he didn't know was that Stella and his stepmother had somehow stacked the deck.

"Does Connie know you paid for her doctoring?"

"No." If it hadn't been for his cousin's big mouth, no one would know outside of Daniel and Juniper. While he'd been chasing criminals all over the states, he'd asked Juniper to use money from his investment accounts to cover Connie's medical expenses, an amount Kyle had never cared to tally. "I sure don't want her to find out. The last thing I want is for her to feel beholden to me." The absolute last thing he wanted was for her to know he'd set the fire that burned her. "She's already balking about us replacing the two dresses she lost."

"She lost more than a couple dresses. Stella told Jake all she brought with her was a single carpetbag. Everything inside it was ripped to shreds."

He cursed beneath his breath. Thanks to his family's meddling she had traveled alone to the middle of nowhere with nothing but his old coat and a bag of charity dresses! His dealings with his sisters told him two dresses wouldn't be near enough. Teaching five days a week and attending church on Sundays, she'd need a minimum of six dresses. Despite Connie's complaints, he knew women tended to be obsessive about such things. Victoria had always been pining for a new whatnot from Mrs. White's shop. His gut tightened at the thought of her ring in Connie's gloved palm. He'd figured it was gone for good and hadn't missed the damn thing.

Connie clearly hadn't expected to see him, and yet she'd been willing to hand over her only possession of real value. She could barter the ring for a year's worth of teaching wages. Now he knew the ring would go to good use—she deserved no less after all he'd put her through.

"Lily's down here in the valley, isn't she?"

"Yeah. She and Rosemary are visiting with my folks."

Raised in San Francisco, Lily Barns had impeccable style.

"Would your wife mind doing some shopping before you come up the mountain tomorrow?"

"Lily is always willing to shop, but are you certain that's the best solution?"

"Can't see why not. Mrs. White will have Connie's measurements. Tell her to pick out four dresses and whatever else she thinks a woman may need."

"I thought you said she was squawking about two dresses."

"I've never known a woman to complain about new clothes. Once it's done she'll be too delighted to fuss."

Juniper didn't look convinced. "If she's the independent sort, she may not appreciate a handout, no matter how pretty."

"Once her wardrobe is full, what can she say?"

"Depends. She got a temper?"

Her big golden eyes and gentle smile flashed in his mind. "Nothing I can't handle."

Her stomach churning with nervous tension, Constance stepped onto the boardwalk wearing the peach dress Stella had insisted on. The light color wouldn't show chalk marks, but she'd never worn a fitted waistcoat. She hadn't been aware that she had any type of figure. The corset they'd strapped on her, despite her protest, defined the curves of her waist and alarmingly lifted her bosom. The ribbed undergarment was a far cry from the binding she'd worn at the mission. She smoothed her gloved hands over the full skirt and gazed down at the toes of new brown boots poking out from underneath.

New shoes. Had she ever owned a pair of brand-spanking-new shoes? She didn't think so. Stella wouldn't relent. Her new assistant had turned out to be as bossy as her older brother, and a sheer delight. An hour after her arrival and she was already indebted to her new employer for the purchase of so many garments. Her entire bag of worn dresses wouldn't have covered the expense of the clothes she wore now, much less the second dress Stella had insisted she purchase.

As soon as she squared her debt, she'd move on.

She adjusted the white sash tied at her chin and glanced up beyond the brim of her new straw bonnet. Kyle stood at the edge of the walk, a few feet away. His casual stance and easy smile caused a startling rush of flutters in her belly.

"I'll take those for you." He stepped forward and reached for the parcels under her arm.

"Thank you," she said, struggling to find her voice as he took the packages. Kyle Darby was every bit as dashing as she remembered—though she had always envisioned him happily married to an equally charming bride. His ring felt like a hot coal in her pocket.

"I brought the wagon over." He turned and stepped into the road. She couldn't pull her gaze away from his easy strides, the muscular lines of his strong back tapering down to a lean waist. He placed her packages in the back of the two-seated wagon. His gaze caught hers and held as he walked back. Sensation shimmered inside her, tingles rushing across her skin. Constance began to rethink that stagecoach ticket. She couldn't possibly work for this man.

The bell jingled behind her.

"You and Stella can sit in the backseat," he said as he took another armload of parcels from his sister.

"Doesn't she look lovely, Kyle?"

His leisurely gaze moved over her new attire and Constance nearly choked on her breath. "She does," he agreed, and turned away from her.

"I'm not so sure a schoolteacher should wear such bright colors," she admitted, following Stella to the wagon.

"You're a schoolteacher, Constance, not a widow."

Kyle grinned and held his hand out to her. "I'll help you up."

She was sure the flutters in her belly strained her corset as she accepted his hand. She hurried to the far side of the padded seat to make room for Stella.

"Hey, Kyle." Two cowboys on horseback reined in beside

the wagon. "Ladies," one said as both tipped their hats to her and Stella. "We'll be riding along."

"We're about ready," Kyle said, and offered a hand to his sister.

"Is your family's ranch in Pine Ridge?" Constance asked as Stella sat beside her.

"No," Kyle answered. "Their ranch is here in the valley but they'll be visiting tomorrow. The men heard about the picnic up at Pine Ridge."

"Picnic?"

"Tomorrow after church, to welcome you," Stella explained. "We thought it would be a pleasant way for you to meet the students and their families before school begins on Monday."

"I see." Stella had put so much work into preparing for her arrival. Constance would stay until they hired a replacement teacher or Stella took over. "And you've arranged a place for me to stay?"

"You'll be staying with me." Kyle stepped up to the driver's seat.

"I beg your pardon?" She couldn't possibly!

"Temporarily," he said, a smile tilting his lips. "Until we finish the living quarters above the schoolhouse. Shouldn't be more than a couple of weeks. My place is closest to the school."

"We have a room all ready for you," Stella assured her. "It's down the hall from mine. We'll be able to walk to the schoolhouse."

"The school isn't in town?" She'd assumed she'd find residence in a boardinghouse where meals would be prepared for tenants.

"Pine Ridge isn't much more than a row of shops in mountainous terrain," Kyle said as the wagon jostled forward. "Homes are spaced across various meadows. We chose a location for the school we felt was accessible to the most students. The apartment above the school has a front room with a kitchen and a separate bedroom."

"We're not a full mile out," Stella told her. "We even have a play yard. The desks arrived last week." Stella talked excitedly about preparations made for the classroom, but Constance barely heard a word as she stared at the broad shoulders directly before her.

Sweet Mother Mary. Not only was her handsome cowboy her employer…she was expected to reside in his home?

The sweet scent of pines bathed her senses, and for the first time in two years, Constance felt a sense of coming home. Reclined against the cushioned seat as the wagon bumped along another winding road, she stared up at towering redwoods reaching toward the waning light of a blue sky. Tall mountains rose up on all sides, hugging the vast forest. After a childhood of drifting across the midwestern plains from one temporary home to another, she'd never felt secure on open ground. While at the mission, the endless miles of dry grasses beyond the high walls reminded her too much of the vast emptiness she'd traveled through during her youth. Montana was the first place to ever feel like home, with its tight mountain valleys and woodsy aromas.

"It's just up the road," Stella said from beside her.

As they rounded the bend she saw the massive log cabin rising up in the center of a green meadow. A wide, covered porch stood out from the front and wrapped around each side. A barn to the right of the house was still under construction.

The men riding ahead of them shouted a farewell as they rode on.

"The school is another half mile on the east trail," Stella said as Kyle stopped the wagon before his house. "Pine Ridge is another mile."

"Good evening." A giant of a man with shaggy white hair stepped from the barn. A smile softened his rugged features as he strode toward the wagon.

"Stella," he said, offering his hand to assist her as she stepped down.

"Thank you. Günter Hagen, this is Miss Pauley, our schoolteacher. Günter's the town sheriff."

"A pleasure, Miss Pauley," he said, his voice carrying a hint of a foreign accent.

Kyle stepped up to Constance's side of the wagon as she stood. "I'll help you down."

Her heart fluttered as she took his hand. "Thank you." She quickly moved to the back of the wagon.

"May I help you ladies wit'da packages?" Günter asked, holding his arms out to Stella as she pulled the first bundle from the wagon.

"You may." She smiled brightly as she piled all of them into his waiting arms. Even Stella appeared short standing beside the tall sheriff.

"You had a nice visit in the valley, I hope?" he said to Stella.

"Yes. Did you miss me?" she asked in a teasing tone.

"Ja. I did."

Kyle stepped between them. "You can go ahead and take those into the house. Second bedroom on the right."

"He forgets I am the sheriff, I think," Günter said, smiling at Constance.

"Sheriff Hagen also makes a fine handyman."

Günter laughed and started toward the house. "The handyman needs to speak with you once your guest is settled."

"Everything all right?"

"Ja. Quiet here. Miss Pauley, you will like Pine Ridge."

"Thank you, Sheriff." The fact that Sheriff Hagen hadn't once glanced toward her skirt gave her hope. Perhaps they hadn't told *everyone.*

Stella brushed up beside her. "We'll visit the school first thing in the morning."

Kyle stayed a few paces behind them, his gaze fused to Connie's petite form. Hours of gripping the reins and resisting the urge to glance over his shoulder every time he heard her voice left an ache in his muscles. The moment he stepped inside the house the succulent aroma of baked chicken and fruit pies seized his attention. Stella and Connie disappeared into a bedroom to the right of the long hall leading to the back door. Kyle dashed to the left, heading straight for the kitchen and his stepmother. Corin met him in the doorway. She smiled at the sight of him. An older version of Stella, she nearly equaled his height.

"You're home!" Her smile faltered. "You're mad," she said, accurately reading his expression.

"I'm *furious*," he corrected, and continued into the kitchen, not wanting their voices to travel into the hall. Pies lined the drainboard and tabletop. The flaky golden crusts made his mouth water.

"I should think you'd be pleased." Corin crossed her arms, drawing his attention to her stubborn stance. "We needed a schoolteacher and Miss Pauley needed a teaching job."

"How did you know Miss Pauley needed a teaching job?"

"Daniel informed us she'd been taken in by the nuns for her recovery. I've stayed in correspondence with Sister Agnes."

"Daniel gave you updates?"

"You refused them."

"I didn't want to get *involved!*" he whispered harshly.

"You brought her here all the way from Montana—"

"Not *here*. I took her to San Francisco for *doctoring*. I deliberately kept myself anonymous."

"She has no one, Kyle. Sister Agnes expressed concerns for her future outside the mission monastery and mentioned she'd taken well to teaching. When Juniper and Lily started plans for the school it seemed the perfect solution. I saw no reason to thwart our plans because you'd come home. You did choose her application."

He recalled the crisp, swirling handwriting that had caught

his attention right off. Miss Pauley had been the most qualified applicant, complete with references. "If you'd already decided, were the other applicants even real?"

His stepmother's downcast eyes answered the question.

"*Corin.* How could you deceive me like this?"

"I didn't set out to deceive you. I tried to talk to you the night you announced you'd be moving to Pine Ridge, and you walked away at the first mention of her. She was injured during your raid and you feel responsible, I understand."

No, she didn't. He *was* responsible!

"I hoped seeing how well she'd recovered would ease your burden. I'm told she's a lovely young woman."

"I'm certain she is, but is she qualified to run a classroom of eighteen new students?"

"According to Sister Agnes she's an excellent teacher. I know you've at least been curious about her."

"That doesn't mean I want her here. She wasn't pleased to discover I'm her new employer."

"How could she not be pleased? You're a good man with a good heart." Corin's tender gaze revealed the unconditional love and pride of a mother, which served to increase his frustration.

Lord save him from the good intentions of his family.

Chapter Four

It's perfect.

Constance stood at the front of her classroom and looked out at the twenty desks spaced across the floor, ten on each side with a potbelly stove in the center aisle. Freshly painted white walls brightened the room. Open windows on each side of the schoolhouse revealed a lush green meadow surrounded by tall redwoods and a beautiful spring day. Her desk sat off to the side of a wide slate board covering the wall behind her. In her fondest dreams of teaching in her own school, she hadn't envisioned such a classroom.

"I think we're all set." Stella placed the last bundle of books on a seat at the back of the room. The founders of Pine Ridge had generously donated a leather book strap for each student. Slate boards and chalk sat on the desktops. She and Stella had written a student's name on each one.

She glanced around a final time. "I believe so."

"We should have just enough time to change and freshen up before the picnic."

Constance was glad Stella had talked her into buying two dresses. After a morning of sorting books and chalk and shuffling supplies, her peach dress was a mess of dust and smudges.

"You've done a wonderful job with the preparations," Constance said as they walked into the narrow coatroom before the front door. "Thank you."

Stella beamed. "I'm glad you think so."

Outside, Stella's parents had set up a long row of make-shift tables and covered them with tablecloths. Ben sat in the shade of a tree, reclined against the wide trunk. Corin leaned against him, wrapped in his arms.

"You'll have to excuse my parents," Stella whispered, her cheeks flushed.

"I think they're sweet." Ben had arrived early that morning and had obviously missed his wife. The moment Constance looked up at his warm blue eyes she'd known he was the father of her cowboy.

Kyle's not my *cowboy,* she silently corrected. Her cowboy was a fantasy. Yesterday she'd seen only glimpses of the gentle man she'd met on the train. From the moment he'd realized *she* was the schoolteacher, his blue eyes had revealed an underlying steel she wouldn't have expected to see in her cowboy. Since arriving yesterday evening he had avoided her completely by hiding out in the stable behind his house.

"All set?" Ben asked as he and his wife got to their feet.

"I believe so."

As the four of them neared the house, she spotted Kyle standing in the yard beside a man of similar height. Their hats tugged low, she couldn't see their faces, but Kyle's relaxed stance and strong build was impossible to mistake for anyone else. They rounded the last bend in the road and she saw a woman standing beside the other man, the top of her head not quite reaching his shoulder. She held the hand of a little girl who couldn't be much over a year old. A pink bow held up a sprig of strawberry-blond hair, the same color as her mother's.

"Juniper and Lily Barns," Stella told her. "They own the lumber camp and started the Pine Ridge community for their employees. Oh, May's with them," she added brightly, and

Constance noticed the young lady with ebony hair and spectacles standing near the wagon.

"Juniper's sister," Stella told her.

Lily Barns turned as they approached, revealing a round belly heavy with child. The young girl let out a happy squeal at the sight of them. She broke away from her mother's grasp chanting a word vaguely close to "Stella."

"Hello, Rosemary," Stella said, rushing ahead and scooping the child into her arms.

The moment they reached Kyle, he gave a round of formal introductions. Mr. and Mrs. Barns smiled in a way that made Constance's heart sink.

"Miss Pauley," they said in unison, the greeting sounding more like an apology. *They knew.*

"Wonderful to meet you," Constance replied, and didn't dare look at Kyle for fear her anger would boil over. Had he told *everyone?*

"Welcome to Pine Ridge," said Lily.

Her husband reached down for the little girl now tugging at his pant leg. "I'm sure glad you weren't hurt in yesterday's stampede."

"Thank you. We've just finished setting up the school. It's a lovely schoolhouse. I'm looking forward to meeting the students today." At least, she had been a moment ago.

"We haven't gotten to see it yet," said Lily.

"We should head on," Juniper announced. "We need to make it home before the picnic."

"Miss Pauley," said Lily, "we'll visit more this afternoon."

"I look forward to it."

Stella and the others followed them to their wagon. Constance continued into the house, devastated by the thought of the entire community knowing of her life's history. She walked into her room, a dented tin canister on the chest of drawers catching her attention. Her salve. *Thank goodness!* Someone had found it at the stockyard. She opened her wardrobe and blinked at a rainbow of shirts, skirts and dresses. For a moment she wondered if she'd entered Stella's room. Her hideous floral dress hung amid the others.

"What in the world…?" She pulled out a light pink skirt and held it to her waist. The perfect length.

Lily Barns's compassionate gaze flashed in her mind, a woman about her size. Had Kyle asked the founder of Pine Ridge to give her clothes? Heat flamed into her cheeks as utter humiliation washed through her. He expected her to parade around the entire community wearing their founder's hand-me-downs?

The front door closed and Constance rushed into the hall. Kyle tugged off his hat and shoved a hand through his dark hair as he let out a long breath.

"Mr. Darby."

Kyle froze. The sight of Connie standing in the hall clutching a pink skirt sent a wave of prickling caution over his skin. Her golden eyes blazed with anger.

"Whose clothes are in this room?"

"Yours," he answered in a casual tone, holding his ground though every ounce of his common sense told him to turn tail and run. Lily had outdone herself, arriving with an alarming number of parcels. Fearful of Connie's reaction, he'd helped her put them away, filling the bedroom wardrobe and dressers.

"You are mistaken," she insisted, the stubborn set of her chin lifting a few notches higher.

"I had Juniper's wife pick out a few extra dresses at the dress shop."

"They're *new?*"

"Of course they're new. Mrs. White altered them to your measurements."

Her eyes narrowed as she stomped toward him. Oh, hell. This was one livid woman.

"You had no right!"

He held up his hands, certain she was about to go for his throat. "You needed dresses."

"I have plenty!"

"You had three."

"Which is more than I've ever owned."

His blatant surprise increased her rage.

"I don't come from wealth," she spat. "But I do have some dignity. Or rather I *did!* I can't imagine what Mrs. Barns must think of me."

"Lily didn't—"

"Choosing clothes for me as though I'm an abandoned street urchin—I won't have it! You will write down the exact cost of those clothes and I will pay you back every cent."

"No, I won't," he countered. "It would take a year of teaching wages to pay for all Lily had hauled up here."

"Yes—you—will," she said through clenched teeth. "Or you will have new dresses hanging in *your* wardrobe."

"Connie—"

She stomped her foot, and damn if he didn't flinch. "You can call me Constance or Miss Pauley. I applied for a teaching job, *not charity!"*

"I never meant it as charity. Think of it as a gift."

"I will not. It's hardly appropriate for you to buy me anything. You had no right to purchase additional clothing without my consent. If fashionable attire was part of your job requirement, you should have stated so in the advertisement."

"I know how women are when it comes—"

"You don't know *me!"*

He couldn't argue that. He hadn't thought there was a woman born who'd be fighting mad over a pile of new clothes. Yet there she stood, five feet of rigid fury.

"You will present me with a statement or you can save your schoolhouse and fancy wardrobe for the next teacher, because I won't be here to have use for them."

"It would take a year to—"

"Then it will take a year." Her gaze burned into him. "I'll send you payments after I leave."

"You're leaving?"

"I suggest you start advertising immediately," she called back on the way to her room. The door slammed shut behind her. Hearing Stella's and Corin's voices approaching from the porch, he made a fast retreat to the safety of his office on the other side of the house. He walked around his desk and tossed his hat onto a stack of paperwork as he dropped into his chair. He felt as though he'd taken a head butt from a bull.

She definitely has a temper.

He leaned back in his chair as a bundle of ruffles and crinoline appeared in the doorway, Connie's white-gloved hands strapped around them. "What's—"

The garments landed on his desk. "These have not been altered and can be promptly returned."

He stood and pulled a long wool coat from the pile. "You need a coat. Mornings and nights get cold up here."

Her fisted hands slammed onto her hips and Kyle's focus shifted to her shapely figure—an observation he'd noted often enough.

"I was in the dress shop," she said, drawing his attention back to her narrowed eyes. "For the price of that one coat, I could have bought three."

"You need a coat. Who cares what it costs?"

"I care! If you had lived your life out of a charity bin you might appreciate the insult."

"I never intended to insult you."

"As if the dresses aren't bad enough." A quaver in her voice revealed something more than anger. To his immediate horror, tears hazed her eyes, tears she instantly blinked back. "You had to tell everyone about my injuries."

"Connie, I didn't—"

"I can see it in their eyes, hear it in their voices when they talk to me, as though talking to a *poor wounded child.*"

"No one is—"

"I've spent a lifetime seeing my reflection through the pity in everyone's eyes. I had hoped this job would be different, a fresh start, a chance to be judged on my own merit. I can assure you, had I known this job was another form of charity *I wouldn't have come.*"

"Juniper's my cousin. My family meddled where they shouldn't have, but they wouldn't repeat something told to them in confidence. No one outside of my family knows your history. You weren't hired out of pity. We had plenty of applicants for your position. I chose you based on your application." Which was true, based on what he'd known at the time.

"You read my application?" Surprise eased the pain in her honey-colored eyes.

"Of course I read it. You have the experience this town needs in a teacher, and likely the finest penmanship I've ever seen. I hired you because I believed you were qualified."

"I *am* qualified. As a courtesy to your sister and all her hard work, I'll give you a month to find my replacement."

She turned and stormed from the room. Kyle collapsed into his chair.

I should be relieved she wants to go. After her reaction to the dresses, he sure as hell didn't want to risk her discovering the extent of his involvement with her treatment in San Francisco. He remembered her words: "I've spent a lifetime seeing my reflection through the pity in everyone's eyes. I can assure you, had I known this job was another form of charity I wouldn't have come."

Her words twisted like knives into his gut. Pity wasn't an image that came to mind when he thought of Connie, not even on the train—hell, not even in that burning house. The moment he'd scooped her into his arms her strength and the concern she'd shown for those who'd left her behind had won his admiration. During the long train ride to California he'd felt an overwhelming protectiveness toward her. Knowing he'd caused her such pain was a personal torture, one he'd worked hard to put out of his mind—until yesterday. Last night he hadn't been able to light a cheroot without seeing her broken skin. He hadn't had a smoke since she'd arrived.

The clothes hadn't been out of pity—he'd bought them out of guilt. In truth, he owed her more than he could ever repay. As had happened in Montana, his shot at a quick solution had hurt her.

Swearing beneath his breath, he stood to gather the pile of rejected garments. Tossing the coat, shirts and petticoats over his arm, he realized the bundle didn't include any of the items they'd stuffed into the chest of drawers.

"Mr. Darby!"

Her hostile voice carried through the house, raising the hair on the back of his neck. *Oh, hell.* She'd found them.

Chapter Five

Pretty as a buttercup in her soft yellow dress, Miss Constance Pauley greeted her students as she charmed their parents with her prim mannerisms and deceptively gentle smile. Watching her crouched down to talk to a girl doing her best to hide in her mama's skirt, Kyle hardly believed she was the same woman who'd made him flinch in his hallway—he'd made his living facing down hardened outlaws, for crying out loud!

The reminder put a twinge in his back. Juniper hadn't found any trace of the vandal in the valley but had taken to wearing his shoulder holster again, just in case trouble arrived. He recognized every face on the meadow, most of them single men from the lumber camp up the mountain. The number of unwed camp workers on the meadow likely outnumbered the students three to one. The moment the mom and daughter moved on from Constance's welcome another lumberjack closed in, fumbling to remove his hat and introduce himself. Not about to be outdone, others gathered behind him.

Constance stepped back, Stella and May flanking her sides. They'd all take heed to stand well back from the deceptively prim schoolteacher.

"They look like a herd of thirsty cattle at a watering hole," Juniper commented as he stepped up beside him.

Kyle grunted an agreement. "She's been using our sisters as a shield."

"Maybe you should step in and help with introductions. You're her host. Folks expect you to show her around."

"I doubt she'd appreciate the offer," he said, as she caught his gaze.

"Whoa," said Juniper. "I felt that singe all the way over here. What'd you do?"

"How was I supposed to know those clothes would turn her into Joan of Arc?"

"I tried to warn you."

"When?"

"At the stockyard. I told you independent women didn't take kindly to gifts."

"Oh, she's insisted on paying me back and gave me a month to find a new teacher."

"She quit? *Already?*"

"That's what she said, and after the thrashing she gave me over the clothes I'm inclined to take her at her word."

"You sure you didn't do this on purpose?"

"I'm not so careless with my hide. You sure can't judge a woman's temper by her size."

"Hell," June said with a laugh. "I could have told you that. You bes' find a way to change her mind."

"Marshal." Abel Williams, a beast of a man with a full black beard, emerged from a group of lumberjacks. The mill foreman was one of many who still referred to him as the marshal. His first trip to Pine Ridge had been to round up the last of the Chandlers, and none too soon. "Miss Pauley seems a fine young lady."

"She does," agreed Jim Grimshaw, the mill manager. "Marybeth and our girl are quite taken by her."

"Glad to hear it," he said, ignoring Juniper's poignant stare.

"Frank wasn't happy to be pulled off the flume line for schoolin'," said Abel, "but he'll do as he's told."

"By the number of lumberjacks standing on this meadow, you best rehire the kids."

Jim laughed. "We've got a full shift working on the mountain today. Every man knows a function like this is bound to yield a crop of single women. Now *there's* a man with courtin' in mind."

Günter dismounted at the edge of the meadow, a fistful of flowers clutched in his hand, track marks from a comb still visible in his usually shaggy hair.

Kyle's stomach clenched at the thought of his Swedish friend wooing Constance. "Miss Pauley isn't here to entertain suitors," he said, while thinking Günter wasn't too tall to be knocked down a few notches.

"You didn't hear?" asked Juniper. "Günter came by the hotel last night and asked for Ben's permission to court Stella."

"And he agreed?"

"Can't see why not. Günter's a good man, and your sister has had a steady stream of suitors for more than a year."

"Stella? She's only—"

"Eighteen." Juniper slapped him on the shoulder. "Welcome to my hell, cousin. Our sisters didn't stop growing just 'cause you were away."

"Where have they all come from?" Constance asked. Each time she stepped from the schoolhouse, the number of men gathered outside seemed to have doubled.

"The lumber camp," said Stella. "Everyone helped to build the schoolhouse so the entire community was invited."

"Stella," May said, nudging her cousin, "look who's here."

Constance followed her gaze and spotted Günter as he strode into the clearing with two of his deputies. Stella gasped and yanked her by the arm, dragging her in the opposite direction.

"Don't you want to greet him?" Constance asked.

"No. I'd rather avoid him."

Her reaction contradicted the friendly exchange she'd seen between them yesterday. Günter had stayed for supper and seemed wholly pleasant.

"Why?"

"Last night we were talking on the porch and I was such a ninny." As she hauled her through the crowd, Kyle's voice rose above the hum of conversations, though Constance couldn't make out his announcement. Stella didn't slow her brisk strides until they reached the far side of the meadow. She looked on the verge of tears.

"I'm sure it wasn't that bad."

"It was. He was being so charming and looking so handsome. I wanted to kiss him so badly, I turned and ran into the house." She sniffed back tears. "He probably thinks I'm a goose, but I can't help it."

"I doubt that. Girls get crushes, Stella." Or so she'd heard.

"Oh, no. I *love* him. I've tested it."

"How on earth does one test such a thing?" she asked, alarmed by the prospects.

"Three years back, he kissed me. Not a friendly kiss, *a real kiss*. It was wonderful, and then he got mad. He said he had no business kissing a fifteen-year-old girl and he stopped coming to the ranch with Juniper. This past year a few young men have courted me. They were all gentlemen, but they weren't Günter. He just looks at me and my stomach turns to butterflies. He can smile in a way that…melts me. He's so charming and easy to talk to—unless I'm making an utter fool of myself," she added bitterly. "I see him so often now and it only gets harder. I don't know what to do."

"You could stop running from me," said a voice from directly behind them.

Stella jumped, nearly knocking Constance over as they turned to see the sheriff standing behind them, a bouquet of flowers in his hand.

"Günter! H-how long have you—"

"Since de' butterflies," he said, affection clear in his eyes.

Stella made a squeaking sound in her throat as her grip tightened, nearly making Constance wince.

"Good afternoon, Miss Pauley. You and Stella will have a full schoolhouse tomorrow. They are serving food now. Kyle has asked for you to join the family on their blanket."

"Thank you, Sheriff."

"Stella, I brought these for you." He held out the colorful cluster of pink and white flowers.

"You brought me flowers?"

"I asked your father's permission to call on you."

Her glistening eyes rounded. "You did?"

"I would be honored if you would walk with me before we join the others." He stepped closer and Stella released her bone-crushing hold, accepting the flowers he offered.

"They're so pretty."

"Not so pretty as you."

They stood there, smiling at each other, and Constance suddenly felt like an intruder. She pivoted and walked toward the schoolhouse. Families fanned out blankets as others lined up along the food tables, filling their plates.

"Miss Pauley." A rough-hewn man in a plaid shirt and red suspenders stepped in front of her and pulled off his hat. "You're welcome to join us."

"Thank you, but I've—"

"Good afternoon, Miss Pauley," said another while more gathered around them until she was surrounded by towering men.

Good gracious.

"Have you chosen a place to sit?"

"She has." Kyle appeared beside her, the steel in his voice mirrored in his hard gaze. "Miss Pauley, I'll escort you to the food tables." He extended his elbow.

The moment she touched his shirt the crowd of men parted like the Red Sea. His hand covered hers as he tugged her close to his side. The possessive move made her belly quiver but she didn't protest. It wasn't fear she felt, though his expression was positively formidable. She felt protected, *safe*.

"Thank you for rescuing me, yet again. I'm not used to such attention."

"I don't imagine the convent had a large population of lonely lumberjacks."

"No," she said, unable to fight her smile.

"I'll serve you," he said, taking a plate from the end of the food table.

"That's not—"

"Yes, it is. With Stella detained and May taking refuge behind her books, I can't run the risk of you being carted off by suitors before the first day of school. I'm your host and I haven't been as attentive as I should."

As he talked he filled her plate from a wide assortment of meats and side dishes, not bothering to ask if she wanted chicken instead of ham, the mashed potatoes instead of fried. "I will admit," he said, adding a sprig of grapes and a roll, "I've allowed my pride to get in the way of my manners. It wasn't my intention to upset you. I'm used to doing what I feel needs to be done." He dug a serving ladle into a bowl of summer squash then paused before glancing down at her. "Do you like summer squash?"

"Yes, though I doubt I can eat all you've already chosen for me."

He cringed. "I did it again, didn't I?"

"If you'd chosen something I didn't like, I would have said so."

His lips hinted at a grin. "Going to go easy on me, are you?"

Suddenly flustered and flushed, she looked away with a curt nod. "So long as you keep our bargain, I see no reason to harbor ill feelings."

"Fair enough. Would you like tea or punch?"

Constance picked up a cup of tea from the end of the table. A girl with dark pigtails popped up beside them and retrieved a cup of punch. A nine-year-old, she recalled, Rebecca Miller. Her bright smile revealed two missing front teeth.

"Hi, Miss Pauley."

"Rebecca," she said as the girl streaked past.

"You've memorized their names already?"

"Stella helped me. You have a lovely family, by the way."

"I suppose they pass muster most of the time."

He was teasing, the warmth in his blue eyes having a startling effect on her pulse. Once they reached his family's stretch of quilts, Constance sat on an open spot of blanket near Lily and May.

Preoccupied with food and conversation, she didn't notice Kyle's absence until much later. Corin and some other women had set out the desserts. Kyle stood a few yards out talking with a group of men. His gaze met hers, his lips shifting slightly, and Constance felt a burst of pleasing warmth. He looked away as a woman approached him, offering a piece of pie—and a flirtatious smile.

"I bet he eats a whole pie to be polite," whispered May. "Jake stayed home with his younger sisters to avoid such foolishness."

"Spring courtship is in the air," said Lily. "Stella is positively glowing."

Stella sat with Günter at the other end of the large quilt, her hand clasped in his as they talked quietly.

"She'll marry him," May said with certainty. "She cried for weeks when he stopped helping with the spring drive, and hasn't fancied anyone else since. I imagine you'll be swamped with suitors after today," she said to Constance.

"Surely not. I came to Pine Ridge for a job, not a husband."

"I feel the same way. All I can think about is going off to school."

She glanced at the stack of books sitting beside her. "Are you planning to go to college?"

"Medical school. We have a family friend in San Francisco who's been sending me medical journals. Kyle's cousin, actually. I believe you know him. Daniel Norwood."

"Dr. Norwood is Kyle's *cousin?*"

May's gray eyes widened. "I assumed you knew."

"No." His cousin? "Was it Kyle who sent me to San Francisco?"

"I think I've said more than I should have," said May.

"You should ask Kyle," Lily suggested.

She glanced over to see him accepting a fruit-filled offering from another flirtatious woman with red hair and fluttering blue eyes.

"I will." She surged up.

"I thought she knew," protested May as Constance made a swift beeline for the circle of men.

"Miss Pauley," greeted an approaching lumberjack.

"Please excuse me." She held up her hand and rushed past him, not slowing until she stood beside Kyle. "Mr. Darby, may I have a word with you?"

Kyle glanced at Constance, surprised by the interruption. He struggled to swallow a mouthful of baked apples. "Miss Pauley, is everything all right?"

"Splendid," she said in a bright tone, but the tightness of her smile conveyed otherwise. "I'd like to speak with you a moment, unless I'm interrupt—"

"Not at all." He excused himself from the conversation and quickly escorted her beyond the hum of conversation. "What's wrong?"

She continued to the edge of the meadow before she stopped, crossing her arms as she looked up at him. "Why didn't you tell me Daniel Norwood was your cousin?"

Oh, hell. "I didn't see why it should matter," he said, wondering who'd sold him out.

"It was you who sent me to California, not Doctor Mason?"

"You were hurt. I knew someone who could help you."

"You didn't even know me."

"Didn't seem to matter when I carried you from that boardinghouse and mattered even less when Doc Mason pulled out his saw, ready to cut off your legs."

Constance gasped, and he realized he could have chosen a far more delicate delivery. "*Hell,* I didn't mean to scare you. The point is, I knew someone who could provide the kind of doctoring you needed. I wired Daniel and he said to send you on, so I did."

She eyed him warily for a long moment. "I was seen by a number of doctors. They told me funding had been arranged and I assumed…"

Kyle shifted uneasily. He didn't want her to know about the money. She'd been ready to tear strips from his hide over the clothes.

"*It was you.*"

"They treated you and you can walk. That's all that matters."

Her brow creased and he waited for her temper to flare. Her tear-glazed eyes caught him off guard. Teardrops glistened down her cheeks, making him cringe.

"Don't cry," he pleaded. "It's not a big deal."

"It's a very big deal." She brushed away the damp trail. "Thank you."

"You're welcome," he said, knowing he didn't deserve the gratitude shining bright in her eyes. "You're not mad at me?"

"How can I be mad at you, after all you've done for me?"

"All I did was send a wire. Doc Mason relayed your personal information to Daniel. I figured the less we knew about each other the better. It was Daniel who told my family about you."

"Generosity runs in your family."

"I wasn't being generous, Constance. You didn't deserve to have your life destroyed by that fire. You didn't ask to be uprooted and shipped across the country. It couldn't have been an easy recovery."

"I'm grateful for the care I was given."

"So am I. Do your legs still hurt?"

She looked away, blatantly disconcerted by the question. "No."

He imagined the scarring was extensive. He had yet to see her without her gloves and had noticed she didn't even remove them to eat. "I suppose you left behind a lot of friends in Colorado?" he asked, wanting to ease the tension between them.

"Not really. Mrs. Farrell kept me busy. But I do like the mountains."

"Judging by all I've heard today, the folks in these mountains certainly like you. If they catch wind that my mistake cost them a fine teacher, they'll likely run me out of town. Can I hold off on advertising for your position?"

Her hesitation was clear before she relented with a slight nod.

"Have you had a nice afternoon?"

"Yes. The students and parents have been wonderful. Those without a child or spouse have been a *nuisance*."

Kyle grinned, appreciating her flat honesty. "Most of the wives here would likely agree, having more than a few bachelors frequent their supper tables, eager for some semblance of family life and home-cooked meals."

"They won't find anything but grammar lessons and the smack of a ruler with me."

He laughed and reached for her gloved hand. "How about I save their knuckles and keep you on my arm while the festivities wind down?"

"Full of pie, are you?"

Kyle couldn't deny the sweetly spoken accusation. "Yes, ma'am."

He tucked her close. Color brightened her cheeks, but she didn't protest. He was certain she would have at the slightest objection. He found reassurance in knowing she'd shove back if he overstepped his bounds. Here he'd been worried a classroom of rowdy students would overrun her, but he was starting to believe Miss Constance Pauley could hold her own most anywhere.

Chapter Six

The school bell clanged as Kyle fitted a windowsill in the bedroom of the living quarters above the schoolroom. A departing wagon kicked up dust beyond the open windowpane, a parent heading back to town. A half mile out, a line of rooftops marked Pine Ridge—where he should be. Monday mornings were the worst, folks tracking him down at his livery or the hotel with urgent business or complaints. He hammered in a nail, wondering how the hell he'd gotten himself into this. A temporary favor to help Juniper out with the town's construction had taken over his life. He'd barely unpacked his saddlebags when the community had nominated him for town mayor. He'd refused. Not that it mattered. As Juniper's appointed overseer, he handled all the gripes and growing pains of a newly forged township.

A hum of activity vibrated up through the floorboards as he hammered in the last nail. Constance's voice rang above the clamor; clear, concise, almost musical as she called her class to order. She'd been a vision this morning, walking into the kitchen in a butterscotch gown, the soft color a perfect contrast to her dark corkscrew curls and emphasizing her honey-colored eyes.

Realizing he'd frozen like a bird dog come to point, he

shook his head and went into the front room for a can of paint. Constance Pauley was the last woman he needed to be setting designs on. Since learning he'd funded her doctoring, she looked at him with a kind of open vulnerability, a trust that made him damn uncomfortable. He didn't want her big doe eyes gazing up at him, mostly because the frankly male portion of his brain saw *opportunity*.

He couldn't be less of a saint. If she were any other woman, he'd be using those smiles to get a little closer...a lot closer. *Not happening*. He'd sooner nail his hands to the wall than make advances on a woman he'd nearly killed. He grabbed a paintbrush from the windowsill and was surprised to see the older boys still standing out in the schoolyard playing ball. They'd laid out their bases with pieces of spare wood.

"Gentlemen," Constance called out from the front of the school. "Is there a problem?"

"No." Frank Williams stood at the center of the ball field, his cap cocked to one side, expressive of his cocky nature. He tossed his baseball into the air and caught it. "We figure since we gotta be here instead of workin' or doin' our chores, we'd play ball. Won't be time for nothin' but chores once we get home."

"I'm quite familiar with baseball," Constance said, coming into view as she stepped into the yard—a ray of sunshine on the green meadow. "We can compromise on outside activities, but right now it's time for lessons in the classroom. If you'll come inside we can begin straightaway."

"We ain't needin' no schoolin'." His buddies closed in around him. "Do we, fellas?"

A low rumble of agreement came from the half-dozen boys standing behind him.

"I see." She clasped her gloved hands behind her back and approached the group of defiant boys. Kyle fought his urge to rush out, not wanting to undermine her authority. She stopped directly in front of Frank, the top of her head barely reaching the kid's chin.

"You are Francis Williams, correct?"

Snickers rose up behind him. His hands clenched into fists. "My name is *Frank*."

"Ah, yes. Frank. Being the oldest student, I had hoped you'd set a good example for the other children."

"I told you, we ain't goin' to school." Frank broadened his stance. Afraid the boy would execute brawn over brains, Kyle turned for the door. The little uprising wasn't anything a threat of his boot to their defiant butts wouldn't fix.

"Are you a betting man, Mr. Williams?" she asked as Kyle reached the stairway landing at the side of the schoolhouse.

Now where the hell could she be going with a question like that? The boy's twisted expression asked the same thing.

Frank pushed a finger under his cap and scratched at his brown hair. "I suppose."

"It may surprise you to know I fancy myself a good ball player." She held her hand toward the boy holding a baseball bat. "May I?"

Toby's freckled face lit with a gushing grin as he relinquished the wood.

Lord Almighty. They were already beat.

Constance stepped back into a batter's stance and gave a slow-motion swing as though testing the weight of the wood.

"I ain't never met a lady who played baseball."

"I've met too many young men who cannot read and write." She lowered the bat, giving Frank her full attention. "Would you say you're an adequate ball player, Mr. Williams?"

"Yeah."

"And the other gentlemen here, are they, too, accomplished at playing ball?"

Frank shrugged. "I guess."

"Splendid." She turned toward the schoolhouse and Kyle eased back, not wanting to intervene just yet. "Miss Darby," she called out. "Send the children back outside, please."

"Wait a minute," said Frank.

"Allow me to make my offer, Mr. Williams," she said, talking over him.

Frank crossed his arms. "What offer?"

"I'm getting to that. Now what about the young ladies?" She gestured toward the seven girls lining up outside the schoolhouse with some of the younger boys in the class. "How would you rank their skill?"

"This ain't no girl's game."

"So, if I were to challenge you to a game, one round at bat, my team against yours—"

"Us against them girls? Wouldn't be much of a challenge."

The kid had a point. Only three of the seven girls appeared to be over the age of six. All of his buddies were ten and over.

"So you accept?"

"Why should I?"

"Very good, to the point of business. I will wager a year's worth of schooling. If we win, you'll come inside and begin your lessons without complaint. If you win, you boys can use our class time as you intended, to play ball."

The kid's eyes popped wide, as did Kyle's. "What about our folks, what you gonna tell them?"

Good question!

"How you deal with your parents is your problem."

Like hell! Their parents were *his* problem. He wasn't about to explain that their sons wouldn't be learning to read because the prim and proper Miss Pauley had wagered away a year of school on a baseball game she had no hope to win.

"Do we have a deal?"

"Miss Pauley?" Stella said, alarm in her voice.

Constance glanced back at her. "Just a moment, Miss Darby." The confidence in her smile kept Kyle rooted in place. *What the hell is she up to?*

"Is you gonna be playin'?" asked Toby.

"Indeed," she said with a nod. "And the five oldest girls.

Miss Darby will serve as catcher and scorekeeper. We challenge you to one inning."

Frank gave a short laugh. "Yer on, lady."

"You will address me as Miss Pauley."

"Miss Pauley," he instantly corrected.

Poor kid. She had him buffaloed and he didn't have a clue.

"Miss Darby will need a mitt."

Only two boys had leather mitts. Both offered them up.

"Thank you, gentlemen. You can be first up to bat. Give me a moment to instruct my teammates." The boys walked toward the plank of wood designating home plate, laughing and nudging as Constance huddled up with the rest of her class. Fully intrigued, Kyle descended the stairs as they took their positions. Stella sat the youngest students on the sidelines while Constance spaced her players around the field. Frank took his turn at bat as his teacher moved to the pitching position.

"One last thing before we begin, Mr. Williams. Do you regard yourself as a man of your word?"

"I sure as heck do!"

She smiled, took a step back, her arm snapping forward so fast Kyle nearly missed the pitch. The ball pounded into Stella's mitt, sending her back onto her butt with a slight shriek.

"I'll be a bang-tailed rooster," he muttered, as shocked as the rest of them.

"Hey!" the kid complained.

"Strike one, Mr. Williams."

"Do I toss it back?" Stella asked, holding up the ball. Kyle swallowed a chuckle. His sister had never played a game of ball in her life.

Tugging on his cap, Frank dug his toe into the ground and crouched lower as he readied for the next pitch—none of which helped him hit her fastball. Within minutes the girls were cheering as they ran in for their turn at bat.

"This ain't fair!" Frank raged.

Constance met him on her way in. "What do you find unfair? You agreed to the terms."

"I didn't know you could pitch like that!"

"I told you I was a good ball player."

Frank took the ball and stomped past her.

Molly Grimshaw was the first batter, her tight orange braids tucked behind her shoulders. She was likely the only girl familiar with the sport, having five older brothers, the youngest her twin. "Hope you boys are ready to get spanked," she called out.

Now there's a girl with sass. He had a notion she bore a striking resemblance to Constance in her youth.

"Molly should be on our team," her twin brother shouted back. "She's more boy than girl."

"Ain't, neither! And I'm tellin' Mama you said that!"

Frank pitched and she knocked the ball past the third baseman. Dropping the bat, she sprinted for first, her classmates cheering the whole way.

"Ha!" she shouted at Toby. "That's how it's done!"

The next girl at bat looked none too confident as she stepped up to the home-plate board. Constance moved in behind her and adjusted her grip. The girl's brown pigtails and white ribbons bobbled with a vigorous nod as her teacher whispered instructions.

Constance stepped aside, Frank raised his arm and the girl closed her eyes.

"Eyes open," Constance told her.

She opened her eyes in time to swing, which was more of a swat, knocking the ball to the ground directly in front of her with a hard bounce. She watched the ball roll to a stop and didn't move.

Molly made a dash for second base.

"Run, Rebecca!" Constance shouted.

Frank's players shouted for him to get the baseball. He scrambled forward and grabbed up the ball as Rebecca hopped onto first base and turned her gap-toothed grin toward her teacher.

Stomping and muttering, Frank went back to his spot. His sour expression darkened when he saw his teacher was next at bat, poised to swing in her fancy full dress and white gloves. None too eager to throw the ball, Frank wiped his brow with the back of his arm.

"Whenever you're ready, Mr. Williams," she called in her pleasant, melodious tone.

Frank scowled, reared his arm back and threw the ball as hard as he could. The bat met it with a sound *crack*. Six young mouths dropped open as the ball sailed high over their heads, disappearing beyond the line of redwoods.

"Be damned," he said, feeling a ring of pride as she charged to first base, her petticoats all aflutter. He laughed as the cheering section went wild. She caught up to Rebecca at second base and took her hand, the two of them following Molly home as a boy finally emerged from the woods with the ball.

Kyle walked toward the front of the school as she met her sulking opponents at the center of the field. He couldn't hear their words over the cheers and chatter, but when she offered her hand to Frank he nodded and shook it.

"Good morning, Kyle," Stella greeted as she ushered the younger children inside.

"Quite a morning."

She grinned and hurried past him. Constance's eyes widened at the sight of him.

"Miss Pauley, congratulations on your victory." He shifted his gaze toward the long-faced boy beside her. "Frank, better luck next year."

"Yes, sir," he mumbled, and shuffled into the schoolhouse.

"Howdy, Marshal," Toby shouted as he ran past.

"Are you a marshal?" Constance asked.

"I was."

"Of course. That's why you were there," she said softly. "I should have realized sooner." She glanced around, but they were alone in the yard. She stepped close, her face leaning up to his. Kyle's gaze locked on her pink lips, and he was hit by a powerful urge to kiss her. "Did you capture them?" she whispered. "The men who tied me up and set the fire?"

Guilt stabbed at his conscience. "We did."

"Good. I have often wondered." Her trembling smile was another blow.

"I don't want to keep your class waiting," he said, easing back.

"We've had a delay, but I believe we have things under control."

"I believe you do, Miss Pauley."

He was the one needing control.

Chapter Seven

A U.S. Marshal. Why hadn't he told her?

She stood in her bedroom listening to the low tone of his voice as he talked to Stella in the kitchen. Constance had gone straight to her room upon arriving home, afraid Stella might ask her to light the stove. She'd taken time to rinse her face and hands and pin stray curls that had fallen throughout the day. She opened the tin canister beside her washbasin and dipped her fingers into the cold herb-scented cream. The soothing balm eased the stiffness in the pink patches on her hands. She pulled out a fresh pair of white gloves from the top drawer of her bureau.

Didn't he think she'd have questions? She'd awakened in California with no one to ask if anyone else had been hurt or who the horrible men had been who'd tried to burn her alive. She could still see his face, the one who'd pinned her down, his dark eyes smiling as ropes burned across her wrists.

Fear shivered through her. Did she really *want* to know more?

Sister Agnes would tell her to let it go, to pray for tomorrow and seek peace. Her advice had helped to stop the nightmares, but much about that day haunted her still. Constance glanced at the unlit oil lamp sitting on the bureau. After supper she'd spend the rest of her evening in the dark. If she was to stay at

Pine Ridge, in that room above the school, it was fear she'd have to face eventually.

She shuddered at the mere thought of touching anything to do with fire, even a match. Certain the stove had been lit by now, she pulled on her gloves and drew a deep breath, ready to offer Stella help with supper preparations.

She followed the glow of lit lanterns toward the heat coming from the kitchen. Stella had already set the table, the white plates and sparkling silverware standing out against a red tablecloth. Stella and Kyle huddled at the stove. Kyle's sister stood a few inches shorter than him, but his shoulders nearly doubled the span of hers. His smooth dark hair touched the top of his collar. Her gaze moved down his leather vest, to a lean waist. Judging by the fit of his denim trousers, the rest of him was just as lean and muscular.

Sweet Mother Mary, she thought, suddenly stifled by the heat in the kitchen.

"Thanks," he said, turning around as he secured a giant nipple onto the biggest bottle Constance had ever seen.

"What are you doing?"

"Going to feed my orphan."

She startled at the unexpected answer. The smooth upward slide of Kyle's lips caused an equally startling reaction.

"My new foal," he explained. "She lost her mother last week."

"She's adorable," Stella said, looking back from the stove. "Take Constance out to see her, Kyle."

"You want to?" he asked. "The stable is out back."

She couldn't resist the thought of watching him bottle feed a baby horse. He opened the door and motioned for her to go ahead of him. As the door shut behind them she felt a pressure on the small of her back.

"Did Frank give you further trouble today?" he asked, seeming unaware of his hand pressed against her, guiding her down the dirt path.

"Not at all," she said, fighting the tremble in her voice. "He even helped to clean the slate boards after school, though I did promise to give him pitching advice at recess tomorrow."

Kyle grinned. His blue eyes, full of warmth and mischief, heightened the surge of tingles low in her belly. "Nothing wrong with good, honest bribery."

His hand dropped away as he reached for the stable doors. Constance sucked in a full breath and strove to quell the current of jitters.

Good heavens.

She stepped inside, breathing in the scent of hay and horses. Expecting to find a dark old barn, the brightly lit corridor surprised her. The large stable housed seven horses. Sunlight streamed in through open Dutch doors in various stalls, creating a warm atmosphere.

"I didn't realize you had so many horses."

"I own the livery in town, so I do a bit of housing and grooming." He walked to the far end. "But this here is my prize." He stepped up to an end stall.

Constance could barely make out the foal lying in the shadows of the far corner. She looked so tiny and lonely.

"Evening, Sunshine." The smooth rumble of Kyle's voice sent tendrils of sensation swirling through Constance. The foal sprang up on its spindly legs. Kyle stepped through the gate and the young horse charged at him, bumping into his chest.

"Easy, now." He crouched down, brushing his hand across its coat in a vigorous caress. In the sunlight her fuzzy golden coat shimmered. The foal nudged him, searching for the bottle he kept just out of reach.

"You're going to be as pretty and ornery as your mama," he said with a laugh, nudging her back.

Constance watched him in amazement. He was so calm and confident, and *handsome*. This was her cowboy, the man she'd met on the train.

Kyle glanced back at her. "Come on in and shut the gate."

She hurried to do as he said. Once inside, she realized the foal was nearly as tall as she was, but it was too late for hesitation. The curious foal bumped right up to her, nearly knocking her back. Kyle's arm braced her, holding her upright.

"Clumsy as she is, you've got to brace yourself."

"Thanks for the warning," she said, smiling as the foal went back to searching for its supper.

"She shimmers. She's beautiful, Kyle."

"Right now she's soft as a mink," he said, his fingers sliding through the fluffy coat. "You should feel it."

He looked at her expectantly, and Constance swallowed hard.

"You got no call to hide your hands from me. I know how badly you were burned. I helped to bandage them up."

"You did?" Heat burned into her cheeks at the thought of him seeing her in such a state.

"I did."

Glancing back at the young horse, she paused a moment, then tugged at her left glove. She brushed her hand over the foal's side. The soft down, smooth as cream, felt so nice beneath her fingers. She glanced at Kyle. His smile was as bright as hers.

"Told you."

"I had no idea they were so soft."

"Not for much longer. It's a shame she'll shed out. She'll likely lose all this light fur and be a dark russet as Blaze was."

When she moved back, he reached out and took her hand before she could replace her glove.

"Don't you get warm wearing those gloves all day?"

Constance felt the color flaming into her cheeks as he turned her hand in his, giving both sides a close inspection before lifting his questioning eyes.

"I suppose," she said in a shaken voice. His thumb skimmed over her sensitive palm as he held her gaze. A tingling sensation vibrated through her entire body.

"Then why do you never take them off?"

She blinked hard, unable to bring herself to answer. He had just seen why! Her heart thundered in her chest as he glanced back at her hand. His thumb stroked the wavelike pattern of skin from her pinky to her wrist.

"Here I was expecting raw bones when you have such pretty, soft skin."

The man is a saint. There was no other explanation.

She struggled to find her voice as tears burned at her eyes. "The patches are shiny and redden if I'm cold or hot. People would ask questions."

Kyle didn't see anything short of a blessing when he looked at that tender pink skin. "You're likely more aware of the redness than anyone else would be." He caressed her smooth fingers, no more discolored than a light blush. "I've never seen prettier skin."

She sucked in a quick breath, her honey eyes surging wide. The deep flush in her cheeks reminded him she'd spent the past two years in a convent and likely wasn't used to anyone touching her with such familiarity, much less a man she barely knew.

He released her hand and she quickly replaced her glove. "I apologize for being forward. I'm just glad to see you've healed so nicely."

The bottle tugged in his arms as Sunshine found the nipple. He quickly tightened his grip and straightened. From the corner of his eye he saw Constance smile.

"Would you like to feed her?"

Visibly fighting moisture from her eyes, she gave a nod.

"Scoot in and get a good grip."

She did as he said, moving in front of him, her gloved hands wrapping around the bottle. "It's warm."

"Just like mother's milk," he said, moving his hands to make room for hers.

Sunshine tugged, fearing she was about to lose her supper. They both stumbled forward. His arm strapped Constance around the middle, all but tucking her between his legs. She struggled to right herself.

Damn it, Sunshine! He struggled to keep from swearing out loud. Holding her to his chest he couldn't help but feel the alluring feminine curves of a woman he damn sure wouldn't mind tumbling into the hay with.

"I'm not trying to be fresh," he said, figuring he should be horsewhipped for the thoughts steaming through his mind.

"I know," she said, her voice strained.

He eased his hold as Constance found her balance. "Got it?" he asked, slowly stepping back.

"Yes." Sunshine settled. With her hold secure, Constance reached out, stroking the foal's muzzle as she drank. She glanced back at him, and her bright smile could have been a shot of whiskey for the way it warmed him.

"I'll, uh, be a few stalls down if you need me."

Silently swearing a blue streak, he set about feeding the rest of his stock. Her soft coos carried through the stable, grating across his senses. By the time he had everyone fed and had closed all the top ends of the outer doors leading to the training corral, Constance was waiting for him in the center aisle.

"You leave the lamps on? Isn't that dangerous?"

"I'm coming back after supper. It will be dark by then." He shut the stable doors and took the empty bottle from her before starting down the path. "Thanks for your help."

She gave a slight smile. The intensity in her gaze told him she had something on her mind.

"Why didn't you tell me you were a marshal?"

And there it was. "Habit, I suppose," he said, the growing curiosity in her eyes tightening the muscles across his shoulders. "I worked mostly undercover, infiltrating bands of outlaws. It's not something I talk about. And frankly, it wouldn't make for polite conversation."

"Were you inside the boardinghouse with the outlaws?"

"No. Ned Chandler was real particular about who he let close to him. I rode with a gang he used for larger jobs. When I got word they were all getting together, I set up the ambush from the outside."

"Was anyone else hurt that morning?"

"Aside from the three dead outlaws, only you."

She frowned, and Kyle tucked his fingers into his pockets, fighting the powerful urge to pull her close. Something in his brain refused to accept he had no right to such liberties.

She walked quietly beside him, her slender eyebrows in a pinch, her golden eyes burning with questions she was hesitant to ask. Waiting for those questions to surface was slow torture.

"If you have something on your mind, you can ask me."

"Ned Chandler, did he have light hair and dark eyes?"

"He did." The fear in her gaze ripped at his conscience. Kyle had been in San Francisco the day he'd received word of Ned Chandler's execution. Had he not been hunting down the man's brother, he would have been in attendance. "He was convicted for a number of horrible crimes and hanged along with the rest of those men."

She tightened her arms around her middle, a visible shiver going through her. "I can't say I'm sorry."

"Don't see why you should be. I wish we had caught them sooner, before they'd hurt anyone else."

"I don't want you to feel bad because of me," she said, her wide eyes full of conviction. "It wasn't your fault."

He knew that wasn't entirely true. He'd been careless, taking the word of others instead of doing the checking himself. It was a mistake he'd been careful not to repeat— one he wished to God he'd never made in the first place.

"Thanks," he said, offering a smile to ease her worried frown.

They reached the back door and he allowed Constance to go ahead of him. She came to an abrupt stop before the door, but didn't reach for the handle. He stepped up behind her and spotted the scene that stopped her. Stella wrapped in Günter's arms, their mouths fused as his hands all but molested her! Not that Stella was fighting him. She leaned up, pulling him closer, and his hands slid down her back, another inch and—

He reached past Constance and opened the door. "If you don't get your hands off my sister, you'll be courting in handcuffs, Sheriff Hagen."

Stella jumped back, her cheeks flushing to a deep pink as she smiled up at her brother.

Kyle wasn't smiling. As they sat down to eat, he took care to place Günter and Stella on opposite sides of the table.

Sitting across from him, Constance noted his mood didn't improve over supper. Neither Günter nor Stella seemed to notice, their gazes mostly locked on each other. She was glad when the meal was over. Everyone helped to clear the table, Günter and Stella washing the dishes while Constance righted the table and brushed crumbs from the cloth.

"What's this?" Kyle asked, starting to lift the lid of a white box stacked atop another near the drain board. Günter snatched them away.

"I brought sweets for my sweetheart."

"Hope you brought enough for all of us," said Kyle.

"Ja, I did." He set one of two boxes on the table and opened the lid. "Mrs. Sorrento's lemon squares. Enjoy." Günter took Stella by the hand. "We will be on the porch."

"You sly devil!" Kyle reached for a powder-coated square. "You're trying to distract me."

"I'm wounded you think such."

Constance watched Stella's beau lead her from the kitchen, Stella's soft laughter echoing through the hall.

"Don't think I won't check up on you," Kyle called after them.

Not about to be caught alone with her brooding host, Constance moved to follow them into the hall. "Good night."

Kyle cut her off. "You can't turn in before you try Mrs.

Sorrento's lemon squares." He held a white-and-yellow square to her lips. "Here, take a bite."

"I don't—" The sweet concoction invaded her mouth. She glared and bit down because she had no choice. The sweet coating gave way to burst of tangy lemon flavor, quickly soothed by a sweet crumbly crust.

"Good, isn't it?" His blue eyes fairly sparkled.

She licked the powdery sweetness from her lips. "Delicious."

He stuck the other half of the square into his mouth and pulled a chair out for her. "A cup of coffee to go with the tarts and you'll swear you're in heaven."

She didn't need coffee. His cheerful company was enough.

Constance sat down as he set the pot and two cups on the table. He slid a small plate with two squares in front of her and began eating his own.

He hadn't brought silverware. Kyle stuck his thumb in his mouth, cleaning off the sticky coating. Discreetly removing her glove beneath the table, she picked up a tart, took a quick bite and tucked her hand back into her lap.

His brow furrowed as he met her gaze. "You don't have to hide your hands from me. They're a whole lot prettier than my scuffed and callused fingers." He held them up, showing off the strong, masculine hands of a man who worked hard.

"You're very kind."

Kyle didn't care for her implication that he wasn't being truthful. "No, I'm not. I'm honest. A kindness that doesn't tell the truth is still a lie. If your hands were disfigured and hideous, I'd say so."

She gaped at him, her golden eyes flaring wide.

"Not rudely, mind you." He reached for the coffee and filled his cup. "Something like, 'that's a damn shame. Best keep them covered when you're out and about.'" He glanced at her delicate hand as she picked up a second pastry. "Not so, darlin'. Your new skin is soft and pretty as a winter's dawn."

She dropped the lemon tart. Quickly tossing it back onto the plate, she wiped at the dusting of sugar on the red tablecloth, her hands trembling ever so slightly. "Thank you for saying so."

Damn. He'd meant to reassure her, not make her nervous.

"Mrs. Sorrento bakes some of the finest foods I've ever eaten and keeps my restaurant packed with customers."

"You own a restaurant?"

"Inside my hotel."

"Why am I staying here instead of the hotel?"

About to fill her cup with coffee, he paused. "Because all thirty of my tenants are lumberjacks taking a break from camp life and likely anxious for the company of a woman."

"Oh."

"We tried to have your apartment ready, but with so much construction going on in Pine Ridge, our carpenters are stretched tight. Stella thought you'd appreciate rooming here with her since she's helping with the school."

"And I do," she said. "I don't mean to sound ungrateful."

"You don't. I wouldn't set you up in a place I wouldn't be comfortable leaving my sister." His elbows hit the table as he picked up another lemon tart and took a bite. "I have to be honest with you, when I hired 'Miss Constance Pauley from the mission,' I was expecting a pruned-up schoolmarm."

She laughed and cupped her hand over her mouth, having just taken a bite of her lemon square. Damn, but he liked that reaction.

"So, tell me, did the nuns teach you to throw a fastball?"

"No. But they did allow me to organize games for the children."

It was easy to see she liked working with kids.

"While I lived on a farm in Missouri I was one of two girls amid six boys. It took all of us to have a decent game."

"Did you like living in Missouri?"

"Not especially. But I wasn't there long." Her lips formed a wry grin. "I wasn't the most dependable field hand."

By the time the dessert box was empty, he knew she'd been born in New York, had lived in nine different homes across the plains and she preferred to talk about his horses or her love of teaching. Which suited Kyle just fine, so long as he got to stare into her smiling eyes.

He realized later, with some annoyance, that Günter's plan had worked.

Chapter Eight

Sunshine whinnied as Kyle entered the stable. Her new nursemaid had fed her before supper. The thought of Constance's delight in the young foal over the past few days brought a smile to his lips. The closer he got to finishing her apartment, the more he thought she'd be better suited to staying here at the house. He sure hadn't minded the past two evenings of sitting with her in the kitchen, hovering over Günter's sweet distractions. His sister's beau hadn't shown up for dinner tonight, and Kyle didn't want to admit he'd been nearly as disappointed as Stella.

He'd completed half his chores when the sound of an approaching horse drew him from the stable. He started toward the house as Günter rode into the yard. Spotting Kyle, the sheriff rode toward the back of the house.

"Evening," Kyle greeted as Günter dismounted. He pulled two small boxes from his saddlebags, brightening Kyle's mood considerably. "You missed supper."

"Could not be helped." He tucked the boxes beneath his arm. "Had trouble in town today. Need to talk to you about it."

"What kind of trouble?"

"Someone broke into the mercantile last night. Andrew stumbled upon the robbery and was knocked out before he got a look at anyone. Didn't take much—dried beef, beans, kerosene and other basic items—no more than two or three men could carry. We found a campsite a few miles north of the town. Could be interlopers fired from another logging camp."

"You didn't catch them?"

"No. Camp was abandoned. But they appear to be traveling on foot, same as whoever was on your place last week."

"You think some out-of-work lumberjack walked out here just to kill my horse?"

"Perhaps he'd meant to steal her. With the newborn, perhaps she attacked him and he panicked."

Kyle shook his head, not buying that scenario. Blaze had been murdered. "I had other horses he could have easily trotted off with if he was interested in taking a mount. Just because we didn't find tracks doesn't mean he wasn't on horseback. There's plenty of ways to cover a trail. They take ammunition?"

"Ja. Rifle and six-gun. I have two deputies keeping watch near the site. Tomorrow I will send the York brothers to finish the floors above the schoolhouse. You come have a look at the campsite."

Kyle gave a nod, knowing he needed to stop in at the hotel and livery as well.

Günter reached into his pocket, then tossed a piece of silver at him.

He caught the tin star.

"You are deputized. Now if you'll excuse me, I have a woman to woo."

"I'll join you."

"Figured you might." Günter chuckled as he shuffled up the back steps. "Been enjoying your evenings with your schoolteacher?"

"We could join you and Stella on the porch."

"No."

"Thought not." He brushed past him and opened the door.

Both women turned as they stepped inside. "Stella, your suitor's here."

"Sorry to be late," Günter said, removing his hat.

His sister rushed to greet him. "I was getting worried."

It was Constance's reaction that captured Kyle's attention, her slow, almost shy smile as she looked from their dessert to him. His chest tightened with an odd kind of tension.

What the hell am I doing?

As Stella and Günter retreated to the privacy of the porch and Constance sat across from him at the table, he knew what he wanted to do—he wanted to sample a sweetness that had nothing to do with baked goods.

He'd never been one to spend time with a lady he didn't have intentions to bed—not that he was opposed to that notion. The mere thought of Constance in his arms made his blood run hot. Problem was, he knew full well what it would take to bed her—a wedding ring.

He wasn't courting her. They simply enjoyed each other's company.

"I'd like to stay after school to tutor a few students with their reading lessons," she said, having barely nibbled on the sugar cookie in her hand. She'd gotten into the pleasing habit of leaving her gloves off at home. "But I'm not sure how receptive their parents would be of me taking time they likely need for chores."

The front door slammed, and Constance snapped straight in her chair.

Stella rushed into the kitchen, her face bright with a smile. Günter stepped beside her, his arm sliding around her waist.

"Look!" She held up her hand. A tiny speck of a diamond on a silver band twinkled in the lamplight. "We're getting married!"

"You just started courting," Kyle protested.

"We've been seeing each other nearly every day for a few months," Stella told him.

"Your father gave his blessings when I asked for her hand last week."

"You asked him for her *hand?*"

Anger darkened his friend's eyes. "Do you have a problem with our engagement, Kyle?"

"I'm—" His sister's stricken expression stopped his protest. "I'm surprised, is all."

Constance rushed forward. "Congratulations," she said, giving Stella a hug. "I'm so happy for the both of you." His sister's happy glow returned as they fussed over her ring.

Kyle offered his hand to Günter. "Congratulations."

Günter was slow to accept. "Thanks."

"So, when do you plan to have the wedding?"

"A week from Saturday, providing your family can attend."

A week from—he hadn't even gotten used to the idea of Stella courting! "You sure that's enough time?"

"I love your sister," he said, pulling Stella close, their eyes glazing as they looked at each other. "Preacher said he can marry us. We want to be together. Why wait?"

"Don't you need a dress and…things?"

"I'm going to wear Mama's dress. We'll send a wire tomorrow to make sure they can come. Constance, would you be one of my bridesmaids? Günter's asked Juniper and Jake, and Kyle, of course."

Great. He liked church weddings about as much as he liked funerals.

"I'd be honored," Constance replied.

Her smile was a tad too tight to be genuine. He knew she wouldn't stay in this house without Stella. And he wasn't about to put her a half mile away from him with a vandal terrorizing the town, which meant they'd best find the interlopers soon or Günter and Stella would be honeymooning in his house. That thought was too disturbing to contemplate.

Chapter Nine

Chalk dust filled the air outside the window as her young volunteers finished cleaning the erasers.

"See you on Monday!" Molly called on her way out of the door.

"I think our first week went well." Stella followed Molly outside before Constance could agree. Their first week had been wonderfully successful. Even in a week, her students had made amazing progress. By next week they'd have—

Footsteps sounded from up above, drawing her gaze to the ceiling as a vision of warm indigo eyes filled her mind. Sensation swirled, stealing her breath. Thumps and bumps had been distracting her throughout the day, making her lose her train of thought more than once. Kyle was back to working upstairs after spending yesterday helping Günter. They'd both made it home in time for supper, and Constance had enjoyed Kyle's company…and the light touches she was starting to believe were a sinful pleasure. No one had ever made her feel these volatile sensations he elicited with a mere glance. The admission brought to mind Stella's description of her "love test."

"He just looks at me and my stomach turns to butterflies. He can smile in a way that…melts me."

Constance didn't even have to see him; the mere thought

of Kyle had her stomach erupting in flutters. His smile could paralyze her mind. His slightest touch, a brush of his hand, a bump of his arm, could stop her heartbeat. After sharing coffee and chocolate cake last night he'd leaned so close— his eyes a hypnotic smoky blue—she'd thought he might kiss her. Fixated by a rush of shock and anticipation, stopping him hadn't crossed her mind.

He hadn't announced any such intention, but there was no point in exposing herself to such volatile emotions when she knew nothing could come from it. Next week she'd move upstairs above the schoolroom, and tonight she was going to bed without dessert.

Realizing she stood in the center of the room, her upturned gaze still fixed on the ceiling, she gave herself a mental shake and started for the door. The sheriff stood beside the road, the late-afternoon sun lighting up his pale hair, his long frame leaning against a horse-drawn cart.

The cluster of colorful flowers in his hand and the grin on his face said he was ready to whisk Stella away. She rushed over to greet him. His arm moved around her as she took the flowers.

"I love them."

"I come to take you to dinner."

"Hey, Günter." Kyle's boots clapped against the side stair-case as he made a quick descent. "You've come to steal my sister away for the evening?"

"I have."

Constance hoped he'd deny his request.

"Be sure to have her home at a decent hour."

Stella looked back at Constance standing on the front steps. "Do you mind?"

"Of course not," she lied.

Günter didn't waste a moment, quickly packing his fiancée into the seat beside him and cracking the reins.

"The place is about finished," Kyle said from beside her.

"Come have a look." He started up the stairs as though she'd have no objections to being alone with him—in her apartment no less!

So arrogant. And impossibly bossy. With a last glance at the road, a cloud of dust all she could see of her deserting assistant, she followed him. She had yet to step foot in her soon-to-be home. Like the classroom, the long outer walls had windows, lighting up the wood floor, a small kitchen and the doorway leading to a bedroom. The thumping and bumping she'd heard must have been the arrival of the cookstove. The cast-iron monstrosity stood on the far wall like a dark unwelcome shadow.

"You don't like it?"

Kyle filled the doorway to the bedroom area.

"Oh, no, this is wonderful. Very spacious."

"Constance?" The question in his eyes was more of a demand.

"I don't cook."

"You can't cook?" he said, his face fixed with surprise.

"I *can* cook. I *don't*. I haven't lit a stove or a match since before the fire. I haven't had to. Meals were provided at the mission."

"This stove is perfectly safe," he said, joining her in the tiny kitchen. "A stove didn't catch that house on fire." His gentle tone increased her embarrassment.

"I know."

"The stove downstairs has been lit each morning."

"Stella's doing."

"Darlin', Stella won't always be here. We get snow all but four months out of the year. Lighting a stove is a necessity."

"I know."

"What are you going to do about it?"

"I assure you I can find a way to deal with it."

"You're hardly hapless, Constance. What you need is practice."

"You think I should *practice* lighting fires?"

"I do. I was thinking we'd go to town for supper, but why don't we eat at the house. You can practice striking matches and I'll help you light the stove."

Alone? With him? *All evening?* "It wouldn't be appropriate for us to be alone at the house."

He arched a dark eyebrow. "We've been alone every evening this week. Quite frankly, I look forward to your company."

She couldn't fight her smile, terribly pleased by his admission. "Stella was home all this week."

"We won't be together the whole time. I have chores in the stable I have to attend. But if you'd rather have Stella help with lighting—"

"*No.* I don't want her to know." It was bad enough she'd told Kyle.

"Honey, having a fear of fire after all you went through is nothing to be ashamed of."

She shook her head. "You understand because you were there. You were in the house, too, and you're not afraid."

Kyle couldn't believe he hadn't picked up on her fear sooner. He hadn't seen her near the stove. Nor had he ever seen her in the front room where a fire burned in the open fireplace most evenings. "I wasn't the one tied to a bed. Plenty about that day has haunted me. You're not alone in that respect."

"Really?"

More than I care to admit. "Honest to God. Let me help you light the stove."

"You think lighting a bunch of matches will help?"

"I'm willing to strike every match in the house to give it a shot."

She heaved a sigh, her tense expression suggesting she wasn't quite so willing. "Okay."

The kitchen reeked of sulfur. A pile of smoking matches sat on a plate on the table, and Constance hadn't lit a single one of them. He'd hoped the five-inch matchsticks used to light the stove would ease her worry about burning her fingers. She stood beside him, an unlit match in her hand, and nearly jumped out of her skin each time he gave a demonstration.

"I feel silly," she said, her frustration and fear as palpable as the burnt matchsticks piled in front of them.

"You're not silly." His lighting-matches idea had clearly been a bad one. "I could hold your hands, help you strike it."

Her fierce glare nearly made him grin. God, she was irresistible, and a refreshing change from the endless line of townsfolk and husband seekers constantly approaching him with a list of favors, wants or ulterior motives. Constance wasn't a woman who liked to have anything done for her. Harboring such a fear had to be at odds with her stubborn nature.

"I've had my share of spills and mishaps and know how fear can play on the mind, growing stronger when not confronted. Once you get past the first strike, the rest will come easier."

Her gaze was skeptical.

"I know from experience. I was fourteen when an ornery bull caught me by surprise. Look here…" He tugged his shirt from his waistband to reveal the pucker of skin where a steer had gored his side. "Damn near bled to death, and I was flat on my back for two weeks. I avoided that pasture for months, until Juniper forced me to go along when that old bull had to be moved. I was scared as hell and damn cautious."

"Kyle—"

"A bullet dug a trench into my side in my first shoot-out," he said, tugging his shirt higher to show the wound.

"Kyle!"

He looked up to see Constance blushing to the roots of her hair, her gaze flickering from his chest to floor.

"Put your shirt down," she said, sneaking another peek.

He couldn't fight his smile. "I didn't mean to offend. The

point is, fear makes you cautious. Caution is good, so long
as you're not crippled by it. You used to light stoves, right?"

She hardly remembered why she was standing in the
kitchen, her mind swooning at images of dark hair over a
bronzed muscular chest. She blew out a shaky breath and
glanced at the deceptively harmless match in her hand.

"I know it will spark," she said. "I'm going to jump. *What
if I drop it?*"

"It's a match, darlin', not a torch. You could step on it,
though it'll likely go out before hitting the floor."

His simple explanation renewed the heat in her cheeks.
"Normally I'd know that."

"Might also help to know a match alone didn't burn that
boardinghouse. Kerosene started the fire. Rotted wood and
sod patches carried the flames. There's not a speck of sod in
this house, the wood is new and solid. *Watch.*" He struck a
match that fast and dropped it. The flame died long before the
partially blackened matchstick hit the floor.

"See?"

His gentle smile eased her nervousness. How could she not
love him? She knew without a doubt he wouldn't allow her
to come to harm.

She picked up the matchbox and scraped the end across
the side, jumping as fire sparked. She stared at the lit match,
watching the small ball of fire slowly creep down the stick.

"Oh, hail Mary—now what!"

"Shake it out, sweetheart."

She did, and laughed with relief as smoke snaked up from
the blackened tip.

Kyle held out a new match. "Ready to go again?"

"Yes," she said, charged with a heady rush of excitement.

After wasting another pile of matches, Kyle led her to the
stove and opened an empty firebox. "Fill 'er up," he said,
standing back. He watched as she arranged the firewood as
she'd done years ago, tucking kindling beneath the larger

logs. She scratched the match and managed not to flinch quite so badly. The glow of embers flared up into ribbons of yellow and orange flames, and Constance shut the door.

"Good job." He gathered her in his arms, giving her a tight squeeze, easing the tremors she hadn't realized needed soothing.

Holding her close, Kyle was reluctant to let her go. She smiled up at him and he felt a true ring of pride.

Lord, she smells good. Wasn't rose water or floral perfume…he couldn't define the earthy, clean scent, but the heated stir of his body confirmed he liked it—too damn much. He released her and stepped back.

"Let's get supper started."

Constance peeled potatoes and carrots while he prepared chicken. With supper roasting, they went to the stable, Constance tending Sunshine as he forked fresh straw into the stalls and brought the horses in from the outside corral. By the time they left the stable, the sun had long since set. He draped his arm over her shoulders as they walked up the path.

"Dark out," he said, as though that gave him the right to tuck her against his side. She didn't object, and he found himself in no hurry to reach the back door.

Once inside the aroma-filled kitchen, he went to his room to find some control and wash up. He took a detour into the front room, lighting the fireplace before he returned to the kitchen. Constance was about to set a second, filled plate on the table.

"We're going to eat in the front room." He snatched the plate from the table and hooked his arm around her waist.

She didn't budge.

"I'd rather not."

He leaned down, touching his forehead to hers. Her eyes widened, emphasizing flecks of brown and gold in rings of honey. She had the prettiest eyes he'd ever seen.

"I thought we agreed the best way to face your fear is to confront it."

"We agreed on the stove, and you're trying to distract me."

He grinned as he straightened. "Is it working?"

"Yes," she said, fully aware of his hand on her waist, the warmth in his eyes, and spirals of sensation. "You're using an unfair advantage."

His smile widened. "And what's that?"

Heat flamed into her cheeks and she glanced down at the food on her plate.

"Just come sit by me," he said, ushering her along. "Fire isn't going to leap out. I promise."

She knew that, of course, had been around plenty of fireplaces—she simply chose to avoid the discomfort whenever possible. She tensed the moment they entered the room, her gaze fused to the flames twisting over the stack of wood in the large stone hearth. They sat on the sofa, their plates on their laps, his arm wrapped securely around her shoulders as they ate.

"I still can't believe my sister is getting married," he said, drawing her gaze away from the fireplace. She didn't mind watching the flames reflected in his blue eyes. "When I left home she was a tiny thing, all braids and giggles. She grew up and I missed it."

"Is that why you came home?"

"I came home for a visit and realized all I'd missed. Our younger sisters are just a few years behind her."

"How old are they?"

"Twelve and fourteen."

As he talked about his family she began to relax, appreciating his warmth and easy conversation as they ate their supper. Finished eating, he set their plates aside and they settled back to watch the fire.

"It's kind of pretty," she said after a long pause of hearing nothing but the crackle of the wood.

"Yeah," he agreed.

She looked up to find him watching her. He tucked a stray curl behind her ear, opening the lid on the thousands of butterflies living in her belly.

"I'm proud of you."

Tears burned into her eyes. He couldn't know what those words meant to her. She'd never been the recipient of such praise.

Her breath stalled as he leaned closer. The light brush of his soft lips over hers sent a wild torrent of shivers across her skin. He pulled her closer, the pressure of his lips coaxing hers apart. At the first touch of his tongue she trembled, and reached for him as pleasing bursts of wild sensation slammed through her. She returned the fleeting touches, and he groaned against her mouth, increasing the intensity of the kiss.

A real kiss, she thought. His hand slid down her back, caressing her body in the same languid, unrushed rhythm, thoroughly melting her against the hard surface of his body.

Saints and sinners, he feels good.

Lost in a haze of sensation, she explored the textures of his mouth, trembling as she threaded her fingers into his silky brown hair. By the time he eased back, she gasped for breath, her mind a haze of sensation as he pulled pins from her hair.

"Kyle?"

Long dark coils tumbled down around her shoulders.

"You have the prettiest hair." He pulled her back into his tight embrace. She went eagerly, hesitation forgotten as she returned his passionate kiss. He surrounded her, consuming her, overwhelming her as he pressed her back against the soft cushions. He shifted over her, his body caressing hers through layers of fabric, every flex of his hips sending a shocking pulse of fire throughout her body. She groaned against his mouth as desire escalated with frightening intensity.

His hand moved up the back of her thigh, caressing the sensitive skin above her stockings. His fingers slipped inside and she realized his hand was beneath her skirt, *exposing her legs.*

She shoved at his shoulders. "No!"

Surprised by the sudden jostle, Kyle blinked down at her, disoriented by the hard surge of desire ravaging his body as he stared down at Constance's wide fearful eyes. He had her pinned to the sofa, her hair fanned out, the ache in his groin pressed to her soft core as he all but wrapped her leg around him.

"Oh, hell." He sat up and brought her up with him. "I shouldn't have moved so fast."

She trembled in his arms, her gaze locked on his mouth, her breathing as hard and heavy as his own. Unable to resist, he brushed another soft kiss across her glistening lips.

"I suppose it's safe to say we're courting."

She stiffened and broke away form his hold as she struggled to her feet. "No, we're not."

"The hell we're not. Con—"

"It was just a kiss. I don't…*good night!*"

She shot from the room before he could argue.

That was a hell of a lot more than a kiss, he thought. Her bedroom door slammed as he struggled with a desire no woman had ever caused in him with just a few innocent kisses. His body burned, his fingers fairly tingled from the feel of her soft skin. He tensed, realizing he'd been grinding against her as though he meant to bed her right there in the front room, when Stella could come home any moment.

"Damn it." He'd only meant to kiss her. He should have known better. When it came to Constance, he only had one speed—*reckless.*

He'd frightened her. Hell, he'd frightened himself. He sat back and shoved his hands through his hair. Her scent didn't help to cool his body. Her initial response had been anything but fearful. He'd tasted the proof in her kisses— she wanted him too. He more than wanted her; he meant to marry her.

The silent affirmation surprised him—and eased a tension that had been building inside him with each passing day. He *wanted* to marry Constance.

He gave himself a good ten minutes to cool down before going after her.

"Constance?" He rapped softly on the door.

She didn't answer. No light seeped under the door into the dim hall, but he heard movement.

"Honey, we need to talk. I'm coming in." He opened the door to her dark room and Constance moved off her bed. Her room smelled like her, like fresh rain. She stood in a stream of moonlight pouring through the open window. The soft glow lit up her thin gown like a paper lantern, revealing all the gentle curves hidden beneath with such clarity he nearly groaned.

"Do you always dress for bed in the dark?"

"Yes," she said, her tone angry.

She had a right to be angry. His actions had been disrespectful, as was openly staring at her supple body when she had no idea her gown was practically transparent in the moonlight. He walked to her bureau to light the lamp. Holding a match to a fresh white wick, it dawned on him how much time Constance spent in the dark. Every morning she'd been dressed and had her hair pinned up well before dawn.

He lit the wick and replaced the globe, casting light around the room.

"You shouldn't be in here!" She stood beyond the foot of the bed, her arms locked over her chest. Her long hair was woven into a single thick braid, draped over her shoulder and the nightdress covering her from chin to toes.

"I'm not going to violate you, Constance. I didn't mean to frighten you. I went too far and, well…I shouldn't have."

"That didn't sound like an apology."

"I'm not sorry I kissed you. Can you honestly tell me you didn't want to be kissed?"

"What are you doing in here?" she asked, the tremble in her voice making him feel like the lowest of creatures. She'd trusted him, and he'd blown it.

"Trying to salvage my mistake. I've wanted to kiss you all

week and have been fighting an attraction that only gets stronger with each day. I told myself I wouldn't act on those feelings, that I don't want marriage, but tonight proved denial isn't working. *I want you,* Constance."

She gaped at him, and Kyle realized he sounded about as cavalier as a barbarian.

"Hell, that didn't come out right. Honey, I want to be with you—I like being with you."

She swallowed hard, the wariness in her golden eyes unchanged.

Damnation, where were the right words when he needed them? Problem was, he didn't want to just sweet-talk her, he wanted to win her as she'd won him.

He strode to her bed and sat on the edge. "Will you come over here? I swear I won't pounce on you."

Her furrowed brow suggested she'd rather sit in a skunk's den, but her foot slid forward. Her gaze wary, she eased onto the edge of the bed, not about to be kowtowed by him. Damn, but he admired that about her. She'd trusted him, had forced herself to face her fear, and now he was being a damn coward himself. He wanted her to stay, in his life, in his bed.

"The thought of you moving even a half mile away… I don't want you to go. And well, I was thinking… Will you marry me?"

Tears filled her eyes as she shook her head.

Her silent denial shocked him. He knew damn well she'd been fighting the same attraction. "Why not?

"I've never felt for a woman what I feel for you. *Marry me.*"

Constance fought the urge to say yes. She loved him so much. "I can't," she said, pressing her nightdress down a bit further so the skirt covered her ankles. There were some advantages to dressing and undressing in the dark—she didn't have to see her legs.

His thumb glided over her cheek, brushing away her tears, which only made them flow faster. His fingers moved beneath her chin, urging her to meet his gaze.

"Honey, I won't be put off by your legs."

"I am," she said.

"I think you care for me."

"I love you," she said, the words escaping her lips.

He smiled and her heart melted. He leaned in, stealing her breath with a light kiss on her lips. "I showed you *my* scars."

"It's not the same." The deep burns had left her shins rippled and pitted.

"I don't believe you," he said, his slow smile equally annoying and endearing as his arms moved around her. "Let me see."

"You don't know—"

"Then let me see." He reached across and pulled her legs over his lap. She gasped as he touched the hem above her ankles. "Can't be worse than my memory of your blistered and broken skin."

She pressed her face to his shoulder.

"Constance?"

"Go ahead," she said against his shirt.

Kyle didn't hesitate. She tensed as her gown brushed across her knees. His long fingers gently grazed her scarred shins.

"Such beautiful new skin," he said, his husky tone adding to the shivers already coursing through her body. "You're beautiful, Constance. *All* of you."

His lips brushed her cheek, her forehead, finding her lips. She didn't try to fight the heat blossoming through her.

He eased her back against the pillow. "Marry me."

His heart swelled as she smiled up at him.

"I…" Movement at the window behind him drew her gaze. Eyes black as coal looked back at her from beyond the glass— the smiling face from her nightmares.

She screamed and clutched at Kyle.

He turned, pushing her behind him as a revolver materialized in his hand. "What'd you see?"

She gripped his shirt. "He was there! You told me you captured him!"

"Who?"

"Chandler!"

Chapter Ten

Kyle's blood ran cold as he glanced back at the dark window.

"Honey, Ned Chandler was hanged in Montana. You sure lighting those fires wasn't too much for you?"

"I know his face!" She pushed off the bed and shoved her feet into the slippers. "It was him!"

A crash sounded at the front of the house, glass shattering. Constance gripped at his arm. He tucked her against his side and rushed to the front room.

Glass shards from the broken window glistened across the floor.

He pushed her against the wall, beside the cover of a hutch. "Stay here."

He eased the door open, the strong scent of kerosene raising the hair on the back of his neck. Farther out, the circular glow of a lit cigar moved like a firefly in the pitch of night. The orange dot brightened as someone drew on the cigar.

Ned. He knew even before the familiar voice sounded from the darkness.

"Welcome home, Darby." He stepped forward in the glow of the porch light, and Kyle's grip flexed on his gun.

"Shoot me and my boys will drop you, leaving your lady

all alone. I've never been one to travel alone," he said, flashing a cold grin.

True enough. Ned always had his entourage close by.

"What are you doing this side of hell?" He didn't have any other question for a man who should have been hanged two years ago. He'd read the execution papers!

"Guess you was too busy killin' my kinfolk to attend the execution."

Kyle couldn't deny the fact. He'd thought he'd rid the world of their entire murderous brood.

"You're not the only one who can take on a new identity, pretending to be someone you're not. A year of answering to the name Duncan, and they let me walk right out," he said with a laugh. "Duncan was kind enough to take my noose. I figured you'd come home at some point." His expression darkened. "It does pay to be patient. I never did finish my business with that little filly."

He'd been at the stockyard. Had he even suspected Ned was alive he wouldn't have allowed Constance to stay in his house.

"You always was the Good Samaritan. Victoria was supposed to seduce you, but you just had to marry her."

He scanned the darkness, fully aware of the cigar in Ned's fingers, the fuel on his porch and knowing at least two others stood in the darkness. The camp Gunter found had been theirs. He had to get Connie out of here.

"Bet you even plan to marry that little cripple."

Rage flared as he stared into Ned's dark eyes.

"Doubt she'd be letting you under her skirt if she knew you set her on fire."

"I didn't tie her to the bed!"

"No, you just set the house ablaze. How's it feel to be on the inside?"

He tossed the cigar, and flames burst across the porch, the rush of heat hitting him like an ocean wave. He slammed the door and turned for Constance. She stood a few paces behind him, her eyes wide with horror. He grabbed her and sprinted for the back door.

"Kyle!"

"Hold on to me!" he shouted, spying flames at a side window as he raced through the hall. They'd surrounded the house. Her legs locked around his waist. Spotting his leather jacket over a kitchen chair, he grabbed it, wrapping the thick leather around her. "Don't look," he said as he opened the back door.

Fire climbed the posts on either side of the back stoop. Connie's hold tightened. His gun drawn, he leaped over the burning stairs. Firelight glinted off something to his right. Kyle fired, shooting a man about to take aim as he came round the side of the house. The man reared back, the bullet taking him down.

Another flash came from the other side as the second outlaw stepped beyond the house. Unprepared, he barely had his gun raised when Kyle dropped him with a single shot.

Seeking the shelter of the darkness beyond the flames, he turned and ran. Reaching a tight cluster of massive redwoods near the outhouse, he set Constance on her feet. She shivered as he tucked her back into the shadows.

"Kyle." He saw the reflection of tall flames in Constance's wide eyes as she looked to the east.

Oh, God. They'd lit the stable.

"The horses!" she cried.

Muffled shrieks carried on the light breeze, his mares screaming, frantic with fear.

"Can you get them?"

He pressed his gun into her hand. "Stay here. If anyone comes near, shoot 'em."

She gave a vigorous nod. *"Hurry."*

By the time Kyle cut through the woods, the stable doors were fully ablaze. Watching for Ned, he opened the wide gate to the corral and ran to the first side door. The second he popped the latch a mare broke free, screeching as she charged out with clouds of smoke. He hurried down the stable, pulling all the latches, the thick smoke choking him by the time he reached the end. In the last stall, Sunshine didn't come out. He tied his bandanna over his mouth and rushed inside, the thick smoke blinding him, stinging his eyes as he stomped on the falling embers. The roof was fully aflame. Smoke whirled like clouds.

Good God. How much fuel had they used, and where was his colt?

She whinnied from somewhere inside.

"Sunshine!"

A fist broke through a dark swirl of smoke, connecting square on his jaw. He hit the ground and the foal ran past him.

"I got your sunshine," growled Ned.

Kyle pushed up as a boot slammed into his gut.

"That's for Billy!"

Kyle rolled aside and jumped up. Ned moved back, his image fading in and out of black swirls like a light-haired devil.

"We keeping score? Because I've got a list a mile long of all the folks you wronged. So come take your lumps."

A rope landed around Kyle's shoulders and tugged him against the center post. The whole burning structure creaked.

"You're not leaving this stable."

Kyle twisted, grabbed the end of the rope and tugged. Ned stumbled forward, right into his fist. A second blow sent him flying through smoke and embers, landing flat on his back.

Kyle tossed the rope off. "If you need to be hand delivered to hell, I don't mind taking you, Ned."

Ned scrambled back, his dark eyes widening with a flicker of fear. "If that's how you want it." He stood up and charged at him.

Kyle blocked his weight and slammed his right fist into his gut. His left fist pounded Ned's chin. The next blow rattled his jaw.

Ned hit the ground and didn't get up.

The roof overhead groaned. He looked up as embers showered down. A section of flames and wood came crashing down. He tried to lunge back but something struck his head. Pain exploded through his skull in a flash of light.

Constance moved through the woods, watching the flames rise higher on the stable. She'd seen Sunshine run out but no sign of Kyle. No one stood outside. As she made her way to the corral, she noticed a spray of embers twinkling like night stars on the ground, as though they'd exploded from inside. Smoke poured out as massive flames lit up the night sky.

"Kyle!" She fanned the smoke obstructing her view. "Kyle!" she screamed again. Heat radiated against her face, fear choking her as she remembered the lash of flames against her skin. Her eyes burned as she peered through the side doors. Beyond the center stall she spotted him, on the ground, unmoving, his blond hair and blackened face clear in the bright flickering light. She called his name. Horses whinnied in the distance. Kyle didn't move.

He's not dead. She had to get him out!

She ran to a water trough in the corral and set down the gun to shrug off his big coat. She dunked the wool and the leather before dragging it over her head. Keeping her gaze on Kyle's unmoving body, she tried to block out her fear as she ran to him. A pile of collapsed roofing burned in a heap just a few feet away from him.

"Kyle!" She dropped to her knees at his side. "Kyle, wake up!" She slung the wet coat over him, using the wool to wipe a layer of dark soot from his face.

His eyes blinked open.

"Kyle!" She coughed, leaning over him as heat buffeted her from all directions.

Constance's voice registered in his dazed mind. Slowly she came into focus: her glossy eyes, wet hair, a wall of fire blazing behind her.

She'd come into the burning stable. Above them, weakened timbers creaked and crackled, about to give way. He sat up, the throbbing in his skull nothing compared to the wild beat of his heart and the need to get her out of there. He pulled the coat over her head and lunged as embers scattered all around them. Rolling to his feet, he lifted her as he stood and ducked through the side door as the rest of the roof came crashing down—sparks and debris spraying him.

He ran to the end of the large corral and dropped to his knees. Both of them collapsed onto their backs, coughing and gasping for breath.

"Con, are you all right?" Kyle rolled over, raising onto his elbow. He pushed her long curls away from her face. The light from the flaming barn turned her eyes to a deep shade of amber.

She framed his face in her hands. "How's your head?"

Did the woman never worry about herself? She was afraid of fire, and yet she'd run into hell's own inferno to save him.

His lips closed over hers, urgent, insistent. God save him, he couldn't help himself. Her arms locked around him and Constance took bold possession of his mouth.

He began to hear voices through the buzzing in his ears. Stella was shouting his name.

"They may need a moment to catch their breath," Günter said from somewhere behind them.

It took another moment for him to release her, both of them dragging for air as their lips parted. Kyle was shocked to see the number of townsfolk standing beyond the fence. He heard shouts of others at the house, yelling for more water.

"What the hell happened?" asked Günter.

Kyle pushed himself up and held his hand out to Constance. "Had some trouble with those interlopers." She sat up and put her hand in his, allowing him to help her to her feet. Her sopping-wet gown clung to her feminine curves, leaving little to the imagination. He quickly lifted her into his arms. Ten little muddy toes poked out from the dirty brown hem of her nightdress.

"You ran into a burning barn *barefoot?*"

"I had slippers, but I lost them."

"Nothing hurts?"

She shook her head and smoothed his hair away from his face. "What about you?"

His head throbbed and his heart still raced fit to burst, but she was in his arms. "I'll be all right."

"I have a blanket," Stella called out, stretching a quilt wide as he approached.

"Thanks." The moment he set Constance on her feet he pulled the blanket tight around her shoulders and hugged her against him. Her strong grip on his waist eased some of the fear still raging inside him. Seeing her face, those flames rolling behind her—

"Anyone hurt?" Günter asked from beside him.

"Two dead out back. Ned Chandler's in the stable on his way to hell."

"A Chandler?" Günter asked.

"The one I arrested in Montana. Billy's older brother."

"Jim found your young foal and is taking her to the school stable. You can stay at my place. Wagon's out on the road. I can take you to the house with Stella and I'll come back."

"Thanks."

"Judging by what me and half the town just witnessed, there will be another wedding to plan."

"I'll marry her, but right now I just want to get Connie somewhere safe and dry."

Constance stiffened against Kyle's hold, his tired tone resurrecting Ned Chandler's voice: "Always the Good Samaritan… Bet you even plan to marry that little cripple."

Kyle had set the fire…and he hadn't told her. Instead he'd made her love him, when his feelings were derived from guilt. She couldn't think of a worse form of pity!

Tears blurred her vision. "No," she said, pushing against him.

"Constance? Honey, what is it?"

"I'm not marrying you." She turned away from their shocked expressions and started walking toward the road. Kyle caught up to her, his hand closing over her arm.

"Con—"

She stopped, shrugging off his hold. "You lied to me."

"When?"

"You made me believe you really cared about me. When all along it was guilt."

"You're wrong."

"You were going to marry his *sister?*"

"Victoria wasn't like the rest of them, but she couldn't stand up to them either."

"Where is she?"

"Dead. She was killed in a shoot-out a few days after she ran off with her brothers."

"That's why you became a marshal, *for revenge.*"

"Partially," he admitted. "Going after Victoria's brothers opened my eyes to the multitude of outlaws just like the Chandlers, not caring who they hurt to get what they want, and not enough lawmen to bring them in. None of this has anything to do with my feelings for you."

"Did you set the fire?"

His pained expression answered her question. "I didn't know you were inside."

"I know that. I wouldn't have blamed you, not for what happened in Montana." Tears streaked hotly across her cheeks. "But I can't forgive you for deceiving me this way."

"Constance—"

"The last thing I want is to be bound to a man who looks at me and sees a victim."

"And I keep telling you, sweetheart, *I'm not that nice.* I've never seen you as anything less than a courageous woman. Honest to God, Constance, I think I fell in love with you in that boardinghouse."

"When I was on fire? That proves it!"

"Not on fire, *fighting* fire. It's in situations like that when you really see inside a person. You weren't shrinking in fear, you were giving all you had and worrying about those who'd left you behind. I love *you,* Constance. The woman who has the gumption to travel clear to the middle of nowhere to teach a classroom full of rowdy timber rats. A woman who races into a burning barn despite her own fear. The same woman who wasn't afraid to call me out when I was insulting and over-stepped my bounds. And maybe," he added, his brow pinched with annoyance, "I like to be saved once in a while. No matter what, I know you've got my back."

She laughed and sniffed at her tears. "I do."

He took a step closer, his arms looping gently around her. "Marry me."

How often had she envisioned her cowboy's bride—and it had never been her. "For two years I believed you were married, and in my mind your bride was *perfect.*"

"And she is," he said, kissing her lightly. "*You* are the perfect bride for me."

Her bright smile warmed his heart. She drew him to her lips and kissed him with a passion that was going to drive him mad before they were wed.

* * * * *

The Shocking Secrets of Regency Rakes

FIVE SEXY HISTORICAL ROMANCES

The Unmasking of Lady Loveless
by Nicola Cornick

Disrobed and Dishonoured by Louise Allen

Libertine Lord, Pickpocket Miss
by Bronwyn Scott

The Unlacing of Miss Leigh by Diane Gaston

Notorious Lord, Compromised Miss
by Annie Burrows

Available 16th April 2010

www.millsandboon.co.uk

millsandboon.co.uk Community

Join Us!

The Community is the perfect place to meet and chat to kindred spirits who love books and reading as much as you do, but it's also the place to:

- **Get the inside scoop from authors about their latest books**
- **Learn how to write a romance book with advice from our editors**
- **Help us to continue publishing the best in women's fiction**
- **Share your thoughts on the books we publish**
- **Befriend other users**

Forums: Interact with each other as well as authors, editors and a whole host of other users worldwide.

Blogs: Every registered community member has their own blog to tell the world what they're up to and what's on their mind.

Book Challenge: We're aiming to read 5,000 books and have joined forces with The Reading Agency in our inaugural Book Challenge.

Profile Page: Showcase yourself and keep a record of your recent community activity.

Social Networking: We've added buttons at the end of every post to share via digg, Facebook, Google, Yahoo, technorati and de.licio.us.

www.millsandboon.co.uk

2 FREE BOOKS
AND A SURPRISE GIFT

We would like to take this opportunity to thank you for reading this Mills & Boon® book by offering you the chance to take TWO more specially selected books from the Historical series absolutely FREE! We're also making this offer to introduce you to the benefits of the Mills & Boon® Book Club™—

- **FREE home delivery**
- **FREE gifts and competitions**
- **FREE monthly Newsletter**
- **Exclusive Mills & Boon Book Club offers**
- **Books available before they're in the shops**

Accepting these FREE books and gift places you under no obligation to buy, you may cancel at any time, even after receiving your free books. Simply complete your details below and return the entire page to the address below. You don't even need a stamp!

YES Please send me 2 free Historical books and a surprise gift. I understand that unless you hear from me, I will receive 4 superb new books every month for just £3.79 each, postage and packing free. I am under no obligation to purchase any books and may cancel my subscription at any time. The free books and gift will be mine to keep in any case.

Ms/Mrs/Miss/Mr ——————— Initials ———————

Surname ————————————————————

Address ————————————————————

———————————————— Postcode ——————

E-mail ————————————————————

Send this whole page to: Mills & Boon Book Club, Free Book Offer, FREEPOST NAT 10298, Richmond, TW9 1BR